To Kath'

Wil

CW01651368

For

Christmas 1995!!

Something in the cellar

In the narrow hallway, she paused outside the door beneath the stairs. Somewhere behind the stout wood, in that gloomy chamber down the worn stone steps, lay the reason for all those mysterious events – the curious, the bleak, and now the deadly – which had gathered in a crescendo around her since she had come to this house.

In four months her life had changed enormously. From sudden isolation to marriage with the wrong man. From fear of loneliness to fear of something worse . . . It was difficult to believe that she had made that first, reckless choice on a beautiful island nearly two thousand miles away . . .

Something in the cellar, which is a change of direction for the author of a number of medical whodunits, is a novel of suspense: a young woman on holiday in Madeira meets a fellow countryman and marries him on returning to England, only to find her new life shadowed by growing suspicions that their modest house is harbouring a sinister secret . . . Criminal activity and murder accelerate to a lethal climax in this gripping story of domestic terror.

Also by Stella Shepherd

Black justice (1988)
Murderous remedy (1989)
Thinner than blood (1991)
A lethal fixation (1993)
Nurse Dawes is dead (1994)

SOMETHING IN THE CELLAR

Stella Shepherd

Constable · London

First published in Great Britain 1995
by Constable & Company Ltd
3 The Lanchesters, 162 Fulham Palace Road
London W6 9ER

ISBN 0 09 474380 0
Set in Linotron Palatino 10pt by
CentraCet Limited, Cambridge
Printed and bound in Great Britain
by Hartnolls Ltd, Bodmin

A CIP catalogue record for this book
is available from the British Library

1

In the narrow hallway, she paused outside the door beneath the stairs. Somewhere behind the stout wood, in that gloomy chamber down the worn stone steps, lay the reason for all those mysterious events – the curious, the bleak, and now the deadly – which had gathered in a crescendo around her since she had come to this house.

In four months her life had changed enormously. From sudden isolation to marriage with the wrong man. From fear of loneliness to fear of something worse . . . It was difficult to believe that she had made that first, reckless choice on a beautiful island nearly two thousand miles away from here . . .

She was early at the pool. Not because loungers were at a premium – there were enough here to cater for any number of dawn-raiding Teutons – but because she wanted her own special corner, a discreet flower-flanked hideaway far from the poolside bar, where she could read her book and watch her fellow guests enjoying themselves.

She placed her bag at the foot of the lounger and furtively pulled from her shoulders the fleecy cotton bathrobe so thoughtfully provided by the hotel. The air held a slight haze, but already the turquoise of the sea behind the palms of the lower garden was deepening, and along the coast the imposing sea-cliff Cabo Girão was sharpening into focus. It was going to be another scorching day. (Madeira will be temperate, but not hot, she had been warned. With those high volcanic mountains, the clouds get caught and drop all their rain. Take a jacket and a cardigan; don't be disappointed if there isn't much sun . . .) Well, they were wrong. She had been here for three days, and the sun had blazed on each of them . . .

'Excuse me, would you like a parasol?' One of the pool attendants had just emerged from the nearby changing-room complex; with one sweep of the eyes over her small, pallid frame he had diagnosed her as English.

'Yes, please.'

'And one for a friend?'

'No, thank you.' He sounded British, too, she noticed. He had a muted northern accent not unlike her own. All the other hotel staff she had met were Portuguese. 'I'm by myself,' she added, then immediately regretted doing so. He didn't need to know that: she could at least have pretended to be part of a group. What if he tried to chat her up?

He retreated to the storeroom and returned with a huge yellow parasol, which he erected at an angle to lend maximal shade to the lounger. 'Two hundred escudos, please.' She handed him three hundred, and he gave a little nod of thanks. 'Watch the sun,' he said. 'People tend to underestimate it.'

She felt embarrassed by her lack of tan. 'I've mainly come to see the island,' she said defensively. 'I shan't be spending a lot of time by the pool.'

'Pity,' he replied, with discernible emphasis.

She fumbled for her book, but he stood there, amused and friendly. 'What have you seen so far?'

'Oh . . . the east of the island. Those funny little cottages at Santana, with the women working at the embroidery.'

'Coach trip, was it?'

'Yes. I'm going to the Botanical Gardens later today, up above Funchal.'

'You'll get a good view of the harbour from there – see the cruise ships, and the yachts of the rich bastards of the world.' He grinned. 'They say that's the best way to see Madeira: coming in from the sea, watching these cloud-capped mountains grow bigger and bigger . . .' He broke off as an inane rippling giggle heralded the arrival of other guests. 'I'm Roy Judd, by the way,' he added quickly. 'And your name is . . .?'

'Bonnie,' she said.

Russell and Amanda, a radiant honeymoon couple from Wolverhampton, erupted into the area moments later, and set up camp on adjacent loungers. *'Dois guardas-sol, por favor,'* called out Russell in an execrable Portuguese accent, then winked at Roy as if to underline a private joke. He turned to Bonnie. 'That's Roy,' he told her. 'He's English, you know. Comes from somewhere near Manchester.'

She nodded, aware of a nostalgic pang in her stomach. Her own early childhood in the north-west had been marvellously secure, with no hint of the cruel upheavals to come. Many times recently she had found herself wanting to retreat there, to regress to the far side of adolescence and opt out of life's vicissitudes . . .

'Well, *I* fancy Tristão,' stated Amanda.

'The waiter?' gasped Russell in mock incredulity.

'That's right. The one who brings me passion fruit.'

'And I thought you were a lady of good taste. Fair enough; if you prefer some dago to me, I shall elope with Bonnie.'

Bonnie gave a tight smile, and wondered if she was supposed to be flattered. Murmuring of a need for exercise, she stood up, padded to the pool's edge and sat down, immersing her feet. She closed her eyes, savouring the coolness of the water and the contrast of the strengthening sunshine on her cheeks and throat. Eventually, clenching her teeth slightly, she slid into the pool and struck out towards its centre with a neat, mechanical breast-stroke. The initial shock of submersion died away; she floated, making lazy finning movements with her limbs, and gradually she felt content, secure in a calm amniotic haven, all anxieties suspended, like her body, in time . . .

Splash! Amanda had leapt in nearby. Russell shouted something, dived in behind her and proceeded to tickle his wife until she shrieked and begged him to stop. Turbulence barrelled across the surface of the pool. Bonnie swam away from their thrashing legs and commenced a slow aquatic circumnavigation. Beyond the tiled pool edge, she could see that the loungers were now being occupied at an increasing rate. The Duponts, a pleasant French family, had chosen a position overlooking the lower gardens; they recognized her, and waved. Near the bar stood a rugged teacher who had introduced himself as 'Dave'.

After three more stately circuits Bonnie climbed out of the pool, towelled herself dry and once more assumed possession of her lounger. She picked up her book, but held it unopened on her lap as she surveyed the scene around her. Two paperbacks lay on an adjacent small table. One displayed a montage of wizards, swords and unicorns encircling a baleful-looking crystal – Russell's choice, presumably. The other was a Danielle Steel romance, more in line with her own ideas of escapism. She herself was re-reading *Rebecca,* the famous du Maurier novel in which a girl rises from inauspicious beginnings to marriage with an enigmatic hero. Periodically Bonnie allowed herself fleeting fantasies about the same thing happening to her . . .

She glanced at her watch. It was just ten o'clock. At this hour for the past two days an elderly lady had picked her way carefully down the slope from the hotel and installed herself, fully clothed, on one particular lounger. A faded-looking companion, perhaps fifteen years younger, had accompanied her, carrying a large basket; she had assisted with the parasol, ensured that the old lady was comfortable, then rummaged in the bag. Instead of the expected picnic, Bonnie had seen saucers brought out, tins of cat-food, a thermos of milk . . . Then the strays had come slinking from the gardens, five or six cats with torn ears and moth-eaten fur, each destined to receive individual attention on the old lady's lap, and food from the companion. Bonnie had been sure that the author of such eccentricity must be English, but on passing the pair the previous morning she had heard them conversing in soft guttural tones.

Even as she mused, the couple appeared, the old lady stooping and limping, yet clearly in command, the younger one hovering, assisting, deferential. Bonnie wondered about their relationship: was the junior partner some relative of limited means, willing to act as dogsbody (or was it catsbody?) in order to experience the fascination of foreign travel? A niece, perhaps? or was she, like the heroine in *Rebecca*, the paid companion to an uncongenial employer? That book had been written in the Thirties, yet there were still such things as companions today, positions advertised in the columns of magazines like *The Lady*. Bonnie knew; she had been studying those columns herself.

Genteel poverty is the worst possible kind, her own aunt had said once. Not that she had considered herself in any way genteel. Bonnie had understood the essence of the frustrated remark: a woman not brought up on bingo, car boot sales and church-hall knees-ups viewed the rapid diminution of her meagre savings as the road to a ghastly uncharted abyss. Bonnie knew that her aunt's dread, like her own, had been the beckoning prospect of some squalid council high-rise whose walls rhythmically bulged in time with the neighbours' reggae music.

She was sure that stress had killed her aunt, only days before that incredible letter had arrived, informing them of their competition success and the prize of a holiday in Madeira. Aunt Rachel had suffered from angina for years, but no one had considered that action was appropriate. Perhaps if she had been a man, a more overt member of the workforce . . . Cynical thought. Bonnie was ashamed. Usually she tried to see the good in people. But it all seemed so *unfair* . . .

She turned again to her book and read for half an hour, keeping her face and upper body in the shadow of the parasol while her pale, slender legs peeped shyly out of the redoubt. A waiter brought her a Sprite in response to her self-conscious signal. There were distant murmurs of German as the dowager and her friend cajoled one of the cats . . .

Russell and Amanda reappeared, noisily towelled themselves dry and proceeded to lather each other with sunscreen products to the accompaniment of much snickering innuendo.

'You going, Bonnie?' asked Russell as she carefully packed up her things.

'Yes.'

'Where you off to, then?'
'The Gardens Tour.'

Gardens. Madeira was often fancifully described as 'a garden floating in the Atlantic', and already Bonnie could understand why. Everything beneath the mountain peaks was verdant, lush, brimming with life and colour. The inhabitants, many engaged in the harsh struggle of farming on forty-five degree slopes, viewed the fertile lava-rich earth in purely practical terms: it would support another harvest of grapes, or avocados, or custard apples, just as the hibiscus by the cottage door supported the lighter items of the family's washing. But Bonnie had more leisure to look, and appreciate. She only wished Aunt Rachel could have shared this with her.

Roy had been right about the view, she decided when she climbed out of the coach at its third stop, the Botanical Gardens, and gazed south over Funchal harbour. Beyond the foreground clumps of impudent Bird of Paradise flowers, red-tiled roofs spilled down towards the shimmering aquamarine horizon, as if the entire town was laying itself out for inspection. Reluctantly she joined the other tourists as they trailed behind their guide, a competent young Portuguese girl who seemed to know every plant by name.

Later still, as they relaxed on the *esplanada*, refreshing themselves with the island's ubiquitous passion fruit drink (Amanda!), Bonnie knew that she didn't want to return to the hotel by coach. She wanted time to linger in the gardens, and to make her own way down to Funchal. With some difficulty she persuaded the tour guide to let her stay on and watched, with a feeling of apprehensive rebelliousness, as her fellow travellers departed like so many lemmings. Failure to conform was a novelty for Bonnie.

Having made her decision, she did her best to enjoy its consequences, and after minutely examining the gardens made a tired but contented progress down the steep hill into Funchal. Even modern builders, she noticed, seemed to observe the old

Madeiran tradition of placing carved birds or beasts at each of the four corners of the roof.

The ground levelled out, and Bonnie took a wrong turning. She knew from the narrow streets and dark doorways that she must have wandered into the Old Town, and spent an anxious quarter of an hour before emerging at a landmark she recognized, a flower-edged ravine where the Ribeira de João Gomes flowed through the heart of Funchal.

Bonnie crossed over a busy traffic-laden bridge, then followed the river towards the sea, her footsteps now slowing. A muscle had begun to tug insistently at the back of her right calf; she realized now that her plan of returning to the hotel on foot was over-ambitious. The Palacio was situated along the coast to the west of the town, well over two miles away, and the heat had left her enervated. She would cheat and catch the hotel's courtesy bus which stopped regularly behind the harbour.

As she drew alongside a row of moored yachts and cruisers – property of the 'rich bastards of the world' according to Roy's elegant description – she spotted Roy himself at an open-air café by the harbour's edge. Seated at an adjacent table was one of the most handsome men she had ever seen. He wore an open-necked white shirt and beige slacks, and the sweep of blond hair above his tanned forehead gleamed like nine-carat gold. Even as Roy appeared to speak to him, he rose smoothly to his feet, glanced at his watch, made a brief reply and strolled away.

Bonnie felt an absurd urge to follow him, but her short lifetime had not equipped her to importune with ease. She had no small-talk, no saucy wit . . . just a strong sense of the rights of other people to peace and space. Sadly she watched as he disappeared round a corner. Some rangy blonde girlfriend would doubtless be waiting at the wheel of a scarlet cabriolet . . .

'Hi, Bonnie,' called Roy. 'Come and have a drink with me.'

She angled towards his table. 'Thank you, but I mustn't stop. The courtesy bus leaves in ten minutes.'

'There'll be another one along. Stay and have a chat. I love hearing news from England.'

Bonnie was tired, and longing for a cool shower, but she felt an obscure sense of obligation. 'I *will* chat, I promise,' she said earnestly, 'but today I have to get back. Perhaps another time?'

'I'll hold you to that,' he smiled, and raised his glass to her.

She returned the smile, her own a little uncertain, and left him with his lager. Crossing the palm-fringed Avenida das Comunidades Madeirenses she needed all her concentration for the traffic, but once aboard the cool, air-conditioned hotel coach she allowed her thoughts to drift. The image of a man's face slowly took shape behind her closed eyelids, and now her mouth began to curve with genuine warmth.

For it was not Roy's swarthy features which she had conjured up: it was the face of the blond stranger.

2

'We're going up to Monte today,' announced Russell the next morning at the pool.

Bonnie lowered her book, momentarily confused. The heroine in *Rebecca* – whose name the author had tantalizingly withheld – was at that very moment ascending the switchback hills above Monte Carlo in a car with the brooding Maxim de Winter . . . 'Monte?' she repeated stupidly.

'You know, the village where they do the toboggan rides – up in the hills behind Funchal.'

'You sit in a wicker toboggan,' put in Amanda, 'and they pull you down a cobbled street with ropes. We thought it would be fun . . . anyway, it's famous, so we've got to go. Come along with us,' she added generously.

'Thank you, but I was planning to go to Funchal this morning,' Bonnie replied. 'I thought I'd look at the market, and buy one or two of my presents.'

As they left her with a cheery wave, Bonnie reflected guiltily that she had given a less than accurate impression of the amount of shopping she needed to do. There were no work colleagues to buy for: she had just been made redundant from her clerical job. Her old schoolfriends had moved away, and Aunt Rachel was dead. There was only Mrs Billington to consider, the neighbour who was keeping an eye on the flat while Bonnie was away. She would appreciate a little gift of embroidery or tapestry.

Turning back to her book, Bonnie prepared to concentrate once more on the heroine's developing relationship with Maxim de Winter, but a shadow fell across the page.

'Good morning, Bonnie.' It was Roy, in his white pool attendant's uniform.

'Hello,' she said.

'Don't worry – I haven't come for the chat you promised: I'm on duty. But I couldn't help hearing you mention shopping, and I wondered if you knew about the Casa do Turista in Funchal. All the local crafts from Madeira and Portugal are laid out on display, a bit like a department store, and you can browse quietly without some of the hassle you get in the smaller shops.'

'Oh – thank you, Roy. I'll bear that in mind. Where is the Casa?'

'You've probably walked past it – it's quite close to the courtesy bus stop. Here . . .' He picked up the parasol receipt issued by his colleague, and rapidly sketched a small street map. 'You going this morning?'

'I thought I would.'

'Well, enjoy yourself. Excuse me: duty calls . . . Would you like a parasol, madam . . .?' He wandered away.

The cool, carpeted rooms of the Casa do Turista were just as Roy had described. This was a more civilized way to shop, reflected Bonnie. She had first tried to give her custom to one of the smaller establishments overlooking the water, but even as she peered into the window the proprietor had leapt out into the street to assail her with a high-pressure sales spiel in nasal, heavily accented English. Had she a credit card? Did she want an embroidered table-cloth (hugely expensive)? He had even seized her wrist.

Here, there was no such coercion, but the beautiful items on display fell outside her stringent budget. Abandoning the embroidery with regret, she moved on to a display of Portuguese ceramics. Two French girls stood in the prime position, whispering excitedly, and beyond them there was a tall man. As the girls withdrew with their choices, Bonnie edged into their place.

With a *frisson* of surprise, she recognized the man, even as he turned his head towards her. He looked at her, half smiled, began to study the ceramics, then looked at her again. 'Excuse me,' he said quietly, 'have we met? I feel I know you from somewhere.'

'I – I saw you at a harbour café yesterday,' she stammered.

'That's right. That'll be it.'

'You were talking to Roy.'

'I'm sorry?'

'Roy. Our pool attendant from the hotel. He was at the next table.'

'Oh – the fellow who asked me the time. Said he'd got water in his watch.' He grinned, a meltingly attractive smile. 'So,' he went on, 'we haven't been introduced. My name's Jeremy Tait.'

'I'm Bonnie Sheldon,' she murmured, awash with muffled feelings of embarrassment. She would never be cynical about serendipity again. She had spent half the night fantasizing about this man, and now here he was, conversing with her. Her treacherous brain, though, had emptied itself of all intelligent social gambits.

'Is this your first trip to Madeira?' If Jeremy was aware of her turmoil, he didn't show it.

'Yes.' My first trip abroad, she almost added, but held her tongue.

'It's my third. I'm mixing business with pleasure, with as much emphasis as possible on the latter.' He smiled again, and they fell to examining the hand-painted jugs and dishes in front of them. She tried to focus on Mrs Billington, but it was difficult with Jeremy so close. Carefully she inverted a small blue and cream bowl in order to read the price label. The price was just within her range, but would Mrs Billington like the bowl? Her flat was cluttered with knick-knacks from all corners of Great Britain, many of the 'Greetings from . . .' variety, but perhaps she had no space for anything else. Bonnie vacillated, her brow wrinkled in concentration.

Jeremy had moved away, but now he half turned and said casually, 'I usually end up buying wine for my friends: it always goes down well, and it's completely typical of Madeira.' He lowered his voice. 'The best quality is in the lodges, of course, but they've got some decently packaged bottles downstairs here – miniatures and the like.'

'It's a good suggestion,' she said. 'Thank you.' She moved to follow his advice, but he remained on the upper floor, and she realized with rueful regret that her bright interlude was over. Well, he had spoken to her. People often didn't. She was one of those pale individuals with no notable features whom it was easy to ignore.

She bought a set of quarter-sized bottles of Madeira wine packed in a wicker basket, and knew that Mrs Billington, who loved sweet sherry, would be delighted. As she approached the cash desk, her attention was caught by a shelf of brightly painted cockerels – O Galo de Barcelos, according to the printed legend. Barcelona? she wondered. No, that was in Spain. This seemed to represent a national symbol of Portugal. She was drawn to the models – like the Bird of Paradise plant they were perky, impudent-looking creatures, the very antithesis of herself. After some deliberation she selected a three-inch high bird as her own souvenir.

Outside once more in the street, she stood in the shade of the building and checked her purchases. Her next destination was the fruit and fish market, and after that, perhaps she would visit the cathedral . . .

A clutch of American tourists issued from the doorway behind her, then she heard a now familiar voice:

'Hello again. Did you buy your presents?'

Her heart began an erratic tattoo. This was ridiculous; she didn't know the man at all. 'Yes. And I bought a cockerel, but I'm not quite sure what it means.'

'Ah. They've got a story about a group of dinner guests in Barcelos. During the meal it was discovered that a pouch of gold pieces had been stolen from their rich host, and one particular guest was accused. He swore he was innocent, but no one believed him. On the verge of being carted off to prison, he shouted that if he was innocent, the cockerel on the platter in front of them would crow. It did, and he was released.'

'Where is Barcelos?'

'It's a small town in northern Portugal, near the coast . . . I say, Bonnie, are you in a hurry? Shall we have a cup of coffee? I know a quiet café not far from here where they have excellent honey cakes.'

'I – yes, that would be very nice.'

As she sat in the cool recess of the café, Bonnie could not believe her luck. Covertly she studied Jeremy's features as she savoured the sweet, spicy cake he had bought. He was perhaps thirty and blue-eyed, with unusual light gilt-blond hair. His easy manner and aura of command would have given away his social position even without the characteristic Home Counties diction. She knew the gulf between them was wide.

'Where are you staying?' he asked her.

'The Palacio – it's a modern hotel out in the banana groves to the west of Funchal. Between here and Câmara de Lobos.'

'I know it.' He nodded approbation. 'Good place – excellent facilities. I think you're wise to be away from the town centre. The Savoy may be elegant, but there's building going on nearby and time-share touts seem to have made that area their patch. They remain aloof from it all at Reid's, of course.'

Bonnie knew of this famous hotel whose guest list from the past read like *Who's Who*: Bernard Shaw, Lloyd George, King Edward the Eighth while Prince of Wales, Churchill . . . She had heard that dressing for dinner was still *de rigueur*, and the beds were made up with pure Irish linen, and tea with Madeira cake was served on a marble terrace at four o'clock precisely . . .

'I couldn't quite afford Reid's,' she joked with a tiny smile.

'Snap,' he laughed. 'Not many people can. That's how they maintain their standards – keeping out the riff-raff. Still, the Palace gets my vote. It's friendly, but formal enough to deter yobs.'

'I like the bathrobes they leave in the rooms,' confided Bonnie shyly. 'White terry robes with a crest on. They actually encourage us to wear them to and from the pool: there's a special lift which avoids the foyer.

'And I like the gardens, too. They're subtropical, all palms and wild flowers, and when you sit in the white wicker chairs and open your book, it feels somehow – colonial . . .' She suddenly realized that he was looking at her appraisingly, a small crimp of amusement flexing his firm lips. 'In the front garden there are lizards,' she rushed on. 'Hundreds of them. Sometimes they're still, like plasticine models, and other times – they dart: brown, green, or iridescent turquoise, so fast they can startle you. I love to watch them basking in the sunshine, but I don't like it when they run.'

'Too much like other creepy-crawlies?'

'Yes. I – I'm not very fond of spiders, and the sudden movement reminds me . . . Actually, that's an understatement. I loathe spiders.'

'Ah. Then in that case I won't tell you what I came across in Crete the other week. Let me just suggest that you don't sit on any stone walls, and you'll live long and die happy.'

Bonnie sipped her coffee, and ventured a personal comment. 'You sound well travelled,' she said.

'It's my job,' he answered. 'I'm a travel writer, and Jewel Ventures have commissioned me to write a series of booklets for their clients. Not the usual lore – hire-car information, craft centres and eating out – but historical perspectives on the culture, and geographical features of interest, and suggestions for places away from the tourist trail.'

'What a lovely way of earning a living!'

'It's more tiring than you might think. There isn't much time to gather all the facts, and you can't afford to breeze around in mental neutral. As for earning a living – it doesn't pay well, but I can't complain, because most forms of writing provide a notoriously meagre and erratic source of income.'

'Have you always wanted to be a writer?'

'I always wanted to travel. My parents aren't thrilled – they think my lifestyle is hopelessly Bohemian. They hoped I'd pursue some safe career like banking, or the law. Still, *chacun à son goût* . . .' He drained his coffee cup and consulted his watch.

'I'm sorry, Bonnie, but I'll have to get a move on. I've got an appointment with a fisherman soon. This has been very nice, though.'

Take me with you, she begged him silently. But naturally he was assuming she had plans, friends waiting . . . 'Yes,' she said. 'Thank you very much for the coffee and cake.'

'My pleasure.' They left the dim, aromatic interior of the café and stood amid the bustle of the street as the late morning sun poured down. 'Well, enjoy your holiday,' he said, proffering his hand. 'You've come to the right place.'

His clasp drove all the strength from her body. 'Good luck with your booklets,' she managed to say, then they both turned in the same direction, and laughed.

'I'm parked up this way.' He grinned. 'I thought you were heading back to the harbour.'

'No . . . I promised myself I'd investigate the fruit and fish market.'

'Oh yes. Not to be missed . . .' Together they ambled to the street corner, then stood in awkward limbo. 'Bonnie,' he began, 'I imagine you've got plans for the rest of the week, but if they're at all flexible, and you fancy seeing something of the island from a car, I'd be pleased to show you around. I'm giving myself tomorrow off. Your mother and father could come too, if they wanted, or your friend, or whoever you're with . . .'

She swallowed. 'I'm here on my own,' she croaked.

His mouth broke into another grin, this one wider and warmer than before. 'And you're not all booked up with coach trips?'

'No.'

'Then what do you think? Shall we explore?'

Bonnie could scarcely find the words to accept.

'You should have come to Monte!' exclaimed Amanda, bounding up to Bonnie as she studied the dinner menu on display outside the hotel restaurant.

'Yes, it was pretty exciting.' Russell brought up the rear with more gravity.

'We sat in this wicker sledge, and two men in hats like straw boaters ran alongside it, controlling it with ropes, and it *rumbled* down this *steep* cobbled road, ever so fast! I was terrified!'

Russell nodded. 'She squeaked,' he said, 'like one of those parrots up near the Botanical Gardens.'

Amanda ignored him. 'Did you go to Funchal, Bonnie?'

'Yes. I bought a present and mooched around.'

'From the look on your face you must have met a handsome stranger.' She giggled to devalue her words, and Russell confided: 'She's fixated with handsome strangers. Having netted one herself, she wants everyone to have their share. Proper little altruist, is Amanda.' He pinched his wife's bottom, and they cooed at each other.

Dave, the hearty teacher, wore a look of pained resignation as he joined the queue behind the newly-weds, but Bonnie found that this time she didn't mind. In fact, she felt replete with benignity.

The red cabriolet swung round the curve of the drive and ground to a halt outside the Palacio's foyer. Bonnie gaped for a moment, then ran to climb inside, aware that everyone waiting for the courtesy bus was watching her.

Jeremy laughed as he sped away westwards, negotiating the twisting road with skill and verve. 'Why did you look so stunned?' he asked her. 'Was it the car?'

'Yes.' It was exactly the kind of car she had envisaged him driving.

'I like the sun on my neck,' he said, misunderstanding, 'but perhaps you would have preferred a sedate little saloon?'

'No; this is lovely.'

He slowed down as they came to a truck obstructing the bend. 'Now, where would you like me to take you?'

'Anywhere you recommend.'

Carefully he overtook the large vehicle. 'We're coming into Câmara de Lobos now: the fishing village where Churchill used to paint. If you want to stop, we can, but otherwise I'll drive through and up into the hills.'

'Carry on,' she said, wanting to put fast, wind-rushing miles between themselves and the hotel. It was just like *Rebecca*, she thought – only this was real. She hung on to the seat belt as the car broke free of the narrow constraints of the village and roared up a steep switchback route which swung now inland, now back towards the coast, gaining height all the while.

'It's useless measuring distances on a map as the crow flies,' said Jeremy. 'You have to multiply by at least four. Madeira doesn't give up its secrets easily.' He indicated the narrow terraces rearing above, cut like steps in the hillside. Here, farmers eked out a precarious living growing grapes, bananas, vegetables or flowers. Not one square foot of land was wasted: every ravine and precipice was lipped by cultivation.

'At least they don't have to bring cattle inside in bad weather,' commented Bonnie.

'No, they let them out when the weather's good.'

She glanced at him uncertainly, wondering if she was being teased.

'Truly,' he said. 'See that hut?' He pointed up the slope to a shack perched at the edge of a terrace strip. 'There'll be a cow in there. The farmers have to lock them in so they don't have a nasty accident . . .'

'You're pulling my leg.'

'No, that's God's truth. The island has a perfectly good dairy industry, and some sheep farming as well.'

Bonnie relaxed as the scenery became starker, less arable. They seemed to be climbing moorland not unlike the Pennines she remembered from her youth. And yes – there was a sheep in the scrubby bracken, regarding the red car with curiosity. Eventually they parked by the side of the road. In a nearby gully, water flowed purposefully along a man-made concrete channel. 'That's a levada,' Jeremy informed her. 'Let's go and take a look.'

They alighted from the car, and Bonnie bounced across the springy turf, inhaling the pure mountain air with delight. 'Dave is always going on about levadas,' she said. 'I wanted to see one.'

'Who is Dave?'

'Another English guest at the Palacio.' She gave a reminiscent grimace. 'He's an Outward Bound type – a science and PE teacher at a boys' school. Every day so far he's set out with a rucksack to tackle a different levada walk.'

'Well, there are plenty to choose from. You probably know the principle: the mountain chain catches the clouds, and it rains like billy-ho, especially in the north. This water all seeps through the porous upper layer, which was volcanic ash, then meets basalt below and wells out again in the form of springs. In the old days it used simply to pour down ravines into the sea and be wasted, but over the years settlers have built up a network of man-made channels to irrigate their farms, most of which are on the south side. More recently still, the Portuguese government began an intensive programme to rationalize water distribution, conveniently tying it in with hydroelectric power.'

Bonnie crouched down and dabbled her fingers in the water. 'I was thinking,' she said, 'that this area reminds me of my old home. I didn't expect to come across moorland here.'

Jeremy sat down on a tussock nearby. 'Where did you live?' he asked.

'Rochdale,' she said. 'A Lancashire mill town . . . My parents used to take me out on Sundays for picnics in the Penines. We'd go to Rishworth Moor, or sometimes out to Saddleworth, and pick whinberries if it was September – bilberries, that is.'

'Or blueberries if you're a Yank . . . Why did it have to stop? Did you move out of the area?'

Long-buried pain stirred deep inside her chest. 'Yes. My parents died when I was thirteen. They were killed in an air crash. I had to go and live with my Aunt Rachel in Dartford . . .' Rough south London accents; new classmates laughing at her own modes of speech . . .

'I'm sorry, Bonnie. I didn't realize.'

'These things happen. It was nobody's fault. A bird strike, they said.' And nine years on, she knew that the unanswered question 'Why me?' would sound self-indulgent.

'Was your aunt too frail to come to Madeira?'

'I'm afraid she died as well. Just a few weeks ago.'

'Oh, heavens . . . I'd better shut up. I'm truly sorry. I didn't mean to upset you.'

'You weren't to know, and I can't go on pretending it hasn't happened. In a way, it's a relief to talk about it.'

'Have you any brothers or sisters?'

'No.'

'Any relatives at all?'

'No.'

'But your friends are helping out?'

'Mm.' Bonnie looked down at the water again. She couldn't mention the loss of her job – not yet. It would seem too much like a ploy for sympathy. The problem of her imminent homelessness was hers, not his. And yet she could sense his interest; he was watching her again, his head cocked slightly to one side.

'Enough about the difficulties I've left behind,' she said, flicking a diamond-drop spray of water from her fingers into the air. 'I'm on holiday, and you're showing me the mysteries of Madeira.' She scrambled to her feet. 'What's your opinion of Monte? Should we go there?'

He levered himself up from the grass and brushed out his trousers. 'It's a village full of steep slopes in the hills above Funchal. Unusual in its way. The church celebrates some legend of a shepherdess seeing the Virgin Mary. Let's see: there's a formal garden where the paths are made up entirely of steps – your legs will insist there are thousands, although there probably aren't. And then of course there's the basket-case run.'

Bonnie giggled, an overswing of the emotional pendulum.

'That's when the tourists leap into glorified laundry baskets without seat belts,' he went on. 'They let two muscular young men jolt them down a cobbled road at high speed, then they spend the rest of the day congratulating themselves because they didn't fall out!'

'Two people from my hotel did that yesterday,' said Bonnie.

'What – fell out?'

'No. Went down the run.' Russell and Amanda: basket-cases

. . . even though she hadn't explained to Jeremy, she felt as if they now had their own private joke.

'Monte will be pretty touristy at this time of year. If you'd like to go, though, we can.'

'No, I just wanted to hear your opinion.' She chuckled again, slowly regaining her equilibrium. 'Where do you suggest?'

'Have you been to Curral das Freiras?'

'No. What's that?'

'It's a village in a very steep valley. The name translates as "Corral of the Nuns" because in the sixteenth century nuns from the convent in Funchal escaped from marauding French pirates and hid in the valley. There was only a narrow mountain path in those days; it must have been a formidable journey – it's hair-raising even today when you can get there by car. I can take you to a vantage point overlooking the valley, if you don't mind a bit of a walk . . . let me see your feet.'

Bonnie ruefully displayed her flat-heeled sandals, chosen for today's outing in preference to plimsolls because they looked more attractive. 'I've got some socks in my bag,' she insisted with the urgency of a small child who feared the withholding of a treat.

'Fair enough.' They returned to the car. 'I'll just show you Paúl da Serra while we're up here.' Jeremy drove past the thinning moorland to a barren-looking plain. 'We're about four thousand feet above sea-level,' he told her. 'Feels funny, doesn't it – you expect mountain peaks. But there's an abrupt drop to the east. You'll see it from the other side when we reach Curral das Freiras . . .'

Eventually he regained the south coast road. They stopped at a neat white-painted inn on the outskirts of Funchal and ate a plain meal of chicken, then Jeremy gunned the engine of the red cabriolet once more and they hurtled into a long steep gorge. 'Hang on to your hair!' he warned, and Bonnie soon appreciated the caution: this road was more alarming than any they had so far encountered. The car lurched from one seventy-degree bend to another, and she realized with excited horror that she would spend much of the return journey hanging above the precipitous drop to the river below. 'Eucalyptus trees!' shouted Jeremy, pointing casually towards the valley floor. Bonnie nodded, but only glanced towards these majestic specimens of the island's flora. Thank God she had taken a travel-sickness pill in the morning.

At last they parked, and Jeremy led the way to a well-maintained path angling gently up the mountainside. As the gradient increased, Bonnie struggled in her flimsy sandals, but kept quiet. Before long, she was rewarded. The path rose again, swinging out of sight to the left; ahead was a crude wooden barrier, and beyond that – nothing. Terra firma had fallen away in a dizzying drop to an emerald valley basin over two thousand feet below. Tiny red-roofed houses were just discernible on the valley floor, which rose on all sides, slowly transmuting to form a sentinel ring of dark mountain peaks.

Jeremy stood at her elbow. 'The only way into that village is via the ravine,' he said. 'You can imagine why the nuns came here for safety.'

'Can we carry on up the path?' she asked eagerly.

'Yes; there's a proper viewpoint not far away. Very safe, plenty of room . . .'

Once they had attained this grandstand, where intrepids of legion nationalities murmured, exclaimed and clicked their camera shutters, Bonnie was fascinated to see wisps of cloud hanging in the air at eye level.

'Beyond those peaks straight across is Paúl da Serra,' Jeremy informed her.

She nodded, and peered once more at the valley floor. 'Could this once have been a volcanic crater?' she asked. 'It looks so deep and round.'

'A lot of guidebooks tell you it is,' he said, 'but recent thinking attributes the depression to erosion from the headwaters of the Socorrides River. I'll have to reflect this in my booklet. That isn't to say, however, that there haven't been volcanic eruptions nearby, leading to the formation of all these high peaks.'

Bonnie groped in her shoulder bag and pulled out a small camera. 'You don't mind my being touristy for a moment, do you?'

'Go right ahead! I took my pictures last time round.' He stepped smartly out of her field of view, and she took a series of photographs from the cloud-brushed mountain crown to the verdant valley floor. As she straightened her back by the viewpoint's sturdy metal railings, she longed to take a shot of Jeremy himself. Just one – something to remind her of a special day. Yet she couldn't ask him. It would seem somehow banal, trite – even a breach of faith. She hesitated. He had wandered to the far side of the platform where the tourists milled, and was half obscured behind an excited American wielding a camcorder. It would be just possible to catch him unawares, but that wasn't playing the game. If he spotted her, she would never survive the humiliation. With a regretful sigh, Bonnie returned the camera to her bag.

'All done?' he smiled minutes later. 'If we head back to the car now, there'll just be time for me to drive you down to the village itself. The road goes through a tunnel in the hillside . . .'

An hour later, they were once more approaching Funchal, and Bonnie knew her treat would soon be drawing to an end. She said nothing, lest an unguarded word should hasten that end. This day had no terms of reference. She didn't know how Jeremy regarded her – passing acquaintance, new friend, what? His behaviour had been affable, pleasant and entirely correct; only once on an uneven portion of the path had he taken her hand for a few brief seconds. It would be foolish and fatal to nurture unrealistic hopes.

'You're very quiet,' he observed, pulling in to park by a small roadside church. 'Not feeling car-sick, are you?'

'No, just tired.' Drat. The very thing she had least wanted to divulge.

'It's all that fresh mountain air – has a soporific effect on people. I was hoping we might get to Reid's in time for afternoon tea, but I'm afraid it's too late now – nearly six o'clock. I'd better take you back to the Palacio – unless there's anywhere else you'd like to go?'

In a flash Bonnie knew exactly where she wanted to be. On each bright morning of her holiday she had padded out to her hotel balcony, past the low table with its complimentary bottle of wine and bowl of tropical fruits, and stared across the water at the imposing bulk of Cabo Girão. She knew it was possible to stand on the headland itself: the Duponts had been there.

Her request seemed to amuse Jeremy. 'To look at you, one wouldn't imagine you harboured such a penchant for precipices,' he said. 'It must be my fault.'

'Yes; you've given me a taste for them.'

Once again, there was a properly constructed viewing area. It was just as well, thought Bonnie as she leaned with some trepidation over the wall to gaze down at the flat sea, blue-grey now, infinitely distant below. There was a small brown streak, almost an artefact, in the motionless pool: a fishing boat, perhaps, returning to Câmara de Lobos with its catch?

'The sea may look calm,' said Jeremy, 'but it can kick up a fair old storm when it wants. Zarco, the earliest Portuguese explorer, found this headland so formidable that he turned his ship back to Funchal. Cabo Girão actually means "Cape Turning" . . .' He seized her elbow as she freed her camera from the bag. 'Be careful, Bonnie. You looked mesmerized just now. I don't want you falling over the edge.'

'Just one picture. Please.'

'If I can hang on to you.'

She felt his hands at her waist as she took time to focus, reconciling the needs of a cactus just below the wall and the base of the cliff eighteen hundred feel below. The firm grip was gone, however, as soon as she had finished, and as they walked back to the car Bonnie knew the crunch was coming. 'I've enjoyed today immensely,' she said. 'You've been the perfect guide, and I appreciate all your kindness.'

He made a deprecating gesture. 'It's been nice for me to have company, especially someone as polite and receptive as yourself. I'm sorry we can't do this again, but on Saturday I fly to the Azores.'

The sick twist of disappointment was acute, but Bonnie somehow kept her voice steady. 'More work?'

'Yes; I'm trying to cover all the main Portuguese territories.'

'When will you go back to England?'

'In a few weeks' time.'

There was a short silence. To her shame Bonnie realized that she was waiting for him to make some offer of renewed contact, perhaps suggest a letter . . . 'Do you live in the south?' she asked, her voice unnatural now.

'Hertfordshire. I'm renting out my home for the summer, but my fiancée's keeping an eye on things, making sure the tenants don't smash the place up.'

He gave her a perky smile, but the word 'fiancée' still clanged in her ears like a death knell. So the world hadn't changed, after all, she thought. At least, not in the way she had just begun to hope.

3

That night, for the first time, Cabo Girão looked sinister from Bonnie's balcony in the Palacio. Beyond the twinkling lights of Câmara de Lobos the headland jutted black and gaunt against the indigo sky; she could well understand the superstitious fears of Zarco's crew.

Bonnie felt hungry now. The prospect of running into Russell and Amanda in the main restaurant, of being quizzed with probing curiosity about the man in the red car, had proved unendurable, and she had possessed neither the heart nor the energy to make alternative dinner arrangements. Wearily she took a banana from the fruit bowl and turned back into the room. With a packet of salted almonds from the fridge in the corner, she completed her lone supper.

The events of the early evening still played in her head like an endless film loop: Jeremy, kind and casual, driving her back to the hotel, helping her out of the car, commenting with a smile as a prismatic green lizard darted across the drive; Jeremy bestowing a brief kiss on her cheek; herself expressing gratitude, wishing him luck, outwardly serene, dead inside. No talk of addresses, or keeping in touch.

The sick weight of disappointment was still with her, and she felt angry with herself for such puerility. He had promised nothing, yet delivered plenty: spent his precious leisure day with a compatriot of lesser means, shared his evident enthusiasm for the island. And how had she reacted? Like a lovelorn adolescent she had wildly extrapolated from his benevolent gesture, even while pretending to herself that her view was pragmatic. You ninny, she thought. The higher you allow your expectations to climb, the further they have to fall.

Through the open balcony door came a bubbling giggle, easily recognizable as Amanda's. Bonnie clenched her teeth, her new-found tolerance dangerously fractured. How old was Amanda? Scarcely eighteen, like her husband. Young, but full of optimism and confidence in the future. Enjoying the holiday of her life fresh from an opulent white wedding glutted with supportive family well-wishers. A sizeable deposit on a neat new semi paid for by those same well-wishers.

Bonnie swallowed as self-pity threatened. Envying others would do nothing to improve her own situation, she knew. Her facts of life were starkly simple: no relatives, no job, no money, and very soon, no home. With a glimmer of insight she wondered if the real reason for the chagrin of the day was not the thwarting of a scarce-begun romance, but the cruel underlining of her own isolation. She had come to Madeira to bury her head in the sand, and instead had found only volcanic cliffs.

'Where've you been hiding?' demanded Amanda at breakfast two days later.

'What do you mean?' asked Bonnie, laying down her spoon.

'We haven't seen you for ages. Not since that handsome blond man spirited you away in his car.' Her eyes sparkled, and she raised the brows suggestively.

'Oh, that. I just went out to look at the countryside with a travel writer I met in Funchal. But he's leaving today.'

'We told Roy, to make him jealous,' said Russell. 'He's been asking about you.'

Bonnie gave a vague smile, and rose to take a bread roll from the vast buffet table nearby. Even after a week at the hotel, and despite the lingering ache of unhappiness, she never ceased to be amazed at the breadth and variety of the spread laid out for the breakfast guests. Myriad types of cereal consorted with bowls heaped with exotic fruits and baskets of bread; ham and cheeses were avidly consumed by the German visitors, while the hot sausages, eggs and bacon served separately were universally popular.

There was also a great vat of ice containing opened bottles of champagne. Those who availed themselves of this facility were usually content to mix a Buck's Fizz, but Russell and Amanda invariably drank the champagne neat. (No wonder Amanda was constantly giggling . . .) Bonnie avoided the area entirely: she had nothing to celebrate.

As the newly-weds settled at an adjacent table, Bonnie spotted Tristão, Amanda's sloe-eyed beau, swinging his narrow hips between the tables as he made his way towards them. He carried a glass of champagne, which he balanced delicately in his left hand.

'*Bom dia*, Tristão,' called Amanda, batting her eyelashes.

'Good morning, Amanda,' he said.

'*Queria café, por favor*,' she articulated carefully, before dissolving into ripples of mirth.

'Just one minute, please . . . Excuse me . . .' He turned sharply to Bonnie and lowered his voice. 'I am instructed to bring you this.' He placed the champagne in front of her.

'Me?'

'Yes.' His face assumed a knowing look. 'You have an admirer.'

For a moment, her heart leapt.

Tristão bent lower, confidentially. 'It is Roy,' he told her. 'I execute his commission.'

'Oh . . .' Roy. Of course. How could it have been anyone else? '*Obrigada*,' she murmured dully.

The waiter nodded, and moved away to smile brilliantly at Amanda, and promise her coffee. Russell leaned towards Bonnie as soon as he had left. 'Amanda's seething with jealousy really,' he said. 'Is Tristão another of your conquests?'

Bonnie was saved the effort of replying by Dave, who strode

up to her table with a determined tread and a plateful of cholesterol-laden sustenance. 'Mind if I sit down?' he asked, pulling out the chair opposite.

'No,' she lied.

He thumped first the plate, then both his elbows, on the table, and regarded her steadily. 'I'm going into the Interior again today,' he said, making it sound like an expedition to rival one of Livingstone's. 'The Levada do Caldierao Verde: takes its source from the Ribeira Grande. There's a waterfall, and a forest route . . . I wondered if you'd like to come along?'

Bonnie was startled; hearty people usually disdained her fragile appearance.

'I heard you walked down from the Botanical Gardens the other day,' he went on, as if in explanation.

'I did, but it was all on proper roads. I don't have the gear for serious country walking.'

'I could take your stuff in my rucksack.'

'I'm afraid it's the footwear; mine just isn't suitable. Thank you for asking, though. I hope you have a successful day.'

Amanda swivelled round. 'We're going to have a lazy day by the pool,' she said. 'Shall we see you there?'

Bonnie sipped her tea and thought rapidly. They meant well, she knew, but their brand of high spirits was not what she needed just at present. There was also the question of Roy . . .

'Perhaps later,' she said.

In the broiling afternoon sun, Bonnie set out from Cãmara de Lobos along the winding road back to the hotel. She felt restless and dissatisfied; the local excursion she had designed to be calming and low-key had been peppered throughout by minor irritations. In Jeremy's red cabriolet the fishing village had been reached in a matter of minutes; on foot, however, there had seemed to be headland after headland between the hotel and her goal, each with its own hairpin bend.

The chocolate-box charm of the village itself had also undergone a subtle transformation. The cheerful sprawl of russet-roofed houses that Churchill had painted forty years before could now be perceived as a collection of hovels, their dim interiors rank with poverty. Groups of beggar children prowled the narrow streets. While tourism was the way forward for many Madeirans, those who laboured in traditional industries had yet to find their lives enhanced.

Bonnie paused, leaning against the wall overlooking a banana grove while she removed her left plimsoll. Something was burning the back of her heel. She peeled away the sock, and twisted her leg round to look. Drat! A livid blister the size of a five-pence coin was forming.

She replaced the shoe and limped onwards, grateful that at least she was not struggling to keep up with Dave on some treacherous levada path in the north of the island. A lorry thundered past, spewing out thick fumes, and a slow stream of cars followed before the road became quiet again. As Bonnie paused for her next break, she heard another vehicle approaching, changing gear for the bend. She turned towards the sea, and out of the tail of her eye saw a small white van swing round the corner.

It stopped a few yards beyond her. 'Bonnie!' someone yelled. The voice sounded familiar, but she hesitated.

'Jump in!' A dark tousled head appeared from the passenger window, and beckoned her urgently.

It was Roy. Still she paused, ambivalent, then realized he could not remain parked on the bend for more than a few seconds. She hurried forward, and the scalding pain in her heel gave a boost to her decision.

'Well done,' he said, pulling away just as a tourist coach snarled towards them. 'You looked as if you could do with a lift.'

'That's true,' she admitted ruefully. 'I've blistered my heel.' She gave a cautious sniff. 'Have you got fish on board?'

He laughed. 'Yes. I've been on a mercy mission for the Palacio kitchens. There was a glitch in their usual supply chain today, so I've picked some up directly from the village. You must see them when we unload – they're ferocious-looking things.'

Within minutes he had parked the van near the concealed kitchen entrance to the Palacio. He opened the door and called

'Leandro!' whereupon a burly aproned Portuguese emerged. On seeing Bonnie, the man gave a little bow, then winked at Roy. 'Your girl, eh?'

'Sim,' grinned Roy, and Bonnie stiffened.

'I heard you,' she hissed as he unlocked the back of the van. 'How dare you say yes.'

'It keeps him happy,' said Roy. 'Now – get an eyeful of these!' He slid out a box packed with ice. Curled in the bottom were four long eel-like fish, jet-black, with staring eyes, gaping jaws and vicious, needle-pointed teeth. 'Espadas,' he said.

Bonnie stared in horrified fascination. 'I saw some of these at the fish market. I didn't realize . . . Roy, I *ate* espada last night!'

'And the flesh was white and succulent – right?'

'Yes. It was delicious. But – ugh! Ignorance is definitely bliss.'

'Hold on a tick while we get these inside, then I want to ask you something.' Rapidly he unloaded the boxes, then Leandro waved a friendly, dismissive arm. 'Leave the van,' he said. 'Tristão can put it away.'

'Obrigado,' murmured Roy, and walked with Bonnie towards the corner of the building.

'I know I promised to talk about England,' she said hastily. 'I shall, really.'

'Good. But that's not what I wanted to say.' He turned to her, his rugged face earnest. 'There's a night-club I know in Funchal . . . good music, not too loud or brash, friendly people. May I take you there tonight?'

In the distance, there was a splash from the pool. Closer to where they stood, one of the waiters from the alfresco bar was laughing with a holiday-maker. Bonnie had already found that the evenings were the worst: everyone seemed to be in couples with something exciting to do. She had even seen through a glass door the German dowager and her companion applauding the hotel's magician with enthusiastic abandonment. Yet she, in her depression, had felt unable to join them.

'I'm not very good at dancing,' she said, 'but yes, I'll come.'

*

Six days later, Bonnie left the hotel's Cristovão Colombo restaurant with a brief wave at Russell and Amanda, and took the lift upstairs to her room. It had been a curious week of peaceful days alone while Roy was on duty, and nights of dancing and fun. She had discovered quite quickly that Roy's background was rough and ready, and his intellectual powers limited, but he seemed so eager to please that she found herself making an effort to respond. It was unfair to contrast him with Jeremy, who had clearly enjoyed a youth of academic privilege; she herself had never shone at the hated Dartford comprehensive school. And if Roy occasionally displayed uncouth little mannerisms, to her at least his behaviour had been impeccable; she had never felt sexually threatened. A warm arm and a good-night kiss had been the sum of his attentions in that department.

Tonight was to be her last night on Madeira. Her bag was neaty packed, and only her travel clothes still hung in the wardrobe. Outside the window, Cabo Girão was still visible in the twilight, solid and unmoved as it had been for centuries, and would continue to be for centuries more. Bonnie, though, would soon have to face all the unpleasant realities she had been avoiding . . .

She slipped a beige cardigan on over her pale yellow cotton dress, picked up her shoulder bag and left the room. She was to meet Roy as usual just along the road from the hotel, so he could avoid any charges of fraternizing with the guests, and she could avoid Russell and Amanda. Presumably they would go to Funchal again, to a small bar or club.

'Hop in,' shouted Roy minutes later, drawing level in his small hired Ford. As she settled beside him, he asked,'Are you game for a bit of a drive?'

'Er, yes,' she answered. 'But the plane leaves early tomorrow.'

'Don't worry, I'll get you back in time. You remember on Tuesday we were discussing the fact that there are no sandy beaches on Madeira?'

'Yes. You told me that the islanders go to Porto Santo for their own holidays.'

'That's right. I was holding out on you, though. There *is* a beach on Madeira – just one, at Prainha, near the eastern tip. I thought we'd have a picnic there tonight.'

'But I've just had dinner, Roy!'

'You wait. The night is young . . .' He drove briskly through Funchal and out along the winding road leading to the airport. He carried on past the tourist complexes at the fringe of Machico, through the village itself, then entered a long tunnel. Eventually the little car emerged into the fading light and skirted another village. 'This is Caniçal,' he said. 'There was a thriving whaling industry here once, but since 1981 there's been a moratorium . . . the former whalers now direct all their energies towards marine conservation.'

Soon they were jolting along a rough track. Bonnie felt strange: the lush Madeiran vegetation had fallen behind them, and lurking in the gloom was a bare landscape of soil and rock. Roy parked the car, swung a rucksack over his shoulders and led her to the edge of the cliff. 'I'm afraid there are a lot of steps,' he said, 'but I reckon we'll have the beach to ourselves.'

It was true. When they flopped down exhausted on the tartan rug he had laid out by the shelter of the rocks, the only sound in the vicinity was the gentle lapping of waves. Above them, the tall cliffs formed a semicircle, keeping the rest of the world at bay.

'Have some wine,' invited Roy, reaching a bottle and two clear plastic tumblers from the depths of his rucksack.

'Oh . . . just a small amount, please.'

He filled the tumbler, ignoring her request, and passed it across to her. 'We're going to have a toast,' he said, 'but first you have to guess which wine this is. No prizes for saying Madeiran.'

'I can't see the colour.'

'No: that would have been cheating. Taste it.'

She took a sip, and let the flavour diffuse across her tongue. A trip to the wine lodge had taught her about Madeiran wine, how it was first created by accident, when a wine cargo sent to the East Indies returned unsold over a year later, and was found to have matured most distinctively in the tropical conditions. She knew that modern companies simulated this process artificially, fortifying the wine with brandy and heating it before ageing it in vats for four years or more. The four main types of wine spanned the spectrum from Malmsey, the sweet dessert wine, to the dry Sercial.

This wine wasn't sweet. That excluded Malmsey and Bual. Neither was it very dry. 'Verdelho,' she said cautiously.

'Spot on!' he laughed. 'So you're a little wino, after all. Anyway, to us!' He touched her tumbler with his own, and lay back on one elbow, drinking his own wine with casual relish; Bonnie sat on the edge of the rug tracing patterns in the sand with her finger. 'You're down tonight, Bonnie,' he observed.

'I was just thinking,' she said. 'I'll never again have a holiday like this one.'

'That's defeatist talk. You've got to think big in life, tell yourself you're good enough for a slice of the cake. Why should the rich bastards have it all their own way?'

Absently she sipped at the wine. Slogans were easy, she thought, but materially improving her lot would take hard work and luck. But Roy was only trying to cheer her up. He knew something of her situation from their conversations during the week – more than she knew about him, in fact.

She felt his hand on her hip. 'Don't suppose you fancy a swim?' he asked.

'I haven't got my costume,' she said, 'or a towel.'

'There's a towel in here. The other doesn't matter.'

She hugged her upper arms as the cool, salty air began to bite. 'I'm sorry, I'd rather not. You go ahead, though.'

'Not without you,' he answered, running the hand down her thigh.

Nervous now, she gulped at the wine. 'Are you working at the Palacio for the whole season?' she asked him.

'My permit expires soon,' he answered. 'I've been here since last winter. I don't know where I'll be next – probably back in England for a while. Perhaps there are some better jobs going now.'

She was aware that he had a chequered history of manual labour, but at least he wasn't a scrounger. 'All work has dignity,' Aunt Rachel had been fond of repeating, and Bonnie agreed with the sentiment. To her relief, Roy was no longer caressing her leg, but was now delving once more in his rucksack. He brought out a white paper package and began to undo the wrappings.

'The rest of our picnic,' he explained. 'I've got bread rolls here, and ham, and cheese. Oh, and a couple of apples. Can I tempt you?'

To her surprise, Bonnie found that she had developed an appetite for food again. She accepted a roll and some ham, knowing it was wise to eat in any case: she had just drunk far more wine than she was accustomed to. Slowly she relaxed as they chatted about Madeira and the places they liked best; she sipped some more Verdelho; he refilled her glass.

The next time she shivered, he slid his arm round her shoulders and she didn't edge away. She felt dizzy and languid, light of spirit, careless of consequence. He made a small joke, and his Lancashire accent was curiously comforting. He leaned to kiss her; tonight his kiss was different. Her mouth felt the fire of fusion, and her own arms pulled him closer.

Only when he tugged at her clothing did the tiny deadened voice of her inbuilt code protest, and by then it was ineffectual, too late. 'I won't hurt you, Bonnie,' he gasped, but he did. Soon the night heat turned cold. In disordered dreams she saw the great whales of Caniçal floundering in their death throes as the harpoons tore out their innards.

Somewhere in the distance there were voices. Bonnie opened her eyes, feeling confused and very sick. Her cheek was pressed to the rug, her limbs were stiff; there was a strange ache deep in her pelvis.

Above, the sky was luminous, cornflower streaked with silver. Alarmed, she sat bolt upright, suppressing a groan as an invisible cleaver crashed into the top of her head. The sea lapped close to their rug; out in the bay was a rowing-boat with three swarthy fishermen, who were talking loudly to each other, sometimes shouting. As she rose, one of them caught sight of her and yelled a few words of Portuguese.

Desperately she turned to Roy, who was lying on his back nearby, yawning and stretching. 'What is he saying?'

He sat up, running a hand through his tousled hair, whereupon the fisherman and his companions became more voluble than ever, laughing and pointing. 'You don't want to know,' he muttered.

But she could guess. Suddenly, all animation left her, and she felt her face grow taut as if turning to stone. She, Bonnie Sheldon, despite all the strictures of her upbringing, had followed the well-worn path of every other stupid girl caught up in a holiday 'romance'. Too much to drink, seduction – this term for those who preferred not to acknowledge the extent of their own participation – then the sour self-loathing which came with the dawn.

As if through a thick glass she saw Roy smile and wave at the men, heard the faint splash of their oars as they pulled out to sea. She felt drained of everything except desolation. She was twenty-two, small, pale and not particularly good-looking. The only thing of value she had possessed had just been squandered, and now could never be proudly offered to the husband she hoped one day to have. Worst of all, she had no one to blame but herself.

Beside her, Roy was packing away the bottle and cups. 'It's ten to six,' he said. 'Plenty of time to get you back.'

'Yes,' she replied, her voice flat.

'You can tell your friends Madeira does have a beach after all.'

'Yes.'

The dead tone roused him, and he crawled forward to peer into her face. 'Bonnie, what's wrong?'

She turned her face away. 'You must think me such a fool,' she said. 'Such an easy . . .' She swallowed, unable to articulate the unpleasant colloquialism 'lay'. '. . . conquest,' she finished up.

'Conquest? What do you mean?' Now he took her chin and gently tilted her face towards him. Above the shadowed stubble of his jaw his brown eyes were searching, intent.

'Don't worry,' she said. 'Just take me back to the hotel, and that'll be the end of it. I won't make a fuss, or send embarrassing letters.'

'What . . .' He looked puzzled, almost angry. 'The *end* of it? Are you serious? Sod it, Bonnie, I want to *marry* you!'

4

'Well, I never said it was the Ritz!'

Roy's tone was defensive as they stood outside 14 Clegg Street, a shabby house in a late Victorian terrace whose faded wall plaque, 'Mafeking Villas', echoed long-gone Empire glories.

Bonnie hastened to reassure him. 'It's fine,' she said, twisting the unfamiliar gold band on her left hand's third finger, 'and it's *ours*!' She stepped back, brushing against the car, in order to assess her new home more fully. The brickwork was etched with a century of industrial grime, and the narrow front garden, enclosed by an equally soot-encrusted wall, was in deep shadow. The tired-looking leaf-green paint on the frame of the bay window was peeling, and one pane was cracked. A thin passageway separated the house from number 16 on the right.

'Yes, it's fine,' she repeated. 'Let's just get our things inside, then I'll make us a cup of tea. Where did you say they left the key?'

Roy gestured towards a lone clay plant-pot by the step, which contained a clump of shrivelled leaves. 'Under there,' he said.

Bonnie knelt, and extricated a small bunch of keys. 'Not the most original of places,' she murmured, thinking of the elaborate security arrangements Aunt Rachel had been forced to employ. She glanced up at Roy, and saw him smirk.

'There isn't much inside to steal,' he said. 'Just a few bits of furniture they wanted to leave. Enough for us to start with. We can buy some more from a junk shop later.' He took the keys from her and unlocked the door, which opened with a squeal. 'Touch of WD40'll solve that,' he added.

Bonnie hesitated outside, wondering if he might want to lift her over the threshold, but he strode up the dark hallway, and she knew the thought hadn't even crossed his mind. Faintly dejected, she trailed behind, but her spirits soon rose as she began to appreciate the potential of the house. It was roomy inside, and reasonably clean; minor details such as discoloured plasterwork and faded floral wallpaper could be overcome with a little work and willing. Upstairs there were two bedrooms. Downstairs comprised the front room with the bay, a generous kitchen, and beyond this, built in to the old wash-house extension, a primrose yellow bathroom. The suite was about her own age, Bonnie estimated, which wasn't at all bad.

One door remained unopened in the hall: a stout wooden door under the stairs. 'Do you think that's a cupboard?' asked Bonnie eagerly.

'Cellar, more like.' Roy pointed to a bolt below the handle. 'See, they did care about security after all.' He pulled open the door as Bonnie pondered the necessity for a bolt in the middle of the house; cool, musty air met their nostrils and a flight of uneven stone steps fell away into the gloom. 'This could be useful!' he exclaimed. 'We could store beer or wine down here.' His fingers groped for a light switch on the inner wall, but nothing happened when he pressed it down. Undaunted, he pattered down the steps, careless of their worn, concave tread.

'You coming, Bon?' he called.

Bonnie hung back as the words echoed in the cavern below. 'There might be spiders,' she said. 'I'll stay here. Do be careful – there isn't much light.'

He turned the corner out of sight, and the sound of his feet was now barely audible. 'It's not totally dark,' he shouted, his voice muffled. 'There's a window with a kind of grille high in the back wall: I suppose it leads to the yard.'

Hence the bolt, thought Bonnie.

'Aren't you coming?' He sounded plaintive.

'No, thank you. You can tell me what's down there.'

She heard him sigh, clump around for what seemed like a full five minutes, then make his way back to the surface. As he emerged into the hall, he held one hand behind him.

'You afraid of spiders, Bon?' There was an odd, cunning look on his face.

'Yes – terrified.'

'That's a pity. I've just seen some real whoppers.'

She shuddered. 'Please close the cellar door, Roy. Let's unpack our things.'

He took a step towards her, leaving the door agape. 'You remember when Saddam Hussein spoke of the Mother of all Battles?' he mused. 'Well, guess what I've got here?'

Her heart jolted. 'Don't tease me.'

'I'm not teasing. Only it's not the mother – it's the father. Or perhaps I should say the *grandfather*.'

'*Stop* it, Roy.'

'Don't you believe me?'

She felt sick. 'No.'

'More fool you!' With a conjurer's flourish and an expression of fiendish glee, he wheeled his hidden hand into view and shook it over her head. There, trapped between his fingers by two of its legs, dangled one of the largest spiders Bonnie had ever seen. She let out an ear-splitting shriek and burst into tears.

Roy swore. From the depths of her panic Bonnie caught a fleeting glimpse of dark arachnoid limbs obscenely writhing before he dropped the creature to the floor and stamped on it. Hot salt water coursed down her cheeks. Helplessly she trembled, ears ringing, while Roy looked on in alarm. He made as if to touch her shoulder, but she jerked away fiercely. 'How could you?' she gulped at length. 'How could you do that?'

'Sod it, Bonnie; how did I know? It was only a joke.'

'But I *told* you.'

'You said you were afraid of them, but I didn't think . . .'

No, she thought, you didn't. You don't understand phobias at all, do you? You're too – insensitive.

'I'm sorry,' he mumbled. 'I'll make that cuppa.' Awkwardly he closed the cellar door, carried a cardboard box in from the car, delved among the contents and assembled the components of the electric kettle. Minutes later, Bonnie was sitting at the kitchen table, darting nervous glances into the corners of the room, her hands cupped round a steaming mug of strong tea.

Roy followed the direction of her eyes. 'There won't be spiders up here, love. At least . . . Tell you what, I'll do a sweep. Right now, the whole house. Floor or ceiling, nothing with eight legs will survive.'

'Thanks, Roy.' She felt drained, yet in need of air. 'Would you mind if I go out while you do it? Just for a few minutes, to explore the locality? Then I'll make up the bed when I come back.'

'Good idea. I'll sort out the hot water system so we can have a bath later.' He gave a lopsided smile, and she replied with a little nod; she still hadn't fully forgiven him for his thoughtless cruelty.

Bonnie left the house and stood in Clegg Street, breathing deeply. The afternoon air was still summer-mild. Down the road, children were playing with a white terrier puppy by one of the doorsteps, but the area was generally quiet. She debated which direction to turn: to the right was the way they had driven, a maze of narrow edge-of-town streets with drab corner shops and old pubs with frosted glass windows. To the left, Clegg Street sloped downwards to a T-junction; across the intersecting road she could see a patch of wasteland and the pointing finger of a distant mill chimney before the ground rose again gently to flaunt a glimpse of Pennine green.

Decisively she turned left. As she passed the children, their Lancashire accents made her smile in recognition. She began to feel once more the sense of home-coming she had experienced when driving north with Roy that morning: the sheer physical impact of nostalgia on seeing dry stone walls, the swell of hill country, the towering hulks of former cotton mills.

As she walked, Bonnie reflected on how that journey had come to pass. Everything had happened remarkably quickly: mere weeks after she had returned from Madeira, Roy had kept his promise and flown back to England. They had agreed to make a fresh start together in an area they both found congenial. While she had relinquished the lease on Aunt Rachel's flat and reluctantly sold the heavy furniture, Roy had lodged here in Holdendale with a friend called Ivor, and made the down payment on a cheap local property. Then he had driven south to marry her in a London registry office, with Mrs Billington their only guest, and one of the staff doing automatic pilot duty as the second witness.

The speed of events had left Bonnie dazed. There had been many fleeting moments of doubt, of suspicion that her judgement was impaired in the aftermath of bereavement, but the spectre of facing life alone was too appalling. She *was* fond of Roy, she told herself. So he was a bit rough at the edges, and didn't always shave, and appeared to read nothing more demanding than tabloid newspapers . . . why should she deserve any better? He had kept his word, that was what counted. He had actually flown home to marry her.

The lower road was called Jubilee Lane. Diagonally across to the left, Bonnie could see a large, red-bricked mill, the Acorn, which from the bright sign near one of the doors and the healthy occupancy of its car-park appeared to be still in use. Straight ahead, though, at the far edge of an expanse of weed-strewn wasteland, another mill was clearly derelict.

Bonnie crossed the road and rambled among the rose-bay willowherb of the open area. She was glad that Roy had found a house so close to the hills. At weekends they would be able to have picnics, just like she used to as a child. And she could pick whinberries, bottle them, make pies . . .

As she turned to retrace her steps, Bonnie saw a row of exposed foundations abutting the pavement further along Jubilee Lane: an old demolition site. She walked along to take a closer look, and realized the site was not so old after all: there was a rawness about the broken masonry, a lack of weathering, which suggested that the houses here had been recently destroyed. She continued for a few more yards and noticed that some of the dwellings on the Clegg Street side were mere empty shells. At the end of the row she saw fireplaces suspended eerily in space, lines where connecting walls had been.

Shrugging her shoulders, she crossed back to Clegg Street, and made her way uphill. The children were still playing with the puppy outside number 25. One of them, a ginger-haired boy with a cheeky, freckle-dotted face, caught her eye as she approached. 'Yer've just moved in, 'aven't yer?' he demanded.

'That's right. Number 14.'

'I'm Darren Schofield. I live in number 18 with me brother and sister. Yer Big Bill 'Eaton's neighbour now, same as us. What's *your* name?'

'Bonnie . . . that is, Mrs Judd.' The words sounded unfamiliar on her tongue. Not Bonnie Sheldon any more, but Bonnie Judd, Mrs Roy Judd.

Darren nodded. 'Watch out fer 'im, Bonnie. 'E's mean when 'e's 'ad a drink or two.'

As she turned into the narrow passageway between her house and number 16, Bonnie was wryly amused. The child's warning, and his election to use her christian name, seemed to indicate that he classed her among his peers. She could imagine an irate householder, lofty in the eyes of a child, berating the youngsters for some minor misdemeanour. Darren obviously thought that she would be similarly at risk . . . So much for her newly acquired adult status!

Suddenly she realized that there was a strong smell of frying in the passageway. Someone was cooking chips – and it wouldn't be Roy. High in the wall on the right was a primitive extractor fan, and almost exactly opposite, in mirror image, was a similar fan leading from her own kitchen. The still air in the confined space between the houses had led to the build-up of greasy fumes.

Bonnie hurried to the back gate which led to her own yard and began to fumble with the rusting bolt. Over her shoulder she caught a glimpse of a tall, scruffy man wearing a red-checked lumberjack shirt in the yard of number 16. Perhaps this was 'Big Bill'. She wondered whether to introduce herself, or whether to wait for him to do so at some future date. His side view didn't look encouraging. As she worked the bolt, Bonnie couldn't resist taking a further peek in his direction. She had heard a soft, bubbling *coo* close by, the sound a dove or pigeon might make, and the brick wall between the two yards was bespattered with droppings. She wondered if . . .

'Seen enough, have you? Was it interesting?'

The stentorian voice was followed within seconds by the appearance of its owner at the gate behind Bonnie. The man with the checked shirt glared down at her, his eyes dark and paranoid, his fists clenched.

For a moment, Bonnie's own voice failed her, then she gasped out a reply. 'I'm sorry . . . I didn't mean to stare.' She swallowed. 'I'm Bonnie Judd. We've just moved in here. My husband is called Roy.' Awkwardly she smiled.

A fraction of the hostility drained from his heavy features. 'Makes a change for folk to be moving in,' he muttered.

She waited, but gracious words of welcome were clearly too much to hope for. 'Are you Mr Heaton?' she asked him.

'Told you, have they? That didn't take 'em long.' He snorted, turned on his heel, and slouched away.

Disappointed, Bonnie continued to juggle with the rusty bolt, and finally managed to free it. She opened the gate and passed through into the flagstoned yard. To her right was a high brick wall with its own wooden gate. She knew from her brief reconnaissance on arrival that this separated their property from a cobbled alleyway which ran behind all the houses in the terrace, parallel to Clegg Street.

Straight ahead, the old wash-house, now a bathroom, projected from the building. On the left, the dingy rear wall of the house completed the enclosure. Remembering what Roy had said about the cellar, Bonnie looked along the base of the wall. Yes, there was indeed a small window protected by a grille; some four inches of dirt-encrusted pane projected above ground level; the rest could be seen through the iron bars of a horizontal grating set between the flagstones of the yard.

She climbed the two steps to the back door, and entered the kitchen. Roy was unpacking cleaning materials into a cupboard beneath the sink. 'Took your time, didn't you?' he observed.

'Sorry. It was lovely and sunny, and I wanted to look around. I'm afraid our neighbour doesn't appear to be very friendly.'

'Which side?'

Bonnie pointed towards the wall with the extractor fan. 'That side: number 16. There's a man there called Bill Heaton. I think he has pigeons.'

Roy made a disinterested *moue*. 'We can take or leave the neighbours,' he said. 'We aren't here for their benefit.'

'No, but it would be nice to make some friends.' She sniffed the air. 'That wretched chip smell is in here now. Do you know, their fan is directly opposite ours in the side passageway!'

'I wonder which genius thought that one up,' mused Roy. 'I suppose it's because the cooker's against that wall . . .' He brightened. 'I know! If this man's as objectionable as you suggest, we'll have Kipper Wars – or Garlic Wars.'

'Ugh!' Bonnie hated garlic. She knelt to look into the cupboard where Roy was crouched. The shelves were stained and sticky. 'Don't unpack any more,' she said. 'I'd better clean inside all the cupboards first.'

'Suit yourself,' he said, and stood up. At that moment they heard a distant male voice call: 'Lorna! Bring the ketchup, will you?'

'Is that your friend?' went on Roy.

'Sounds like him. We'd better be careful what we say: they might hear us!'

'Nah. Only if we bellow like he does.'

They pottered about the house, arranging their few belongings, making up the bed, hanging their clothes away once Bonnie had dusted out the wardrobe. Roy had very little baggage – 'Travel light, travel easy' – and Bonnie herself had been able to salvage few of Aunt Rachel's precious artefacts. A row of books, a crystal vase, a framed watercolour, a portable sewing machine, a few pans and some tableware were all she had allowed herself to bring, apart from private letters and papers; the rest had had to be sold.

A little smile played around her lips as she took a folded lambswool scarf from her suitcase and unwrapped the gaudy cockerel from Madeira. She remembered Jeremy telling her the legend of the cockerel as they stood outside the Casa do Turista. Handsome Jeremy . . . She wondered where he was now. Was he still trawling the Portuguese territories for interesting facts, or was he home with his fiancée in Hertfordshire? How surprised he would be if he heard she was married! She could still scarcely believe it herself. But there was no danger of his finding out . . . they had never exchanged addresses.

As she placed the model on the mantelshelf in their bedroom, she heard Roy clumping up the stairs. 'By the way, Roy,' she said when he appeared, 'I meant to tell you something. A lot of the houses on Jubilee Lane seem to have been demolished recently.'

'Jubilee Lane?' he murmured vaguely.

'That's the road at the bottom of the hill.'

'Oh, down there! Yes, I heard about that. They were slums: they'd been condemned for years. Don't worry. Our house is sound enough.'

'So the solicitor did the search, or whatever?'

'What d'you take me for, Bonnie?' With some irritation he flung the holdall he was carrying on to the bed. 'Christ, I'm starving! We haven't eaten properly since breakfast. Let's go and get some fish and chips.'

'Is there a shop nearby?'

'This is Holdendale, girl. Of course there's a chippy nearby. There's probably one on every street corner.'

He held out his hand to her, and she grasped it like a child. Jubilee Lane was forgotten. She, too, was more than ready to eat.

An orange pool of light spilled beneath the thin curtains on to the bedroom floor. Bonnie moved to accommodate the contours of the lumpy mattress, her limbs weary with the exertions of the long day. Beside her, Roy's eyelids blinked in the semi-darkness.

'I brought Aunt Rachel's sewing machine,' she said. 'I could run up some proper curtains for that window if you think we can afford the material.'

'Later, when we've got a bit of money.'

'I'll look for a job first thing on Monday,' she promised. She knew Roy had already found employment, thanks to his friend Ivor. He would be working in a timber yard.

'There's an agency that deals with your kind of skills,' he said. 'Ivor gave me their address. There's a good chance of you finding something, if you're not too choosy.'

Ivor again. 'We owe Ivor a lot,' she said. 'We should invite him for a meal once we're sorted out.'

Roy sniffed. 'You're too late. He's moved on to Newcastle. It was his job in the timber yard. But I showed my gratitude in the pubs while he was here.' He rolled over, and their conversation ceased.

Drowsily, Bonnie contemplated the soft light from the street lamp. Her thoughts slid back to the balcony in Madeira, to the twinkling chain of lights leading over the hills to Cabo Girão. Then, so much had been uncertain. Her whole future had been a dark abyss, a source of genuine fear. Now, though, she had a home in her childhood county, a companion, the prospect of a job. Everything mapped out with a new pen. And if the feelings of uncertainty annoyingly persisted, then that was just the newness of it all . . .

5

'I'm Hazel, this is Jayne. And you know Mr Fisk, of course.'

Hazel, a mildly overweight woman in her late forties, looked pleasant enough to Bonnie. Jayne, nineteen or so with fountains of obviously dyed red hair, wore plenty of mascara and an ignorant expression. Apart from Mr Fisk, the manager, who was ensconced in the office next door, the three females comprised the entire office staff of the light engineering firm. Bonnie's role would be that of glorified accounts clerk.

'Tell us about yourself, Bonnie,' commanded Hazel.

'Well, er, there isn't a lot to say . . .'

'Come on, don't be shy. Tell you what, I'll kick off. I'm divorced, thank God, and my daughters live with me. I've been here at Gradwell's for nearly ten years. Jayne joined us last year.' She flicked an encouraging hand towards Jayne. 'You're much more Bonnie's age than I am. Tell her where the fun can be found in Holdendale.'

The teenager shrugged. 'There's the Palais. Me an' me mates go dancin' there every Sat'dy night. An' there's the Odeon. Or the bowling rink. There's plenty goin' on.' She spotted Bonnie's wedding ring. 'You married?'

'Yes.'

'Where's yer engagement ring?'

'Er, we didn't get round to buying one – it all happened rather quickly.' She felt herself blush as Hazel's gaze swung down to fix on a point just below her waist. 'That is, we met on holiday. In Madeira. And by the end of the holiday we decided to get married.'

Hazel was impressed. 'Now I call that True Romance!' she said. 'I've lost count of the number of likely lads I've met abroad who've promised the earth, then vanished like cockroaches when the Rentokil man comes . . . Well done you, Bonnie. What's his name?'

'Roy.'

'And what does he do?'

'General jobs. He's in a timber yard at the moment.' Bonnie sensed their disappointment, and reflected how glad she would have been to have described Jeremy to them, had events turned out differently. Then she felt ashamed. She was fond of Roy, her rescuer, and if her heart didn't exactly glow at the opportunity to speak his name, the fault was hers, not his. She *would* learn to be satisfied, once they had settled down to carve a niche together.

At lunch time, Bonnie went out with Jayne to collect meat pies from a nearby corner shop. A row of crates on the floor held a variety of carbonated drinks.

'Sarsparilla!' she exclaimed. 'Oh, and dandelion and burdock. I *must* buy a bottle . . . one of each.'

Jayne looked at her oddly.'Can't you get those in the south, then?'

'No. It's *years* since I tasted them.'

'They're made by a local firm,' supplied the shopkeeper in his warm northern voice. He handed the pies, wrapped in a white paper bag, to Jayne, and the girls set off along the street back to the office. As soon as they were once more with Hazel, Bonnie fell upon her pie.

'Look at the depth of the filling!' she marvelled. 'They're like nothing else in the whole country. No Cornish pasty or pinky-grey Midlands pork pie can touch them.' She poured a slug of sarsparilla, after offering it to the others, and drained the glass with a sigh of pleasure.

'You sound like an exile come home,' observed Hazel.

Bonnie pondered this statement. 'Yes,' she said. 'That's how it feels.'

That evening, Roy took her to the King's Head, a spartan pub within walking distance from their home. It had frosted glass windows and deeply grooved wooden tables; a handful of framed photographs of the pub darts team adorned the mush-room-coloured walls.

'Whoever named this pub had a rather horrible sense of humour,' whispered Bonnie as they sat down.

'Why?'

'The picture outside shows Charles the First . . .'

No recognition dawned on Roy's face, and Bonnie had to quell the niggle of irritation she felt. She had already found that any allusion to matters not strictly practical, nor concerning sport, tended to meet with blankness. And Roy was never interested in hearing the answer, either. She would have been pleased to have shared her knowledge with him, but to him it was just a waste of time. Still, Charles the First! Surely *everyone* knew about that . . .?

'What can I get you?' asked Roy.

'Oh . . . ginger beer, please.'

'Right you are.' He left her to join the smoke-wreathed crowd of regulars at the bar, and Bonnie surreptitiously looked about her. In general, she was not keen on pubs, but she didn't want Roy to establish a habit of coming on his own. She knew from Madeira that he enjoyed his alcohol, and suspected he would need little encouragement to over-indulge if she wasn't present as a moderator.

In one corner, two young lads played a clanking pinball machine, while beneath the frosted windows, three women in their thirties with low-necked blouses were drinking gin. Across the room, silent and alone, sat a middle-aged man. His heavy features were seamed with melancholy as he nursed his pint of bitter. He wore a brown raincoat despite the warm stuffiness of the room.

When Roy returned to the table, it seemed to Bonnie that they had caught the man's eye. With a sixth sense she felt his long, measured stare, though when she turned towards him his gaze had moved to the tall glass he held. Some sad old regular, she thought, assessing the newcomers.

Roy stayed at the pub long after Bonnie would have wished to go home. Though he remained relatively taciturn, the atmosphere around them became rowdier. The man in the brown raincoat, who had risen from his table at least four times for replenishment at the bar, had now begun to stagger. As Bonnie fiddled moodily with her empty glass and coughed in the solid wall of smoke, she was just able to make out above the general hubbub the barman's kindly refusal to serve him this last time.

'Not now, Stan. You know you've had enough. I'm just about to call time, anyway.' The man made an ill-tempered rejoinder, and lurched out of the door. The thick haze felt lighter for his leaving.

On the Thursday evening, Bonnie discovered she had no meat stock cubes. She set out to the local store, nominally a newsagent's, which kept long hours and a wide variety of provisions. Just outside, she heard light footsteps on the pavement behind her.

'Excuse me . . .' It was a woman, a slender woman of twenty-eight or so with brown eyes and long dark hair tied at the nape of her neck. Her face, which was handsome and somehow artistic, was pale except for the blurred purple-yellow of a fading bruise above her right eye. 'Are you the lady who's moved into 14 Clegg Street?'

'Yes,' said Bonnie.

'I'm Lorna Heaton, from the house on your right.' She held out a hand with long, shapely fingers as Bonnie murmured her own name; briefly they cemented their new acquaintanceship.

'This is a very useful shop,' smiled Lorna. 'I'm always forgetting to buy things, or only remembering them when I'm at work.'

'Do you work near here?' asked Bonnie.

'At the Acorn, down the hill. We make clothes, mainly for mail order.' She glanced up as a small thin woman stepped out of the shop laden with groceries, a cigarette clamped firmly between her jaws. 'Madge here works at the Acorn, too. Madge, this is my new neighbour, Bonnie.'

'Bonnie Judd,' she amplified. 'And my husband is Roy.'

Madge cackled. 'Yer sound like a southerner to me. Got yerself into a nice area, 'aven't yer? Still, yer won't 'ave ter put up wi' us fer long.'

'Don't be naughty, Madge,' said Lorna. 'Bonnie – you must let me know if I can help you with anything. Local facilities, or whatever. I do my heavy laundry every Monday just round the corner from here, and I go to the library on Saturdays . . . Are you working yourself?'

'Yes,' said Bonnie. 'I do clerical work for a small engineering firm on the Blackmoor estate.'

'Oh, that's across town.'

'Yes – I go on the buses. I can't drive.'

'Cars!' snorted Madge. 'Who needs 'em?'

'We do,' said Lorna, and Bonnie giggled. Already she felt an affinity with this woman, despite knowing so little about her. Perhaps it was the stamp of spirituality in her face, or the simple mention of the word 'library'. She decided then and there that her own destination on Monday evenings would be a certain launderette.

Over the weeks that followed, as the summer sun began to wane and the shadows lengthened in the small front garden of 14 Clegg Street, Bonnie's life divided itself into three distinct compartments: her work, her time with Roy, and the brief periods she was able to spend with her new friend.

Work was tedious, but tolerable. Hazel was inquisitive and Jayne woefully short of grey matter, but Bonnie was able to please them by sharing her photographs of Madeira. They exclaimed over the rich mauve blossoms of the jacaranda trees, the cloud-capped mountains and the views of Funchal harbour.

The shots of the valley at Curral das Freiras particularly impressed them; Bonnie said nothing of Jeremy, but remembered with a pang of regret how she had failed to capture his image for her secret store of mementoes.

There were some photographs of Roy, though. The longer she lived with him, the more puzzling she found his disposition: he spoke a lot of 'bettering themselves', yet already she had found that he was inherently lazy. On evenings when he didn't go to the Taphouse (whose beer he claimed was superior to that of the King's Head) he slouched in front of the television, or read the occasional tabloid paper. For some reason, though, this inactivity didn't seem to relax him. Bonnie thought she could sense a suppressed air of anticipation, of biding his time in some way.

His attitude to her ranged between indifference and flashes of affection, such as the time he bought her the crateful of dandelion and burdock which now resided down the cellar. At night, he rarely seemed interested in consolidating their relationship; only when he had been drinking did he roll towards her and start grappling with her nightclothes; inevitably these were the times she found him least attractive.

Then there was her friendship with Lorna. Bonnie's first instinct had proved correct: here was someone whose mind was of a similar cast to her own. It wasn't a matter of intelligence – Lorna was almost certainly brighter than she – but of consonant tastes. They liked similar novels, history, textiles, anything connected with nature . . . Lorna told her where a bus could be caught which led straight up to the moors beyond Larch reservoir, where one could ramble with the wind in one's hair, and find whinberries when the season was right.

By tacit consent they never met in each other's homes. A wave over the back yard gates was about the sum of their communication in Clegg Street. But the scented steam of the launderette enclosed a different world. Here, they sat together on the bench and talked for hours, easily and naturally. The only subject which was never even touched upon was Lorna's past, and her life with Bill.

'Watch out fer Bill 'Eaton,' Madge hissed at Bonnie once when they met by chance near the shop. 'E's got a right bloody temper on 'im. Lost one of 'is blasted pigeons last year, and two days later Mrs Schofield's cat were found wi' a broken neck . . .'

How had Lorna become involved with someone like Bill? Madge volunteered dark snippets of information: they weren't married; Lorna's previous boyfriend had been violent; she seemed to forgive Bill anything.

Bonnie listened and felt a cold flutter deep beneath her ribcage. If some facet of Lorna's personality made her cleave to unsuitable men, what did that say about Bonnie herself? By the sound of it, Lorna at least loved her man. Bonnie was trying hard to hang on to the warmth and tenderness she had felt for Roy when he had offered to marry her. She needed to build on these feelings before they slipped away entirely, or worse: revealed themselves as impostors all along, gratitude wearing a different face.

Bonnie was sitting with Roy at the kitchen table, eating pork and orange casserole, when there was a light tap on the front door. She laid aside her cutlery, walked through the gloomy hall and opened the door.

Lorna stood there with a book. 'I didn't know whether to try the back or the front.' She smiled. 'Either seemed a liberty. But I thought you might like to borrow this – we were discussing it the other evening . . .'

Ah, yes, thought Bonnie, reading the title *Daniel Deronda*. The only other George Eliot novel she had read was *Silas Marner*.

Roy appeared in the kitchen doorway, wiping his mouth. His stance was hostile.

'This is Lorna, Roy,' said Bonnie hastily, wondering why she should feel guilty. The introduction should have been the other way round. 'She lives next door with Bill.'

He nodded briefly, and vanished again. Bonnie felt her cheeks flame.

'Keep the book as long as you like,' urged Lorna, giving no sign that she saw anything amiss.

'Thank you.' Bonnie glanced towards the roadway; Roy's old

white Escort was parked against the kerb, but the Heatons didn't have a car. Bill rode a blue and silver three-speed bike, which he sometimes left propped in the passageway between the houses. There was no sign of him in the vicinity.

She longed to add something, even a simple invitation to come and have a cup of tea some time, but she felt inhibited by Roy. 'The back door is fine,' she said. 'That's for the chosen few.'

'Good.' Lorna lifted her hand in valediction, went out through the front gate and turned left.

Bonnie retraced her steps to the kitchen. 'Lorna's lent me a book,' she said to Roy. Taking courage, she went on, 'You might have been more friendly.'

For a moment his eyes darkened and his nostrils flared. He gave her an odd, searching look. Then he shrugged. 'I don't think it's a good idea to get too pally with the neighbours. I've seen Bill Heaton, and he's a bit of a thug. Besides, we won't be here for that long anyway. When we've a bit put aside, we'll get somewhere better . . .'

He was back on his familiar theme of 'some day my ship will come in'. Bonnie was in no hurry to move. She had grown to like their house, and was proud of the small improvements she had been able to make with the minimal resources at her disposal. Only the cellar intimidated her, but she had no reason to go down there herself.

As if in telepathy Roy crossed the kitchen floor, knelt by their second-hand fridge and groped among the contents. 'Sod it,' he said. 'No lager.' The rest was stored down the cellar. 'I'm going for a four-pack,' he announced. 'Want one of your bottles?'

'Yes, please. This one's nearly finished.' She watched as he took a red flashlight from a nearby kitchen drawer. 'Roy . . .?'

'Yeah?'

'Wouldn't it be wise to mend the light down there some time? The steps are so uneven; I don't want you breaking your neck.'

'Hardly seems worth it,' he murmured, walking through into the hall.

Bonnie shuddered as she imagined his descent into the cellar, the hollow echo of his footfalls, the baleful presence of the resident arachnids. Not for anything would *she* go near that hell-hole . . . her mind recalled endlessly the obscene, wriggling trophy that Roy had plucked from its depths when they first moved in. If she ever came across another one so huge, she couldn't answer for her reaction. People would probably have to cart her away in a strait-jacket.

On Saturday Bonnie and Roy breathed a sigh of relief at the advent of weekend freedom. They had a leisurely breakfast of Weetabix, grapefruit and bacon, and made plans for a shopping expedition.

'I've been thinking,' said Roy, draining his coffee cup. 'Bloke at the yard told me where you can get a good deal on coal if you buy in bulk. Perhaps we should get some.'

'The weather hasn't turned yet; it's barely autumn.'

'No point waiting for the price to go up. We'll be using it soon enough. There's only that little electric fire in the front room.'

Bonnie considered: it would certainly be cheerful to sit by dancing flames as the nights drew in, and they were already using expensive electricity for the water in the immersion heater. 'All right,' she said. 'If you think we've got the money.' Roy controlled the household accounts, and gave her weekly cash for housekeeping.

'It'll be an investment,' he answered. He stood up from the table. 'I'll go now while you wash up and tidy the place. We can go to Asda this afternoon.'

'Oh, *do* let me come.' Bonnie didn't get many trips in the car.

'There's no need. You're not strong enough to help me with the stuff.'

'Please, Roy. It'll give me a better picture of Holdendale; there are whole areas I don't know yet.'

'If you insist. I'll have to check the address in the Yellow Pages, though.'

They didn't have a telephone themselves. The nearest one was half-way to the launderette, at the junction between Clegg

Street and Barlow Road. Bonnie bought a newspaper while Roy stood in the phone box, one of the few remaining traditional red ones, scribbling details on the back of an envelope.

The depot proved to be a scruffy little place near an abandoned railway siding. It offered coal, coke, smokeless fuels and charcoal for barbecues, most of these prepacked in sacks or bags. While Roy and a burly assistant swung bags of Coalaflame into every cranny of the Escort, Bonnie studied the prices and tried to work out how long their supply would last.

'Coal would have been cheaper,' grumbled Roy as they drove back.

'But smokeless fuel is better for the environment. Thank you for getting the other.' He didn't often follow her suggestions. She kissed his cheek; it was bristly beneath her lips. She wished he didn't always let himself go to seed at weekends.

Roy heaved the first bag out of the car unaided, and staggered along the passageway with it. He waited while Bonnie struggled with the bolt to the back gate, then dumped the bag on the ground. When the rest lay stacked alongside, he glanced around, panting. 'Pity we haven't got a shed. We could put a few where the dustbin is just now, under that concrete slab. Or there's the cellar . . .'

They went inside, washed their hands and had a quick snack of coffee and toast before driving to Asda for the weekly shopping. It was late in the afternoon before they addressed the problem of the Coalaflame again.

'Reckon it should be in the cellar,' stated Roy. 'It's a pity I can't just pour the stuff through the window. As it is, I'll have to carry it down the steps.'

'Don't have an accident,' begged Bonnie. 'Let me help you.'

'I can manage.'

'I'll hold the torch at the top of the steps.'

Roy switched on the hall light and pushed open the cellar door. 'There's no need,' he said. 'I can see well enough. There'll be some light through the grille at the bottom . . .' He went to the yard, lifted a bag chest-high and blundered towards Bonnie, who was still hovering. 'Make me another cuppa, there's a good girl.'

She smiled and returned to the kitchen. Minutes later, the kettle was bubbling and Roy had moved four of the bags down the cellar. Idly she poured the scalding water on to the small pyramid of tea leaves in the pot, and stirred with a spoon. Then she became aware of an angry voice nearby.

Someone was shouting at somebody else. Bonnie couldn't make out the words, but the tone was unmistakable: as the tirade rose in volume and pace, she knew the speaker was working himself up into a passion of fury . . .

She bit her lip and glanced up at the fan in the wall. Just a few feet away, Bill Heaton was berating Lorna, and there was nothing she could do to help. Shivering, she hugged her arms. The voice paused . . . She heard two separate, explosive monosyllables, then silence . . .

Bonnie felt a sick thumping in her chest. She was afraid for Lorna, who was no match for six feet two inches of gnarled malevolence. Had Bill hit her again? What if he had really hurt her?

Recovering from her trance, Bonnie crept towards the doorway to the hall. 'Roy?' she called in a low voice, then louder, 'Roy?'

'What is it?' Crossly he appeared at the bottom of the steps, brushing coal dust from his hands.

'Please come up.'

'I'm arranging the bags where it isn't damp. Hold on a minute.'

'Please, Roy.'

Sighing, he stomped up the steps. 'What do you want?'

'It's Bill. He was yelling at Lorna again. I'm frightened, Roy: he sounded really venomous.'

'Bonnie, for heaven's sake. We can't get involved in someone else's domestic problems. If Lorna doesn't like it, she knows what she can do.'

Fear stabbed Bonnie, a momentary knowledge of her own insecurity without Roy. Suggesting that people should leave home was easily done, but the actuality was savage . . . 'It sounded worse than the other times,' she murmured.

Roy folded his arms. 'What exactly do you want me to do? Go

round and threaten to bop him on the nose? It's not our place to interfere, Bonnie. Get that into your head, or Bill and Lorna won't be the only ones to fall out.' With that threat he marched outside for the next bag, leaving Bonnie feeling worse than ever.

Next morning, Bonnie's vague sense of apprehension was accentuated by a hangover. Roy had repented of his burst of hostility the previous evening, and taken her out to the cinema. The film, *Jungle Warfare,* wasn't exactly what she would have chosen, but still: it was the thought that counted. Afterwards, they had eaten a Chinese meal, and on arriving home Roy had poured her a drink from one of his souvenir bottles of Madeira wine. It was Bual, rather sweet, like his clumsy gesture. She had felt obliged to drink it all. She remembered giggling to him that things tended to happen when she drank Madeira wine, and his reply that he certainly hoped so. The rest was hazy, but now there was an empty glass on her bedside chest-of-drawers. She felt a strange pang of guilt when she saw *Daniel Deronda* lying just behind it.

Normally, Bonnie liked to go to church on Sunday mornings while Roy pottered around with the papers. Today, however, she felt achy and heavy-headed, and even if she hurried, she would miss the start of the service. Perhaps it was just as well: they might come up with something unpalatable about being one's brother's keeper . . .

Clegg Street was quiescent throughout the day. Bonnie saw neither Lorna nor Big Bill. She wasn't surprised: Lorna had pride, and if she was in fact sporting a new bruise, she would be keeping a low profile, especially among the people who cared. Certainly someone was in residence at number 16: their wall fan whirred gently in the passageway, though Bonnie could detect no cooking smells.

It was a grey day, though no rain fell. Roy buried himself behind the papers, uncommunicative now, snappish, even. From early afternoon he watched television, breaking off his attention only to accept a tray of food or a drink.

Bonnie wished she had the energy to walk out into the hills.

There were few buses on a Sunday, and she couldn't drive the Escort. Maybe one day she would buy a bicycle: she had been quite skilful on two wheels as a child. Now she prowled restlessly around the house, wasting the day, actually looking forward to Hazel's gossipy account of her weekend's trivia.

Monday was even greyer, and now a thin drizzle did filter from the heavens, laying a sullen sheen on the pavements, streaking the dusty window panes. Bonnie longed for an honest-to-goodness downpour to refresh the air, but it never came; flaccid clouds hung over Gradwell's, releasing an occasional tentative splatter, while inside the building tempers fluctuated with the humidity level. Jayne had a cold, Hazel's ex-husband was starting a new family, and Mr Fisk grumbled endlessly about an account which had been lost to a rival firm.

The journey home provided no release. People in the bus queue, normally so placid and uncomplaining, were fractious; when the bus arrived – late – a group of youths jostled Bonnie so violently that her shoulder bag ended up in the gutter. In Barlow Road a cyclist sprayed her with muddy water from the only puddle in the entire district, and when she let herself into 14 Clegg Street she found a pile of greasy dishes on the draining-board.

'I came home for lunch,' explained Roy from the depths of their second-hand sofa in the living-room. The jabber of the television competed with his words; his eyes never left the screen as he spoke.

He made no effort to wash the dishes, either before or after Bonnie had prepared their supper of macaroni cheese. She knew that to ask him would be to provoke an argument; Roy might be ill-educated, with few coherent thoughts on important world affairs, but his views on the role of women were clearly defined. Bonnie sighed, and took the familiar path of least resistance. At least tonight was laundry night: she would be able to escape the brainless intrusion of non-stop television for a couple of hours, and hopefully meet Lorna.

At seven thirty she carried a bagful of sheets and towels up Clegg Street and across Barlow Road to the launderette. Two teenagers were just leaving; it was otherwise empty. By nine fifteen Bonnie was folding her clean towels with a mixture of relief and unease: relief because the humidity of the day had made this chore a strength-sapping trial of stamina, unease because Lorna had not turned up.

Returning a sadly buckled paperback to her bag, Bonnie glanced at her watch. No, Lorna wouldn't be coming now. She never missed; Bill must have hurt her where it showed. Bonnie felt an uncharacteristic surge of anger, and wondered if she dared call round at number 16 on some pretext. Roy would disapprove, but he needn't know. More inhibiting was the prospect of alienating Lorna herself . . .

Darkness had now fallen, and the glow of each street lamp was reflected in the pavement's thin residual sheen of moisture. Bonnie crossed the road, turned left at the corner shop, and halted.

Half-way down Clegg Street, in the immediate vicinity of her own home, were the flashing lights of two police cars. Beyond reared the broad white back of an ambulance. Bonnie broke into a run, despite the weight of the linen, and as she approached her front gate she saw with a horrible sense of suspicion fulfilled that the activity was centred on number 16. Lights blazed on both floors; the silhouettes of strangers appeared at windows and disappeared again . . . Outside, men in police uniform milled with a sombre air.

Bonnie saw that her own living-room curtains were drawn. Roy would be inside, getting his fix of electronically processed noise, oblivious to the tragedy only a few feet away. Swallowing, she forced her trembling legs to carry her to the nearest policeman. He had a round face and looked no older than she was. 'Excuse me, please,' she whispered, 'but what has happened?'

'An incident in this house, madam. I'm afraid I can't tell you any more just at present.'

'Please, I – I live next door, number 14. Bill and Lorna are my neighbours. Are they all right?'

He appraised her with more interest. 'Your name is . . .?'

'Bonnie. Bonnie Judd.'

'And you say you live next door? Someone will come and see you shortly, to ask you a few questions.'

'Please – is Lorna all right?'

'Someone will see you shortly, madam.'

She turned away, sick with dread, and as she did so, a figure flew out from the shadows beside the ambulance.

'Bonnie!'

It was Madge, a cigarette hanging uselessly from her lower lip as her mouth worked and writhed.

'He's killed her, Bonnie.'

Bonnie's legs lost the last of their strength: she sagged back against the garden wall.

'Did you hear me? Lorna's dead in there. The bloody bastard's killed her!'

6

'When did you last see Mrs Heaton?'

In the event, the round-faced constable himself had rung Bonnie's door bell at ten thirty; now he perched on the living-room sofa with an equally callow-looking colleague. Roy sat in a chair nearby, a small frown between his eyebrows.

Bonnie knew from Madge that 'Heaton' was a courtesy title. 'I'm not sure if they were married,' she said apologetically.

'Do you know her real name?'

'I'm sorry, no. Madge might be able to tell you. The lady from number 3. She was outside here earlier. She works . . .' She swallowed. '. . . worked with Lorna, down at the Acorn Mill.'

'Number 3,' he murmured. 'Did Lorna have any children?'

'No.'

'So . . . when did you last see her?'

'It was Wednesday evening. She was bringing in some clothes from the washing line in the yard. She waved at me over the gate.'

'And you didn't come across her at all after that?'

'No. That is . . .'

'Go on.'

'Well . . . I may have *heard* her. I heard Bill shouting at her late on Saturday afternoon. At least, I think it was Bill. It sounded like him, and he was always yelling at Lorna.'

'Where were you, Mrs Judd?'

'In the kitchen. I was making tea while Roy stacked away some coal we'd just bought. Our fan in the wall is virtually opposite next door's, and in certain conditions we can hear across the passageway.'

The policemen exchanged glances. 'Their fan was switched on?'

'Yes.'

'May we see your kitchen?'

'Of course.' Bonnie led the way, and for some minutes the young constables prowled with flashlights between the kitchen, the yard and the side passage.

'Did you hear any exact words?' they asked on returning inside.

'No, but the tone was very hostile – frightening.'

'What about you, Mr Judd?'

'I'm afraid I was out of earshot.'

'The fan at number 16 is switched on right now . . . Can either of you recall whether it was on yesterday?'

'Why, yes,' said Bonnie. 'I thought that meant . . .' Her voice trailed away. She had taken it to mean that someone was at home on Sunday. But there had been no cooking smells at all. Had the fan never been switched off . . .?

Once more she felt the draining physical weakness she had experienced in the street. She remembered those final staccato shouts. *Had she actually heard Lorna being murdered?*

'When did she die?' she asked the round-faced policeman.

'That's still being established.'

He wouldn't tell her anyway, Bonnie felt. Not until all the other facts were clear. 'Who contacted you?'

'The Schofield family from number 18.'

She nodded wordlessly, reluctant to ask any more.

Roy cleared his throat. 'I only saw Lorna two or three times myself,' he said, 'but she had a bruise on her face the first time. Madge told my wife that Bill was violent.'

The policeman made another note in his book. 'When did either of you last see Bill himself?'

'Thursday evening,' said Roy. 'He let some of his pigeons out, and we watched them flying over the rooftops.'

'We called them "the squadron",' added Bonnie softly.

'You're sure you haven't seen him since the shouting episode on Saturday?'

'Positive.'

'Does he work shifts?'

Bonnie coloured. 'I – I'm sorry, I don't know what he does. He often arrives home shortly after me in the evenings – around quarter past six.'

'Has he got a car?'

Roy shrugged. 'I've only ever seen him on a bike. Someone came with a van to collect a box of pigeons the other week: I think they were going to a race.'

The young constable asked for details of the bicycle, of Roy's place of work and of Bonnie's, all the while scribbling in his own personal shorthand. He then stepped into the hall with his colleague, thanking them for their assistance.

Cool damp air greeted them as he opened the front door. The street was quieter now, although Bonnie could see the rear portion of a police car from her position in the hall. She didn't know if the ambulance still waited outside number 16, or if there was now an anonymous white van. She didn't really want to know.

Suddenly, there was a commotion. A man in a brown raincoat lurched through the gateway to stand blinking and swaying just outside the front door, supporting himself by holding on to the gatepost. 'What'sh going on?' he demanded of the two police officers.

'Now, Stan. It's nothing you need involve yourself in. You get home to bed.'

The man straightened his back and glared at the constable. '*Shirr* to you, you young punk. They should teach you to show reshpect . . .'

'Very well, sir. We suggest you go home now, and get some sleep.'

'Sleep? Fah!' he snorted, his eyes peering now into the lighted hall; they fixed on Bonnie and narrowed; she edged behind the broad back of the constable.

'Come along now, sir . . . let me help you . . .' The more junior constable made as if to seize the man's elbow, but he was violently repulsed. His colleague turned to Bonnie and apologized, telling her that detectives would be calling in the near future.

As they bundled the man firmly but gently out into the street, Bonnie caught a fragment of their own conversation: '. . . just a domestic . . .' She felt a stirring of fury. What crass machismo! Didn't Lorna count for anything? Didn't it somehow reflect on all of them if a man slaughtered his helpless common-law wife a few feet from their neighbours?

Already tinny sounds were coming from the living-room: Roy had neatly removed himself from the situation. Bonnie's fingers curled in frustration. She wanted to protest, express her outrage to him. And she wanted to inform him of something else . . .

The inebriated man who had just stared at her so intently was the same drunk they had encountered in the King's Head.

'It were me! I found 'er!' Darren Schofield broke away from his group of cronies and ran up to Bonnie the next day.

'Mrs Heaton?' she asked unwillingly.

'Yeah. I were playin' with me ball out back after tea. It went over the wall into Big Bill 'Eaton's yard. I knew 'e'd be mad, so I crept through 'is back gate and 'ad a look. But I couldn't find it. I thought it might have bounced up on the pigeon loft.

'Big Bill's bike weren't there, so I reckoned 'e were round the pub. I thought I'd ask Mrs 'Eaton if I could climb up the loft . . .' Darren took a big breath. 'I knocked on the back door, and it swung in . . . I saw 'er straight away. She were lyin' on the kitchen floor all sprawled like, an' 'er face were all purple, and there were these marks across 'er throat . . .'

Strangled, thought Bonnie. Poor Lorna.

Darren hadn't finished. A scenario that might have given another child six months of screaming nightmares had provided him with much fine bragging material.

''Er eyes, Bonnie: they were open! Not *fully* open, but – yer know. An' 'er *tongue . . .*'

'That's enough, Darren!'

He looked sulky; clearly there was more to tell. As a child of twelve or so flashed past on a gleaming green mountain bike, Bonnie seized the opportunity to change the subject. 'I like your brother's bike, Darren. Is it new?'

'New last Christmas – well, second-'and. *I* want a bike, too. I 'ad one, but it got bashed up, and anyway, it were too small. But me mum an' dad won't let me 'ave another. It's not fair: they say I 'ave to wait and do jobs and earn the money.' He darted her a sly glance. 'I wish Big Bill'd left *'is* bike. No one would've wanted it . . . I could'ave taken it off their 'ands.'

'That's very public-spirited of you, Darren.'

'"Waste not, want not",' he chirruped, evidently echoing sentiments expressed by his elders.

Bonnie smiled wryly to herself, and gave him a valedictory nod. As she turned into the passageway separating her house from number 16, however, she found Darren at her heels once more.

'You know what, Bonnie? When I found Mrs 'Eaton, she'd been dead for days.'

'You're just guessing, Darren.'

'No, I'm not. Them detectives told me mum and dad. So there!'

Bonnie's sense of guilt about Lorna refused to abate. If anything, it became sharper as the week wore on. Her polite British attitude of non-intervention, of keeping oneself to oneself, now seemed tragically flawed. Because of it, she may have missed clues to the build-up of the final crisis between Lorna and Bill;

at the very least it was responsible for Lorna's lying dead on her own kitchen floor, unmourned, for over two days.

'You can't go blaming yourself!' admonished Hazel when the subject was dissected in the office over tea and custard tarts. 'You said you'd only known her a few weeks. You aren't responsible for her having a victim's nature. She'd never have left him, whatever you said.'

'And even if you *did* 'ear the big row when 'e actually strangled 'er, you couldn't 'ave got there in time to save 'er.' Jayne's contribution was sage, but her eyes were round; they followed Bonnie all day, as if living next door to the scene of a violent death had somehow invested her with celebrity status. It didn't make Bonnie feel any better. She had only told her workmates what had happened when the local paper had printed a florid account of the murder, complete with address. She had needed the relief of talking to someone, and Roy was such a brick wall at present. Now she regretted it.

Back home, she tried to reach out to Roy, to stem the incipient sense of isolation which seemed to be affecting them both. It astonished her to recall that only three months earlier she had been single, and terrified of the future. Now she was beginning to suspect what would then have been unthinkable: that worse situations existed than being alone.

'I'm off to Old Trafford this afternoon,' announced Roy abruptly the next Saturday. 'Blackburn Rovers are playing away; I've always supported them.'

'Oh . . .' Bonnie was torn between the genuine hope that this might cheer him up, and a feeling of chagrin because she was so cavalierly excluded. 'May I come along?'

He gave her a pitying look. 'You can't get tickets just like that! Sorry, Bon, but I'm going with the lads from work. You wouldn't enjoy it, anyway.'

She shrugged, and didn't press the point. If he didn't want her company, then he was right: she wouldn't enjoy it. By the time he left the house, her sense of hurt had already blunted into mere resignation.

Bonnie went out herself half an hour later, carrying a small stack of library books for return or renewal. The branch library Lorna had first shown her was only fifteen minutes' walk away. A man leaned in the passageway alongside Madge's house, reading a paper. Though his face was concealed by a broad, trilby-style hat – almost a fedora – there was something disconcertingly familiar about the brown raincoat he wore. Bonnie hurried past.

Once at the library, she took her time and browsed pleasurably in sections she would normally have ignored. After finally making her choices, novels by Mary Stewart and Winston Graham, she then lingered in a nearby wool shop before visiting the newsagent's. Whether the loiterer was a sad derelict, a weirdo or an innocent passer-by, she was giving him ample time to have moved on.

She turned into Clegg Street and felt an immediate sense of relief: he had gone. The street was full of noise and children. With a spring in her step she approached her garden gate, noting with approval the health of the pot plants she had installed by the front door. She reached in the shoulder bag for her keys, then suddenly the back of her neck began to tingle.

Someone was watching her, she was sure. Slowly she straightened up, and glanced around. The nearest group of children were playing a game strongly reminiscent of blind man's bluff. Bonnie had heard that the local school dinner ladies were helping to pass on the old traditions. As she watched, a blindfolded boy lunged at the circle of children surrounding him, and caught a squirming victim; he wrapped his hands round the little girl's throat and yelled 'Yer dead!', whereupon she assumed the blindfold and took his place in the centre.

'Bill 'Eaton's gonna get yer, get yer, get yer,' chanted the other children, dancing round. Bonnie felt sick. She turned again to the door, but the impression of being observed persisted. Once inside, she drew the bolt, left her books in the hall and glided upstairs. Edging along the wall to her bedroom window, she peered out into the street.

Diagonally opposite, down the road beyond the children, was a black car she had never seen before. A man with dark hair crouched in the front seat, staring towards her house, but she could make out no further details. It might have been the man from the passageway, it might not. As the children's gleeful refrain reached her ears through the single glazing, she shivered: this watcher could even be Bill Heaton himself.

By six thirty Bonnie was becoming impatient. Roy had promised to return immediately after the match, and there was no sign of him. He didn't need to wait at crowded bus-stops: he had the Escort.

She had spent the remainder of the afternoon tackling domestic chores, even hanging a few hand-washed clothes out in the yard once the black car had disappeared. There was a slight breeze; she propped open the kitchen door and let the air circulate. She felt mentally relaxed now, but thirsty with the physical exertion. Roy hadn't replenished her dandelion and burdock supplies in the fridge; perversely that was the one drink she now craved. Orange squash simply didn't appeal.

Hurry up, Roy, she thought as she peeled potatoes for their meal. Seven o' clock passed, then seven fifteen. This was ridiculous. If it wasn't for the spiders, she would go and fetch a bottle herself.

Could I? she wondered. Was it really so outrageous an idea? Only her own phobias had kept her from the cellar so far. If she hurried down the steps and avoided brushing against the wall, what were the chances of coming into contact with a spider? *Realistically*? Very small indeed. Almost infinitesimal. And if she didn't linger, the risk would remain minute . . . Resolutely Bonnie strode to the kitchen drawer which housed the red flashlight. The torch wasn't there. She scrabbled among the adjoining drawers and cupboards with increasing irritation, but no success. How typical – just when she had made up her mind to act!

She paused in the hall, considering. There was still some residual daylight outside: it would provide low-key illumination for the cellar via the grille and window. As for the steps . . . if she put on the hall light and left the door open, that might just suffice . . .

Quickly, before she could lose her new-found courage, Bonnie pressed the hall light switch and pushed open the cellar door. The stone steps angled down to the left, paralleling the staircase above. She could just make out the brick wall at the bottom. Taking a large breath, she began to descend.

One, two, don't turn your ankle, don't look up, don't let your arm touch the wall . . . Bonnie gained the flagstoned floor safely, and turned sharp left into the bulk of the cellar. The light was dimmer than she had expected: she had forgotten how filthy that little window was. Cautiously, she assessed her surroundings. Across the floor, in the darkest corner of the cellar, was an alcove piled with bulky shapes. As her eyes became more used to the gloom, she saw this was where Roy had stacked his Coalaflame; two of the bags had split, and lumps of fuel were scattered across the floor. Buckets and old tools lay nearby, presumably debris left by number 14's previous owner.

Inches from her foot stood a mound of lager cans, and beyond this was the crate of mineral drinks. Keen now to return to ground level as soon as possible, Bonnie leaned forward to extricate a bottle. As her fingers closed round the neck of the nearest one, she heard the distant thump of a door.

'I'm down here, Roy!' she called, obscurely relieved. 'I won't be a minute!'

There was no reply. For a few seconds all was quiet above, then a sound reverberated close by which caused a wave of sick terror to surge through her body.

It was the slamming of the cellar door.

7

Bonnie stood up stiffly, feeling her eyes grow huge as she fixed them on the high window with its feeble filtering of light.

'Roy?' she quavered. Her heart began to thud. 'Roy?'

In the unnerving silence, she turned back towards the walled-off steps and with hollow apprehension peered round the corner; yes, instead of the angled oblong of light from the hall there was now darkness. Somehow the door had slammed to.

Pulling in her shoulders to make them as narrow as she could, Bonnie crept up the steps one at a time, her fingers brushing the treads up ahead with nervous brevity, in order to assess their height. Near the top she called again, but still no one came. At last, she was within reach of the door. Outside, it had an old-fashioned handle: there had to be some part of the latch she could seize on this side.

A thin bar of light lent faint illumination to the front of her shoes, but the door itself was uncompromisingly black. She knew there were horizontal wooden cross-pieces above and below the latch; Bonnie inched her hand forward at waist-height; the fingers sank into something gossamer-soft and sticky. With a cry of disgust she recoiled, and her shoulders hit the rough brickwork behind.

Bonnie jerked away from all unseen contacts and stood in the darkness, motionless except for the deep shudders which periodically shook her small frame. If the door was covered in spiders' webs, nothing on earth would induce her to grope blindly for the latch. She would rather stay here indefinitely.

'Roy, *please,*' she whimpered, but it was a forlorn request. He wasn't home yet; doubtless he was out boozing with his friends, having forgotten or disregarded his promise to return promptly after the match. Face it: she was trapped. Whatever malevolent gust of wind had caused the door to slam had incarcerated her as effectively as if the bolt had been drawn.

To slam . . . Suddenly Bonnie felt her heart suspend its beating, then accelerate furiously as if to make up for lost time. She had heard the thump of a distant door at the back of the house several seconds before the cellar door itself had swung shut. She knew the back door had been unlocked, but no longer open; she had attributed the noise to Roy. But Roy was not here: he would have responded to her shouts by now. *So who was in the house?*

Immediately a vision of the raddled-looking man in the brown raincoat took shape in her mind, the man who had stared at them so intensely in the King's Head. Was he ransacking their personal possessions at that very moment? He wouldn't find much . . . Or was it someone entirely different? *'Bill 'Eaton's gonna get yer, get yer, get yer . . .'* Could Big Bill have slipped back to fetch belongings from his house, and succumbed to the temptation of some opportunistic pilfering from his erstwhile neighbours? Surely he wouldn't dare while even a hint of daylight remained?

Bonnie's eyes turned slowly down to the right, to the bottom of the steps where the pallid reflection of light from the grille round the corner had shrunk to a mere suggestion. Yes, he would dare. The people nearby would be having their evening meal, or watching some quiz show on television, or making preparations for a night out on the town. He could sneak from a car to the passageway with minimal risk; even safer was a quiet entry via the back alleyway.

Whoever the intruder was, he must have heard her yelling for Roy. So he had stepped through into the hall to identify her whereabouts, and the draught had caused the cellar door to slam . . .

Stop fooling yourself, Bonnie, she thought. She had heard the back door close before she called out. Where was the draught supposed to have come from? And in any case, could a passing air current really have made any impression on the heavy, inward-hanging cellar door?

There was only one conclusion. The door had been deliberately slammed. And that was a pointless gesture unless the bolt had also been drawn . . .

Bonnie clenched her fists. She knew now with utter certainty that she was indeed imprisoned here, confined by more than her own phobias. Highly agitated now, she crept down the steps towards the pathetic residuum of daylight, fearful of stumbling, of making any more noise.

At the bottom she could only just make out Roy's pile of lager cans. The light trickling through the grille was a sullen pewter grey. Only in the darkest corner, by the coal alcove, were there any tools she might use as a weapon, and Bonnie was loath to probe that particular area: the coal sacks looked menacingly humanoid in their umbral shapelessness, like bodies left to fester. The loose coal might also crunch beneath her feet.

Bonnie found that her legs seemed to have made their own decision to stay put. She stood rigid, lips parted and dry, eyes staring unseeingly towards the grille while her ears strained to pick up the lightest nuance of sound. If the door burst open, she would rush to the tools and fight for her life . . .

Slowly her knees stiffened, her skin grew cold, the cellar turned black. No one came. Not even Roy. Perhaps no one would ever come . . .

'Bonnie, where the hell are you?'

Bonnie jolted, and blinked. She had been in a kind of trance, brought on by fear, and nervous exhaustion.

'Stop pissing about!' The voice was muffled, but close by.

'Roy . . .' It came out as a miserable little croak. Swallowing, she tried again. *'Roy!'*

'Bon?'

'I'm in the cellar.'

'I can't hear you.'

'I'm in the *cellar*!'

A handful of seconds elapsed, then she heard a rasping click and the door was thrown open. She hurried to the bottom of the steps and looked up to see Roy's head and upper body leaning out from the hall.

'What's going *on*? The house is cold, there's no sign of dinner, and I find you down the bloody cellar!'

She ran up the steps to squeeze past him into the blessed normality of the hall, smelling beer fumes on his breath. 'I was locked in!' she retorted. 'I've been there for hours. Didn't you just undo the bolt?'

He looked astonished. 'What?'

'The bolt. I was shut in. Someone came when I went down to fetch a dandelion and burdock, and they slammed the door!'

'Well . . . the door was shut, all right. But it wasn't bolted. Just on the latch. But what do you mean, someone came and slammed the door?'

Bonnie explained, feeling a growing sense of confusion as his expression hardened into scepticism.

'Rubbish, Bon,' he said when she had finished. 'What a story! Big Bill Heaton coming back to the scene of the crime. He's probably in Scotland by now . . . You must have left the back door open, and a sudden draught shut you in.'

'It was open, but I distinctly remember closing it,' she insisted. 'And look at the weight of *this* door!' She rapped against the stout wood with her knuckles. 'It wouldn't flutter around like paper.' She felt angry now, in her relief.

Roy shrugged, clearly unconvinced. 'I can't fathom why you were down there anyway, without a torch. I thought you couldn't stand the place.'

'I can't . . . I'm never going back. There was enough light when I first went down, but not after the door slammed. I didn't take the torch because I couldn't find it. It wasn't in the kitchen drawer.'

'Sorry, Bon, I think that was me. I went to get something from the car boot the other night, and I must have left the torch out there . . . Hey, cheer up.' He patted her shoulder. 'Sorry you've had a rough time. I stopped off for a few drinks, or I could have helped you sooner . . . where are you going?'

'Upstairs to check if anything's been stolen.'

The bedroom was exactly as she had left it. Bonnie rapidly inspected her books, her few clothes, her precious souvenirs of Madeira: all were *in situ*. When Roy confirmed that the living-room was undisturbed, she acknowledged the fact with much less interest. The television could go, for all she cared.

'So – no burglar,' announced Roy brightly.

'Mm.' For his benefit, Bonnie didn't disagree. He had already set his mind against her interpretation of events. But as she made a late supper of ravioli, her own instincts refused to waver. Someone *had* been in the house, she was sure. The reason was as elusive as his identity . . . Next time she might not be so lucky.

'Ey, me brother told me a good joke yesterday,' said Jayne ten days later. 'Paddy goes ter this buildin' site lookin' fer a job. 'E's in the foreman's 'ut, givin' 'is particulars, when the foreman interrupts 'im, leans out of the window an' yells "Green up" 'E then asks Paddy ter carry on, tell 'im about 'is previous experience an' so on, then 'e 'olds up 'is 'and, opens the window again an' shouts "Green up!" This keeps 'appenin', until Paddy eventually asks 'im why 'e's callin' out "Green up!" all the time . . .' She leaned forward, totally intent on her colleagues. 'The foreman said, "I'll tell yer why. There's two of yer compatriots out there, layin' turf."'

Hazel gave a snort of laughter, and simultaneously Mr Fisk appeared in the open doorway. 'I don't approve of ethnic jokes,' he said stiffly. 'At Gradwell's we try to foster an egalitarian milieu.'

For the first time, Bonnie noticed the hooked shape of his nose above the spindly moustache. She watched silently as Jayne pulled a creative array of faces at his retreating back.

'No sense of humour, that one,' said Hazel as soon as her boss's office door closed with a huffy little click. 'There's nothing wrong with a bit of fun in private. The world's full of jokes about stupid Sassenachs and whingeing Poms. What we don't hear can't hurt us . . . I say, I've got another one . . .' She lowered her voice. 'How many Irishmen does it take to change a light bulb?'

'Dunno,' said Jayne.

'Bonnie?'

Bonnie gave a slight shake of her head.

'A hundred – one to hold the bulb, ninety-nine to turn the house round!'

Jayne spluttered, and clapped a hand over her mouth as Hazel gestured for lower volume. 'My go,' she hissed. 'How do you sink an Irish submarine?'

'I know that one,' said Hazel. 'Knock on the hatch . . .'

They carried on in this vein like schoolgirls, growing increasingly rowdy, before Hazel broke off and eyed Bonnie across the desk. 'What's the matter?' she asked. 'You look like a wet Monday.'

'Sorry. I was just worried about Mr Fisk.'

'Nonsense. You've been broody all morning. Want to tell us about it?'

'Oh, it's nothing. I was just thinking about a girl who married the wrong man . . .'

She knew it now, beyond any doubt. And what was more, Roy knew it, too. They had nothing in common, no philosophies, no standards, no hobbies. For her part, Bonnie knew that she had been fond of Roy, had made vows in all sincerity and had tried to make his life pleasant. Every day she tried. But Roy made no reciprocal effort, unless it was for reasons she now regarded as suspect.

After the cellar episode, she had been briefly heartened when he had suggested a Sunday outing of her choice. He had taken her to Tatton Park in Cheshire, a haunt of her childhood, where its two meres, its fifty acres of garden and even larger deer park always offered something new. The clean air and the tranquil Japanese Garden, with its pagodas, lakes and bridges, had restored her spirits and given her new hope. But the very next day Roy had reverted to the demeanour that was now typical: inert and surly, repressive yet somehow on edge himself. On the Friday he had come home drunk, and Bonnie had dared to remonstrate.

Roy had glared down in a black fury, reminding her frighteningly of Bill Heaton. He hadn't married her to be nagged at, he had shouted; he wouldn't stand for much more. Goaded by a need for answers despite the unpropitious timing, Bonnie had asked him point-blank why he *had* married her . . .

She couldn't forget the way his mouth had snapped open on the word 'because', only to close again, swallowing the rest of the reply unborn. He looked stunned and somehow chastened, as if he had nearly divulged something irrevocable. After a long silence he had given a heavy sigh, and murmured, 'I liked you better when you were stupid.' Then he slouched upstairs to bed.

Hazel was still watching her, eyes astute.

'It was a film I saw,' improvised Bonnie hastily. 'The man clearly didn't love his wife, so you were left wondering why they'd got married. Unfortunately, I missed the end . . .'

'There must have been a *purpose,*' pronounced Jayne, her interest captured. 'P'raps 'e needed a son an' heir, an' was about to be disin'erited if 'e didn't provide one. Or maybe the girl 'erself 'ad money, an' 'e wanted to get 'is 'ands on it. Or property. I saw a film like that once: one o' them old black an' white ones. This con-man married Ingrid Bergman, then tried to convince 'er that she was goin' mad, so 'e could get control of this big London 'ouse an' 'er aunt's jewels. Was that the film?'

'No, it wasn't *Gaslight,*' said Bonnie. 'It was quite modern, and the girl had no possessions at all.'

'Perhaps she was a route to British citizenship,' suggested Hazel.

'No; her husband was English himself.'

Jayne frowned for a minute, then exclaimed in triumph. 'I've got it!' she cried. 'Life insurance!'

At ten past five, when Jayne had made her noisy exit from the office, Hazel took a seat across the desk from Bonnie. 'I know you're unhappy, love,' she said. 'It doesn't take Einstein to work out that it was Roy you were talking about. Want to get it off your chest?'

Bonnie hesitated. She had not been brought up to spill all her woes to friends and acquaintances at the least provocation. Her father, in particular, had been a great exponent of stiff upper lip ethos. Yet the domestic pressures that had been building up for weeks were making life intolerable. She might have confided in Lorna, but Lorna was dead. There was no one else to tell.

To her dismay, she found that her own lips had begun to tremble, and tears were welling beneath her eyelids. Hazel's brisk kindness had completely disarmed her.

She turned her face away. 'Oh, Hazel,' she choked. 'I'm such a failure.'

Half-way to the pie shop at lunch time the next day, Bonnie realized that she had taken no specific order from Jayne. Guessing was unwise: Jayne's preferences varied with the weather, her mood of the morning, and her mother's likely choice of food for dinner.

Retracing her steps past the hangar-like units of the industrial estate, Bonnie slipped into Gradwell's by a side door. She was feeling relaxed, more balanced than at any time since her marriage. She had discussed her general misery with Hazel, and received good advice: men were different; marriage was always a compromise, but the majority still succeeded . . . Lorna's death must have been depressing . . . In time, everything would come right.

As she approached the office, Bonnie noticed the door was slightly ajar, and heard Hazel's voice in low, intense conversation.

'Well, I thought, what do you expect? I didn't say that, of course, but we all know what men are like – the bastards. They want a housekeeper, that's what, preferably one who can bring in a bit of money as well. They love to play The Little Emperor around the house, and cut up rough when they don't get their own way.

'But really, she was asking for trouble right from the beginning. Holiday romances are notorious for distorting your judgement. Poor Bonnie must have been desperate for a boyfriend . . .'

Mortified, Bonnie crept away. And as the day wore on, transmuting Hazel from traitor to trimmer in her estimation, she knew that after ten weeks of life in Holdendale, she herself remained totally alone.

8

The crisp nip of autumn air teased at Bonnie's cheeks the following Saturday, but she was undaunted. She felt rebelliously delighted, window shopping in Manchester's King Street without Roy's knowledge or permission.

He had left the house that lunch time with a newly acquired blue and white scarf, muttering 'Eward Park – Arsenal,' from which Bonnie had deduced that Blackburn Rovers were playing at home to the London club. Within minutes she had set out on foot for Holdendale's modest railway station, just over a mile away, and caught the next train into Manchester. 'God helps those who help themselves,' Aunt Rachel had often reminded her – and that had not been a reference to shoplifters. Bonnie knew that it was up to her to create her own treats.

Emerging from Victoria, she had planned to visit the Arndale Centre and work her way round to Piccadilly Gardens, but the elegant shops of St Ann's Square and the Barton Arcade waylaid her. Now, three hours and a cup of good coffee later, she was still in the same vicinity, having stayed to examine the bold glass structure of the Royal Exchange Theatre, built inside the historic Cotton Exchange.

As she admired floaty Indian garments in the window of a clothes shop, she glimpsed the reflection of a smartly dressed young woman crossing the pedestrianized street behind her. Bonnie turned slowly through ninety degrees to take a closer look. The woman walked with long, confident strides. She wore a black micro-skirt and a saffron jacket with prominent black lapels; her figure was easily equal to this outfit, yet her most striking feature was a splendid mane of rich chestnut hair.

For a moment she glanced towards Bonnie, as if aware of her interest, but then her gaze veered away as she homed in on

Boodle and Dunthorne's jewellery display. Bonnie held her breath; there had been something very familiar about those leaf-shaped brown eyes, the straight nose and narrow lips. Amidst the jostling crowds of Manchester she had not expected to come across a face from the past, but her north-western childhood had rendered such a chance encounter at least possible.

Someone from school, surely . . . She wrinkled her brow and sucked against her teeth, desperately trying to think who would fit the bill. No one from her own class in Rochdale had been so striking, unless – yes, it was: Sandra Kershaw.

'Sandra?' The word was out before Bonnie had given the matter any more thought. Suddenly it seemed like serendipity to run into someone she knew, someone untainted by the dark stain of Clegg Street or the humiliating gossip at Gradwell's.

The girl paused, looked up, but said nothing. Bonnie's wave of certainty ebbed muddily away. Sandra Kershaw had been pubertal when Bonnie had last seen her, with a well-fleshed torso, rounded jowls and a heavy chin. This girl's features were taut and clear-cut. Yet the hair was surely unique. Sandra's crowning glory had just grazed the shoulders, and her fringe had been cut as if with a guillotine . . . this hair, though longer and curlier, was nonetheless identical in strength, lustre and colour.

'Is it Sandra Kershaw?'

The girl, who had been about to move on, gave a faint exhalation which sounded resigned. 'It's Cassie,' she said. 'Cassie Kershaw.'

Ah, yes. Her full name had been Cassandra, but at school she had favoured 'Sandra'.

'Rochdale High School . . .?' said Bonnie tentatively.

'That's right. You're Bonnie Sheldon, aren't you? You look just the same.' In view of her own vastly improved appearance, that was probably no compliment. 'You went down south, didn't you?' she went on as Bonnie nodded.

'Yes. Dartford.'

'I remember. Your parents had an accident . . . I'm sorry.' She spoke in brisk, matter-of-fact tones, as if to her accidents and deaths were an everyday occurrence. 'You back here for a visit?'

'No – I've moved to Holdendale. I got married in July.'

'Congratulations.' The sharp brown eyes rested momentarily on Bonnie's ring finger, then slid as if by association to the infinitely more expensive contents of the jeweller's window. 'I'm looking at rings myself . . . Tell me about your husband.'

Bonnie gave a brief verbal sketch of Roy, emphasizing their meeting on Madeira in preference to his personal attributes.

Cassie laughed. 'I'll have to include you in one of my more frivolous features – holiday romances that actually work. People can't get enough of the "human interest" stuff, you know.'

'You're a journalist?'

'Sorry, yes.' She didn't look sorry – proud was more accurate. 'I work for the *Manchester Herald* – Features Department. The offices aren't very far from here.' She waved a vague but well-manicured hand in the direction of Deansgate.

'Oh – do you commute from Rochdale?'

'No; I live in Manchester now. I share a flat near Platt Fields Park. I started off on the *Rochdale Gazette*, though, doing bread and butter journalism straight after my GCSEs. I didn't see the point of hanging on for A-levels or a degree: in journalism you learn best on the job. I was indentured, of course, and I passed my Proficiency Test without any trouble . . .'

Bonnie glanced at her teeth, and saw that they looked quite genuine. She didn't understand everything Cassie was saying, but could fathom the gist. The Sandra Kershaw she remembered from school had also been able to talk effortlessly about herself, her successes and aspirations. She had won the English Prize twice running, and had displayed confidence, stamina and analytical skills. The best reporters, though, needed the tact and patience to draw out the other person's story. Bonnie had an uncomfortable feeling that she had already been sufficiently probed, assessed and found wanting.

'Must go: I've got an appointment,' finished up Cassandra, consulting an attractive little Cartier watch on her left wrist. 'Nice seeing you again.'

Bonnie hesitated. Inadequacies apart, it was strange how cheering she had found this unplanned encounter. At school, her clique and Sandra's had been light years apart: oil and water, radio waves versus gamma rays. All the bold, smart girls had been in Sandra's set, while the oddballs, the awkward and the shy seemed to find common cause with Bonnie. She had never expected to regret the loss of *Sandra's* company. Yet just now, she looked on Cassandra as a slender thread anchoring her to a past when everything had seemed normal – wholesome, even. Cassie might know how to contact other schoolfriends, people more congenial . . . If she moved on now, the thread would snap, the past would be lost, and all the grey barrenness of the present would rush into the vacuum. 'Do you ever visit Holdendale?' she asked.

'Not as a general rule, but as it happens I'll be out there this next Thursday researching an article . . . Why?'

'Oh . . . I just wondered if you'd like to come to dinner, that's all.'

Immediately Cassie's face told her that the offer was inappropriate. 'I mean tea,' she amended rapidly. 'Afternoon tea, when you've finished your investigations.'

'Well, that's very kind. Why not?' If Cassie found the idea a tooth-grinding imposition, at least she was now hiding her reluctance. 'I'm writing an overview of the region's industrial decline, with special reference to the cotton and textile industry. Let's see: I'll be at the Moss Mill at two o'clock, and the Acorn at three fifteen.'

'I live just up the road from the Acorn. 14 Clegg Street.'

'We'll say four thirty, then.'

Back at home, Bonnie's buoyant mood of defiance towards the still-absent Roy underwent a serious deflation as she appraised the house. Despite her best endeavours, she knew it must look squalid to the eye of an outsider. The living-room curtains needed to be a much lighter colour . . . that crack in the plasterwork should be hidden by a picture or a plant . . . she had recently noticed an odd, musty smell in the hall . . .

Returning from the nearest garden centre on the Sunday, Roy watched with an ironic curl to his mouth as Bonnie attempted to improve their environment with a lush collection of pot plants. 'If you're so worried about what your friend'll think, I don't know why you invited her in the first place,' he commented.

'I told you, I knew her from school. I want to talk about old times.' Bonnie moved a Calathea back and forth along the mantelpiece, assessing its optimal position.

'This Croton had better stand by that window . . . I don't like strangers around the house, Bonnie. I thought we'd decided that.'

You did . . . 'Cassie won't be staying long. She'll probably have left before you come home from work.'

In the event, Cassie was still on the premises when Roy returned the following Thursday evening. She had arrived on the dot of four thirty and paused just inside the front door, her stance faintly theatrical. 'This is a nice little place. I love terraced houses – all that history.' She wore long, loose black trousers this time, belted at the waist, and a turquoise sweater, sharded with black, which accentuated her enviable figure.

'You know I've been looking at the mills,' she continued as Bonnie led the way inside. 'A lot of the older terraces were built by the mill owners especially for their workers. They provided community centres, as well. I don't think Clegg Street was associated with the Acorn – the date's too recent – but I reckon the lower side of Jubilee Lane was. I say, doesn't the mill have fascinating architecture? That acorn-shaped water tower at the top will have been an emergency supply for the sprinkler system . . .'

Bonnie was only half listening: she was wondering whether the fare she had provided was correct in quality and quantity. After the expense of the pot plants, she hadn't dared to buy anything exotic for the sandwiches. Smoked salmon would have been very nice, but she had been obliged to settle for cucumber, and egg and cress. Next to these on the tray were a small pyramid of freshly baked scones with jam and cream, and beyond these a chocolate cake. There was only just room, with the teapot and crockery; anxiously Bonnie wondered whether she should have used the kitchen table, where she and Roy normally ate.

'I've been trying to write a broad review of the region's industrial decline – what happened to the spinning and weaving companies once the cheap imports flooded in: did they fold, did they hang on grimly in a reduced form, or have they managed to rise and blossom like the phoenix from the ashes? Some have survived by diversifying – the Moss Group, for instance. Moss plc make both specialized furnishing fabrics and products for the NHS – surgical pads, cotton wool balls or whatever. They're still fighting. The Acorn, though, uses mainland European and Far Eastern fabrics for most of the clothes they assemble . . .'

For a reporter, Cassie found no difficulty in talking. Bonnie reflected ruefully that it was her lot to be of no interest even to a journalist. At the same time, though, she was relieved not to be questioned too closely about the nature of her work, or her relationship with Roy.

'Do have a scone,' she said, proffering the plate. 'Have two.'

'Just the one, thanks,' said Cassie. 'I've got to keep myself in trim. I do aerobics twice a week. Are you with a club?'

'No. I like walking, though . . . Trish Packham was very athletic, wasn't she? Do you ever hear from her nowadays?'

Bonnie's clumsy attempt to steer the conversation towards old schoolfriends met with prompt failure. Since her move to Manchester, Cassandra had kept up with none of them. Perhaps this was the point at which Sandra had become Cassie.

'I'm doing other articles as well, of course. Sometimes the features are themed, like my "anniversary" series. Some are prosaic: "Ten years since hypermarket Z was opened – how has it affected traffic patterns and the livelihoods of local small traders?" Some have a mystery element: "Five years since the RPC raiders went to ground – the quest goes on." The titles will be snappier, of course, but there's the gist . . .' She broke off as the back door thumped lightly.

'That'll be Roy,' said Bonnie. She wondered nervously if he would choose to sulk and stay out of sight because Cassie was still in the house. Perhaps that might be preferable to open hostility.

Muffled footsteps through the wall. A faint gurgle of pipes.

Five minutes later Roy entered the room, his face freshly scrubbed, his hair neatly plastered down.

'You must be Cassie,' he said easily. 'I'm Roy.'

Cassie paused, her cup half-way to her lips. She stared at him, recognition and uncertainty struggling for pre-eminence in her mahogany eyes.

Slowly she placed the cup and saucer on the table. 'Don't I know you?' she said.

9

Roy had always reacted badly to catechisms. There were broad gaps in his past life that Bonnie had failed to persuade him to fill. Yet now, to her surprise, here he was tolerating a string of quite impertinent questions from Cassie, his manner pleasant, even forthcoming.

'. . . So you see, we can't have met,' he finished up when his school life, chequered employment in Preston, and decision to follow the sun by working abroad had all been aired. 'I was in Preston, you were in Rochdale. Unless you came over to some of our pubs and night-clubs . . . No? Then I don't see how . . . unless it was somewhere like Manchester, and I think I would have remembered.'

His eyes raked her figure appreciatively, dwelling on the swell of her bosom. Bonnie felt embarrassed for Cassandra, but her guest was unperturbed. 'You ever been married before?' she asked Roy.

'No. I wasn't in a hurry for the old ball and chain . . . Pax, Bon, I'm only joking. I suppose I was waiting for the right girl.'

'Then you lost no time,' observed Cassie.

'No virtue in hanging around once I'd found her, was there? We didn't have anyone else to consider.'

Bonnie felt a bleak little pain in her chest at these words. The hollowness of the first sentiment, the sad truth of the second. She knew beyond doubt that if her family still lived she wouldn't now be going through the puppet motions of living, bound by wedlock to an indifferent stranger.

Cassie had unleashed a slow smile at Roy, the tawny gloss she wore making her narrow lips seem more generous. Her eyes roamed down his body in a parody of his own predatory assessment, and he didn't seem to mind at all.

'More tea, Cassie?' Bonnie, hot and nervous again, managed to spill a quantity into the saucer.

'I'll get you another saucer,' said Roy, springing up. 'By the way, Bon, what is this tea? It's fancier than the usual.'

Bonnie gritted her teeth. 'Darjeeling,' she said, her pretence exposed.

He winked at Cassie. 'In your honour, evidently.'

She gave a small bow of the head, while Bonnie sat by the tea-tray, contemplating murder. The conversation ebbed and flowed, moving away from the personal to safer topics like the hat-making heritage of Stockport. Cassie was in no hurry to leave, and Roy was showing none of his usual irritation.

'Do you use one of those pen-names?' he asked when at last she rose to her feet.

'A *nom de plume*? No: my by-line's simply Cassandra Kershaw.'

'I shall look out for your articles.'

Bonnie reflected that now was the moment when she should make innocent reference to his usual choice of reading material, and the deductions one could make regarding his actual ability to read. But she kept silent. Petty revenge wasn't her style. That was why people like Roy always rated themselves winners in juvenile point-scoring competitions of their own making.

Cassie roared away in a red Citroën, and Bonnie carried the crockery through into the kitchen. There had undoubtedly been mutual interest between her husband and her guest; what she had yet to determine was whether or not she actually cared.

Roy lounged in the doorway. 'I bet Cassie looks good in a short skirt,' he said. 'She's a nosy bitch, though.'

It was Saturday morning when the letter arrived. Bonnie had knelt down in her dressing-gown to scoop up the scattered circulars littering the lower hall; when her hand alighted on a long, official-looking envelope with PRIVATE AND CONFIDENTIAL printed in the upper left-hand corner, she was at first puzzled.

'Anything for me?' yelled Roy from upstairs.

The letter was addressed to her. 'Er, no,' she called back. 'Just junk mail.' Apart from the odd bill, that was all they usually received.

She padded through into the kitchen and put the kettle on, then stealthily slit open the envelope with a vegetable knife. The content of the single white sheet inside was word-processed, except for the flamboyant signature at the bottom. 'I need to see you soon. Suggest café in Royal Exchange on Monday, one o'clock. Ring me via the office if you can't make it, otherwise I'll see you there. *Don't tell Roy*. Cassie.'

What on earth did that mean? Bonnie read it again, frowning, then slipped the paper and envelope into the pocket of her dressing-gown as she made two mugs of tea and placed them on a tray. Was this some caprice of Cassandra's, some idea for one of her articles coupled with the arrogant assumption that Bonnie could just drop all at work on Monday and travel into the middle of Manchester? Persuading Mr Fisk to allow flexible hours this last Thursday had been difficult enough.

Don't tell Roy . . . That italicized sentence worried her, imparting a sinister tinge to the entire missive. Yet it could simply mean that Cassie was planning a surprise for him.

Bonnie carefully carried the tray up the stairs. The air of elaborate assignation could be explained easily enough. 14 Clegg Street had no telephone, and she had given Cassie no precise information about where she was employed.

'Thanks, love,' said Roy, sitting frowstily in the bed. He sipped the tea. 'What's that paper poking out of your pocket?'

'Oh – just a shopping list.' Bonnie half turned away from him. 'I like to write things down as I remember them.'

'Well, you can add beer and HP sauce.'

'Will do.'

As soon as he had gone to the bathroom, she glanced down at the pocket. A thin white rim of the envelope was visible; it must have worked its way upwards as she climbed the stairs. Hurriedly Bonnie hid the letter among the mended cottons in her underwear drawer. She would decide what to do about it later.

Bonnie craned her neck to gaze at the ornate ceiling diagonally above the chair where she sat. This large Victorian building, once a bustling cotton exchange, now hummed with life of a different sort. The cafeteria within its walls was standard enough, apart from the wide selection of drinks offered, but the theatre-in-the-round, which she had admired the weekend she met Cassie, was truly unique. There was something almost surreal about the juxtaposition of cupolas and stately columns with the theatre's starkly modern shallow cylinder of steel and glass.

She nibbled at her sandwich, glancing to left and right, unsure from which direction Cassie would come. She had felt obliged to buy something, as the cafeteria was popular and it would not look right to be monopolizing an empty table. Now she hoped that Cassie wouldn't be late; it would be difficult to hold the fort here. For her sake, Bonnie had taken the afternoon off from Gradwell's; travel by public transport was very time-consuming.

From Cassie's point of view, she conceded, the Exchange was a sensible enough place to meet, and Cassie knew that Bonnie was familiar with this part of the city centre. But it had been a substantial journey. And now Cassie *was* late. Only by ten minutes so far, but it was enough to occasion Bonnie a small niggle of annoyance. The issuer of such a peremptory summons should have had the grace to be on time.

Gimlet eyes watched her at the table. Two middle-aged ladies, come into town for a matinée, perhaps, were waiting for her to relinquish her place. Bonnie sipped slowly, eking out her tea. Twenty past one. Come on, Cassie.

She scanned a leaflet she had picked up in the bookshop nearby, but all the while she was aware of the ladies hovering, ready to swoop. Both were well-built and looked unused to standing for any length of time; soon Bonnie's nerve cracked and she surrendered her table to them. If Cassie didn't like it, she should have been punctual.

By two o'clock, Bonnie was restless with anxiety. Had she got the rendezvous wrong? Surely not: there was only one Royal Exchange. If the letter had been in her handbag she would have checked the instructions again by now, several times over, even though she knew the words by heart. But it wasn't in her bag; it was nestling in the wild rose scent of her underwear drawer, between two worn cotton vests.

Trying to look nonchalant, she studied an adjacent display of blown glass vases, then loitered by the top of the steps leading out into St Ann's Street. Cassie would come from this direction, unless she had been in the very centre of the town that morning. Perhaps she had been delayed by an interviewee . . . Perhaps she had been working at home, and her car had broken down . . .

As the minute hand of her watch crawled past the six, Bonnie knew that Cassie wasn't coming. She had forgotten – or changed her mind, and not even sent a message. With a brief spurt of decision Bonnie pattered down the steps and strode through the thronged streets towards Deansgate, but as she neared the *Herald* offices her bold tread began to falter. It would be humiliating to have to stand at some reception desk and ask for Cassie. She was probably enjoying a gourmet lunch with her boyfriend at this very minute . . . Feeling angry and foolish, Bonnie halted. All she wanted to do now was return home by the least arduous route possible. A train, or two buses? She opted for the train.

Back in Clegg Street, weary from the fruitlessness of the day, Bonnie craved a bath. To her surprise, the water in the immersion tank was quite hot. The power would only need to be switched on for a few more minutes.

In the bedroom she stripped down to her underwear then began to ferret in the drawer for clean clothes to put on afterwards. She saw Cassie's letter, read it again, then crumpled it up and threw it in the waste basket. Slipping on the dressing-gown which hung behind the door, she made her way to the primrose-coloured bathroom in the old wash-house extension.

Bonnie sighed as the rose-scented water came up to the sides of her chin. Her toes peeped out from a lacework of foam just beneath the taps. She heard a vague thud behind her in the house. The letter-box, perhaps? Forget it. Forget Cassie and her whims. There were other ways to track down the whereabouts of her old schoolfriends . . .

She mused in a state of dreamy suspension for nearly half an hour, adding more hot water twice. When the skin of her fingertips began to macerate, she guiltily sprang out of the bath and towelled herself dry. Water gurgled down the plughole, and somewhere in the background was a splattering sound, like rain.

Bonnie opened the bathroom window, which faced the yard. Immediately, the splattering sound became louder. She could see little due to the steam on the pane, but a downpour seemed to be going on outside. That in itself was odd, because the day, though cool, had been bright and cloudless.

Donning her dressing-gown and slippers, Bonnie hastened to the kitchen window for a better look. A thin column of water neatly bisected the view, falling sheer from some point high out of sight to splash against the flagstones of the yard. A spreading pool of water hungrily sought out the cracks, while subsidiary runnels probed the hollows and uneven areas with inexorable fingers.

She unlocked the back door and peered anxiously up at the roof. The source of the cascade appeared to be a narrow pipe jutting out just below the eaves. Something to do with the attic, she supposed. Was it serious? She knew nothing of plumbing, but the pipe was presumably some sort of overflow, and water was pouring out with considerable force.

She ran up to the bedroom, where her clothes were laid out on the bed. What an appalling day this was turning out to be. The attic was as forbidding a prospect as the cellar to an arachnophobe, but Roy wouldn't be home for another hour yet and the problem felt urgent. As she pulled a dark jumper over her dripping hair, Bonnie heard sinister bubbling noises directly above. Dragging on her only pair of trousers, she hurried to the landing.

The trapdoor to the attic was dangerously sited above the stairs, and Bonnie had never been inside before, but fear of a devastating flood lent her energy and ingenuity. She prodded at the high trap with a broom handle, forcing the spring catch to open. Glimpsing the aluminium rung at the edge of the opening, she fished for purchase with a makeshift hook; to her relief she was able to pull down the entire ladder in creaking, juddering stages.

Bonnie climbed until her head and shoulders were inside the cool darkness of the attic. The source of the gurgling was now very close at hand. In the gloom she could just make out the solid shape of a tall lagged tank over by the chimney breast.

Without light she could go no further. When she had collected the broom, Bonnie had found that the torch was missing once more. Now she scanned the immediate area for a switch, in the faint hope that there might be a light fixture here in the attic. As she darted nervous glances up at the angle of the roof, which was blunted by an array of filthy cobwebs, something brushed against her shoulder.

She screamed, and tensed, then identified the cause of the alarm: a piece of knotted string hung down from a beam above, where a single light bulb protruded starkly. Hardly daring to hope, she gave the string a tug . . . the bulb lit up.

With new urgency now, Bonnie climbed the last few rungs and stepped gingerly on to the floor of the attic. There was a boarded walkway down the centre; unless the wood was rotten, that would support her weight. She crept along, bent double, well aware that the crannies above were colonized by eight-legged fiends grown huge by years with little disturbance.

Near the tank there was another string, another bulb. Yet again there was light, and Bonnie began to believe that her fortunes might be changing. The cistern stood high on a plinth; though padded round its circumference to protect from frost, it was only partially covered at the top by a grimy sheet of polystyrene. Cautiously Bonnie edged this aside, and peered into the interior . . .

It was a shock to see the water level so near the top. From the outside dimensions of the tank, Bonnie knew the depth was scarcely two feet, but in the poor light of the attic it looked much deeper. Dead flies floated on the viscous-looking surface. A ball cock wallowed sluggishly beneath, like a moribund jellyfish; the valve at the end of the lever arm was shapeless with corrosion.

Desperately, Bonnie tried to work out what was happening. Water was entering the tank and its level was now unregulated because the float valve had jammed. The excess was pouring out through a pipe leading straight through the wall above the back yard; she could still hear the distant splashing sound. So where was this overflow pipe?

She could see the dull gleam of copper where it snaked across the attic floor, randomly camouflaged by the glass fibre insulation lying between the joists. It then turned through a right angle and vanished in the polythene-covered padding around the tank. Bonnie looked back at the scummy surface of the water beneath her. Surely that was the level where the overflow would be found . . .

With a sick twist in her gut she understood why the pipe was no longer visible from the inside. The water was already *above* the outlet: its capacity was inadequate, and it was merely delaying disaster.

Now she could make out the opening, three inches down. There was no time to run downstairs for rubber gloves. Taking a noisy lungful of air, she forced herself to grasp the slimy ball float and wiggle it around. For a few brief seconds she thought she had released the valve, but the tank water continued to rise. She tried again, and knew she had failed.

She would have to turn off the water supply. At least three pipes led into the tank from below, but Bonnie could see no sign of a stop tap. There would be one somewhere on the ground floor, but where? It wasn't under the sink, she knew that much. *Roy* would know . . .

With a final glance at the sinister water level, Bonnie fled the attic. Clattering downstairs, she paused only to collect some small change from a dish on the hall stand before leaving the house and sprinting up the road. The telephone box was blessedly empty. She seized the Yellow Pages and riffled through the book until she reached the section on timber yards.

She had never telephoned Roy at work before. He wouldn't be pleased, but he would surely realize that this was an emergency. She dialled the number of Wilson's Timber and tapped her foot impatiently as she waited for someone to answer.

'Hello, Wilson's.' A surly-sounding man.

'Hello. I'm sorry to bother you. I'm Roy Judd's wife. I need to speak to him urgently.'

'Who did you say?'

'Roy Judd. I'm his wife.'

'There's no one of that name working here right now.' His tone was cagey.

'There is . . . there must be. He started in July. Please – it's a plumbing emergency.'

There was a pause, then a sigh. 'I'm sorry, Mrs Judd, but we can't help you. Your husband *was* with us but he left some weeks ago and we've had no further contact.'

'But – '

'I'm sorry, Mrs Judd. Goodbye.'

10

'Where have you been?'

Roy paused in the act of pulling off his jacket and stared stupidly at Bonnie. 'What kind of question is that? I'm not late, am I? In fact, you're home early.'

'I've been here since quarter to four. I was taking some time off.' With an effort, Bonnie controlled the anxious sharpness in her voice; a defensive Roy was unlikely to provide answers.

Casually he hung the jacket in the hall. 'So what's your problem?'

'There was a plumbing emergency. The ball float jammed in that tank up in the attic . . . the overflow couldn't cope and water was about to flood into the house.'

'You fixed it?'

'I didn't. Mr Schofield came and helped. He says the valve should be replaced.'

'Fair enough. We owe him one.'

'Roy . . .' Bonnie followed him back into the kitchen. 'It was quite alarming at the time, with all the water pouring into the yard and the tank level rising . . . I ran up the road and tried to ring you at Wilson's.'

'Oh?'

'Look at me, Roy. They said you weren't there. They said you hadn't been there for weeks.'

He gave a half-shrug. 'Someone made a mistake.'

'They didn't, Roy. It's only a small place. They know who their employees are. Please tell me what's happened.'

'Nothing's happened.'

'Roy – please.'

He flushed and began to fill the kettle with water, an unusual gesture in itself.

Bonnie laid a gentle hand on his arm. 'Roy . . . I thought we got married to share things. I'm not judging you, I only want to know. They said you'd left, but was it their fault?'

Slowly he put down the kettle and stared out of the window. 'There was a bloke at the yard,' he said. 'A right psycho. Hated my guts right from the start – and I hated him. Personality clash, if you like. It all blew up one day; I got my cards.'

'Roy, I am sorry.'

'I've been doing bits and pieces ever since, in between trips to the DSS and sessions at the Job Club. There just isn't the work around. But don't worry, I'll get something soon.'

'Of course you will.' Bonnie hugged him, and after a moment's hesitation he reciprocated. As she drew back, though, her compassion was skewered by a shard of fear. She knew so little about their financial affairs: Roy handled everything. All she knew with certainty was the paucity of her own salary. Were they already behind on their mortgage loan repayments?

'Let me help with the budgeting,' she proposed minutes later as they drank their tea. 'I've been such a passenger – I don't even know how much we pay for the mortgage each month.'

'There's no need for you to be involved in our accounting,' he said. 'You've got your household jobs, I've got mine.'

She swallowed. 'But are we behind with our payments to the bank?'

He met her gaze steadily. 'No, we're not. My savings will tide us over. You're not to worry about this, Bonnie. Tell me you won't.'

He needed her vote of confidence, but Bonnie was not given to lying. His news had further shadowed an already dispiriting day; security was once more slipping away . . .

She forced herself to smile at him. 'We'll manage,' she said.

It was a week of strained atmospheres. On the one hand, here was the explanation for Roy's recent edginess and moods. His self-esteem must have suffered badly; Bonnie suspected he had hoped to conceal the job loss until he had found new employment. On the other hand, his refusal to involve her in financial readjustments had left her floundering in the dark. How long *would* his savings last? She had none of her own. Should he be drinking so much beer? Should they sell the car?

Bonnie could voice none of these questions to Roy. She could well remember the manic glare in his eyes on the sole occasion she had dared to challenge him for being drunk. Instinctively she knew that even mild suggestions of a strategy for domestic economies would provoke the same result. She would do anything to avoid that.

Each night, she lay awake thinking as Roy snored and grunted. Lorna must have lived like this: 'walking on eggs', afraid to discuss anything frankly. Why did they submit, join in the conspiracy? Were they so very afraid of being alone?

But there was the irony. To all intents and purposes, Bonnie was already alone. Lorna was dead (a rat-faced detective had called on the Tuesday to ask if they had seen anything further of Bill), Hazel could not be trusted, Cassie had treated her like yesterday's plaything . . . And Roy himself, her husband, whom she could touch if she stretched out her hand, was the most distant of all.

Between the piled shelves of Asda, Bonnie made mental calculations as Roy thrust an armful of baked bean tins into their shopping trolley. She could covertly cut down on a number of items, buy cheaper brands, make fewer dishes with meat . . . Roy wouldn't notice. But trying to prevent him from offsetting all her savings when they reached the liquor section was another matter altogether. She didn't relish the likelihood of a public argument.

'I thought we might walk up into the moors this afternoon,' she ventured. 'The weather's so fresh, we'd enjoy it. There might even be some whinberries to pick.' She knew his soccer team was down in Norwich.

'You go if you like. I don't fancy it.'

'Please. I'd love you to come, and it would do you good.'

'I said I don't fancy it!'

At the drinks section, the trolley jinked and vibrated as Roy clanged five four-packs of strong lager down on to the wire mesh. Bonnie said nothing.

She set off at two, wearing a quilted jacket, cord trousers and leather lace-up shoes. Crossing Jubilee Lane she felt that something was different about the houses along the road, but didn't stop to investigate. She cut across the patch of waste ground, forging through nettles and the prolific rose-bay willowherb, and gained the upland road just beyond the abandoned mill.

September was almost over. The weather was dry with a soft, cool breeze, and clouds sporadically skimmed past the face of the sun.

'Shall we have a picnic, Bonnie?' In the deep recesses of her

brain, Bonnie could hear her mother's girlish voice. Games and picnics had been as much a treat for her as for the child. Indeed, who would willingly grow up? Life as an adult held nothing but burdens.

As she breasted the first rise of these Pennine foothills, Bonnie paused to look back over Holdendale, sprawled like a huge terracotta crab in the valley basin behind her. The swaths of dereliction on this side of town were, she knew, to some extent offset by the relative newness of the units in the industrial estate where she worked, yet Holdendale still struggled to shake free of its dependence on the old industries and adapt to the changing patterns of the modern world. The queue at the DSS and Roy's recent experiences were proof enough of that. As was the empty mill below . . .

It reminded her of the engine houses of long-defunct Cornish tin mines, ivy-clad sentinels on cliff-tops and moorlands, strangely romantic in their windswept isolation. This cotton mill, which had once clicked and whirred with the activity of scores of spindles, was now a similar monument to a lost era. Unlike the Moss Spinning Group ('diversify or die,' Cassie had quoted their managing director as saying), it had failed to adapt. Perhaps its workforce had hung on to the old ways with Luddite insistence. Or perhaps the unwelcome Cotton Industry Act had signalled the end. Whatever the reason – cheap labour abroad, unfair competition, subsidies, dumping – the life of this mill had slowly ebbed away in one long attrition. Only the shell remained, a square hulk with a thousand broken window panes and a tall chimney – still intact. To Bonnie this was not the accusing finger of a corpse, but a straight back, an echo from the dignity of the past.

Down on the valley floor a green bus was trundling along the strip of road past the Acorn Mill, like a tortoise bettle out for a gentle stroll. It swung left and began to ascend the slope towards Bonnie; with sudden decision she turned to locate the nearest bus-stop. Lorna had told her of beautiful walks five miles or so into the moorland: the bus could take her there.

Seventy yards up the road a woman with a bulky shopping bag was standing outside a lonely stone cottage. She held out her arm stoutly as the bus swept past Bonnie, and with squealing brakes the vehicle slowed to a halt. Sprinting, Bonnie was just in time to embark before the doors closed. She heard the woman say, 'The reservoir,' and watched her proffer a pound.

The driver addressed his next passenger. 'Where to, love?'

'The reservoir, please,' echoed Bonnie. It sounded nice and open, at least. She took a seat at the back as the bus lurched on its way, and saw the deserted mill slowly retreat behind the hillside until only the top of its chimney remained visible. Perhaps one day it would be the subject of a steeplejack spectacular, a dramatic demolition in front of gaping crowds. That might even be the sensible thing to do – yet somehow she hoped that the powers that be would leave it alone.

The reservoir was clearly a popular walking area for local people. An established path ran close to the water, and three bench-style picnic tables were situated in an adjacent curve of the hillside which had been levelled and gravelled over. There was some limited car-parking space.

The air was cooler up here: more vigorous. As Bonnie took great breaths through her nostrils, she saw the woman from the bus plump herself down on the nearest bench and fumble in the bulging shopping bag. Picnic first, thought Bonnie, amused. Then maybe a walk if there's time . . . Moments later she acknowledged herself mistaken. The woman lifted a tiny dog, a chihuahua, from the depths, clipped a lead to its collar and set it on the ground. It gave a yap of delight, and she proceeded to follow the furiously pumping little legs at a leisurely pace.

Bonnie chose the alternative anticlockwise route, because the handful of other strollers seemed to have chosen the same route as the woman. Alone on her side of the reservoir she could walk at her own pace, and muse. On Sundays, the whole place was probably teeming with families.

The reservoir was man-made to follow the natural contours of the land, not large enough to have become a water sports centre and not essential enough to the strategy of North West Water to have been fenced off with barbed wire. Indeed, Bonnie had heard that Holdendale's supply came from the Lake District sixty miles to the north. Its quality had been the first thing she had noticed on returning to Lancashire. Clear and pure, it bore little resemblance to those scummy, kettle-clogging offerings from the south's chalk downlands.

After a mile of robust walking, Bonnie paused to watch the water surface ruffle in the breeze. When the sun escaped from its cloud veil and the wind abated, she could see the sloping walls of the reservoir, with their cobbled pattern of stone, disappear into a layer of silt on the reservoir bed. The water, its surface three feet below where she stood, looked about four feet in depth. That meant it was actually deeper. Something about refraction, she remembered vaguely from school.

An object lying in the sediment caught her eye. It was an old pram, rusting and distorted. A little further along was something blue. What a pity people had to use this lovely spot as a rubbish dump! As she approached this second piece of jetsam, Bonnie saw that it was a bicycle, an old-fashioned roadster. It had a frame of cobalt blue with silver forks; the wheels were steel. The rear wheel was partially buried in silt, but it seemed to have its full complement of spokes, as did the fully visible front wheel. The chain was there, the brake cables, gears, saddle . . . no attempt appeared to have been made to cannibalize any parts. Despite its age, it looked too good to throw away. Someone like Darren Schofield, two or three years older and taller, could have made good use of such a bike.

Bonnie frowned as she lifted her gaze to stare assessingly across the water. Whoever had dumped this bicycle had wheeled it almost half-way round the reservoir. A wastrel with more money than sense would not have taken the trouble. Perhaps it had been stolen by a joyrider. Yes, that seemed likely. There was a saddlebag down there in the murk, a flap of bottle-green nylon.

Bottle-green nylon . . . Surely Bill Heaton had carried a saddlebag like that. And his bike had been blue . . . Everyone had assumed that Bill had left the area on his bike, then abandoned it and hitched a lift somewhere, to London or

Scotland . . . Was this the same machine? Bonnie couldn't be certain. It might be a vital clue for the police, or it might be a wild-goose chase. Would he really have left it here? Suddenly she wished that Roy was with her. Like most men, he took notice of mechanical details while Bonnie only registered vague parameters like shape and colour. He would know.

There were no landmarks close at hand, but Bonnie judged that she could find the spot again, especially if she located the pram. With one final look, she set off along the path and soon met up with people coming the other way.

The woman from the bus was now carrying the chihuahua; she nodded in response to Bonnie's tentative smile. Behind her, a couple of teenage boys scuffled and bantered with each other, but made no move to block her path. In the distance, a child flew a kite while an elderly man watched.

At the far corner of the reservoir, another footpath branched left towards the moorland proper, away from this grassy transitional area. Bonnie turned and began a slow ascent, feeling the soul-expanding vigour of freedom as she climbed. The mysterious bike was thrust to the back of her mind: she wanted to concentrate on the springiness of the turf beneath her feet, and the carpet of heath just ahead, the possibility of whinberries on the nab. In her pocket were two plastic bags; it was late in the season to find the sweet berries, but hopefully not too late.

Each horizon led to another. Holdendale had slipped from sight long before the reservoir, so now there was nothing but swelling uplands at all points of the compass, sometimes grass, sometimes broad stretches of peaty wasteland. On the breeze came the liquid keening of a curlew, and Bonnie glimpsed the bird wheeling over a hollow with its gull-like flight.

After an hour she had still found no bilberry plants. She had kept to the beaten footpath, doggedly persisting in the belief that after all this climbing she must soon come upon a view . . .

Abruptly, she did. From the shoulder of this particular hill the edge of a valley unfolded obliquely ahead. There were farm buildings and scattered cottages; a ribbon of road wound through the valley floor. If she found a sensible way down,

Bonnie thought there might be a bus back to Holdendale from here. But she wasn't sure. Perhaps it would be wiser to retrace her steps . . .

A man was striding towards her from the high ground to the right. He wore an olive-green pullover and cords, a russet bodywarmer and tweed cap. As she stood, her thin blonde hair flapping in the wind, he began to angle down the hill towards the nearest farm.

She saw the pink of his cheek as he raised his head to glance across at her; he took two more paces, looked again and stopped.

'Good Lord,' he said. 'It's little Bonnie!'

11

'Jeremy!' Bonnie was stunned. Of all the people she might have expected to encounter here on this windswept moor, he was the least likely.

'The very same.' He took a step towards her and tilted the cap back, showing his face. 'Bonnie . . . would you believe it? I could have sworn you told me you lived in Dartford.'

'I did. I moved here. I live in Holdendale now.'

'A fresh start, close to your old stamping-ground? Good for you. I must say I think it's pretty invigorating up here. I'm renting a farmhouse while I get my notes in order and the text written. There are still tenants in my Hertfordshire place. I thought I'd get right away from there.'

'Is, er, your fiancée with you?'

'Helena?' He gave an ironic laugh. 'No. She called off our engagement – said I'd spent months travelling and was already looking for an excuse to globetrot again. She's right, you know. I've got itchy feet: I can't help it.'

'I'm sorry, though,' said Bonnie.

'Don't be. I deserved it. And if I'm honest, I feel relieved. I really wasn't ready.'

Bonnie hovered, a prey to mixed emotions. From the sound of it, all the pressure had been Helena's, even though she had been obliged to give up in the end. But what of Bonnie herself? She had hardly been the unwilling victim of ineluctable forces. So easily had she made the mistake of her life, and now standing mere feet away was a major reason to regret it.

How handsome he was, with those strong white teeth and the healthy glow of exercise in his face! It was as if they were once again on the tussocky moorland west of Paúl da Serra, she explaining how it reminded her of the Pennines she had known as a child. Perhaps he had come up here to see for himself, the traveller's instinct ever active.

'Either your companions are very slow, or you're here on your own,' he remarked.

'I'm alone, but . . .' She needed to say, 'I'm married,' but the words stuck in her throat.

He waited, then gave a little nod. 'Right. Well, I was just going back to the farm for some tea. It's the stone building over there, with sheep on three sides. Would you like to join me?'

Still she couldn't tell him; it felt like a shameful secret.

'Come on, make a lonely writer happy.'

'Since you put it like that . . .'

'Good.'

Bonnie had expected a spartan interior, to match the farmhouse's weathered outer aspect, but the rooms were surprisingly luxurious.

'I'm renting it furnished,' Jeremy explained. 'It used to be a working farmhouse, but now it's a businessman's second home. The pastures here belong to Lower Clough Farm down the valley.'

'It's lovely,' said Bonnie sincerely, admiring the satinweave curtains of the sitting-room, the subtle peach and blue shades of the upholstery. The kitchen was enormous, with an Aga, a stained pine table, and plentiful matching cupboards.

'That blasted thing,' he said, pointing to the Aga, 'may be

every middle-class housewife's dream, but it certainly isn't mine. I do my cooking on those rings in the corner.'

Bonnie laughed, imagining endless stir-fries; she couldn't envisage Jeremy as a baked-beans man.

'I've converted one of the bedrooms into a study,' he continued. 'The view from the window encompasses most of the valley. If I'd had any wit I'd have used the other room for work. I can sit staring out for hours, getting nothing done!'

'Have you written up your Madeira booklet yet?' she asked shyly.

'No. I'm still sorting out which photographs I want to use.'

'May I see them?'

'Of course. They're in a bit of a jumble, though. Let's have tea first.'

It was when she reached out to take a cup from him that his eyes fixed on her left hand. 'Nice ring,' he commented.

'Yes. I . . . got married in July.'

'That was quick work. Congratulations.' He spoke lightly, but Bonnie felt herself blush.

'You, er, you met him,' she floundered. 'Just briefly. By the harbour in Funchal. The man who asked you the time.'

'Sorry, I . . . oh, yes. Ray, didn't you say he was called? The pool attendant.'

'Roy,' she corrected him, then found to her horror she had nothing more to say.

'So you're living in Holdendale,' he went on easily, leaning back in his armchair and crossing one cord-clad knee over the other. 'What does Roy think of the north?'

'He's Lancastrian himself . . .' *We've got that much in common* . . . 'He knows this general area quite well.'

'Not a walker, though?'

Bonnie forced a smile. 'He supports Blackburn Rovers.' Jeremy needn't be told they were playing at Norwich.

'Ah, never get between a man and his soccer team. I must admit I escaped that particular bug. Helena would say it didn't make much difference . . . Here, have some of this shortbread while I fetch the photographs.'

He returned with maps, leaflets and a batch of prints. Bonnie, after wiping her fingers assiduously, examined the pictures with great eagerness.

'This is the Nuns' Valley!' she exclaimed. 'But you didn't take it from the viewing point.'

'I had to avoid angles which thousands of tourists could replicate.'

'Oh, look at these! What vivid orchids . . . and these – how dramatically you've captured the cliffs, all dark and steep with the little road winding along the very edge . . . Is this the north coast?'

'Yes: the road near Porto Moniz at the north-west tip. I'm not a trained photographer, though; I haven't done the subjects full justice.'

'You have. Your pictures really give the flavour of the island.' Bonnie studied each print carefully, then returned to one which held special appeal. 'I like this one the best.'

Jeremy leaned forward to see, and was puzzled. It was an innocuous shot, a tract of scrubby moorland with a single, startled sheep just to the right of centre. 'That could be here,' he said.

'That's why I like it.'

He raised his eyebrows, but she didn't explain. When he had driven up into the hills to show her the levadas, she had felt such a sense of homecoming. Part of it had indeed been the joy of a moorland terrain after the dreary flatnesses of England's south-east, but an equal part had been the pleasure of his company and kindness.

'It was taken near Paúl da Serra – you remember Paúl da Serra, don't you, that flat, tundra-like plain? I thought so. Did I tell you they planned to build the airport there, only to discover that it's covered in cloud over fifty per cent of the time . . . They had to create a site in the south instead.'

'Across a horrid little spit of land!' said Bonnie with feeling. She well remembered the plane banking to approach the runway, her realization how short the runway was, the scream of reverse thrust on touch-down, the white-knuckled alarm of most of the passengers . . . While Amanda had emitted a burst of reflex squeals, Bonnie had been forcibly reminded of the manner of her parents' deaths.

'The pilots are superb,' Jeremy was saying cheerfully. 'They get used to landing like that, and setting off again with just enough fuel to reach the bigger runway on the next island, Porto Santo . . .' He stood up. 'Let me clear these dishes away, then we can talk some more.'

As he disappeared into the kitchen, Bonnie idly opened one of the maps. It was an ocean-floor map, giving an entirely new perspective to the tiny dots of land people normally saw from the surface of the sea. There were great mountain chains, plateaux, rifts, so much topography hidden under fathoms of blue. Madeira looked sinister here, a dark, steep mountain with a siren crown of green.

She checked her watch as Jeremy returned, and was suddenly appalled. What would Roy be thinking? She had 'gone for a walk', not specifying any duration, but the time was now five fifty and she still had to find the nearest bus-stop. 'I must be getting back,' she said anxiously. 'I have to put the dinner on.'

'Of course. Let me give you a lift.'

'No . . . no, thank you.' She felt instinctively that Roy would be furious if she rolled up in Clegg Street with Jeremy. 'I need to find out where the bus-stop is for next time. That is, I might be walking in this general area again . . .' Mentally she cursed herself. Whatever she said sounded wrong. Now he would think she was angling for another invitation.

'You don't drive?' he asked.

'No. Could you tell me the quickest way to the main road from here?'

He sighed. 'Bonnie – let me drive you home. It's no trouble.'

'Thank you, but I'd rather take the bus – honestly.' She knew she could have asked him to drop her off somewhere away from Clegg Street, but he was too astute to be fooled. He would have stayed to watch her enter her own front door.

'The next bus goes in half an hour,' he said. 'I know – I see them from the study window.' He helped her on with her jacket;

as she reached in the pockets for her gloves, one of the plastic bags fell out.

'I was hoping to pick whinberries,' she said, 'but I didn't find any.'

'There's a tangle of blackberry canes in a corner of the garden here. The fruit's bang on ready – black and sweet. You're welcome to pick some. There is time.'

Bonnie gratefully accepted the offer, aware that the spoils might provide a slender excuse to Roy for her tardiness. Afterwards she accompanied Jeremy down a narrow, rutted lane, while sheep bleated in the surrounding fields.

'Are you happy with life, Bonnie?' he asked her unexpectedly as they turned into the main road and approached the bus-stop.

'Yes,' she answered after a split-second pause.

'I'm glad.' They walked a few paces in silence, and she could feel his assessing gaze.

'You're sure you'll be all right on the bus?' he asked as the tall green vehicle hove into view along the road.

'Quite sure. Thanks ever so much for the tea. I've really enjoyed myself.'

The bus drew up with a rumble of diesel engine. As the doors swished open, Jeremy bent to kiss her cheek. 'Goodbye, Bonnie,' he said, then thrust a small folded paper into her hand. 'That's my telephone number,' he whispered. 'You know where I am . . . Ring me if you ever need a friend.'

The living-room at Clegg Street was a mess. 'What time do you call this?' demanded Roy when Bonnie stepped inside and nervously eyed the squalor.

'I didn't mean to be so long. I was looking for whinberries out beyond the reservoir, but I didn't find any. I got these, though. They were growing near a wall.' She showed him the blackberries, a poor enough excuse for five hours of absence. 'I'll make us a crumble tomorrow,' she promised.

'What about tonight? No food on the table, no clue as to when madam will deign to return . . . What were you *really* doing, Bonnie?'

Bill Heaton's bicycle flashed back into her memory. 'I spent some time at the reservoir,' she said carefully, 'and I came across something strange. Do you remember Bill's bicycle? The blue and silver roadster that disappeared when he did? Well, I saw a machine which looked amazingly like it at the bottom of the water. It even had a green saddlebag like his. I wondered whether we should call that detective who was here last week.'

'What, to tell him you've seen some old junk on a reservoir bed? I think you'd be done for wasting police time.'

'It *wasn't* old junk. It was in good condition. I never looked at Bill's bike particularly closely, but the overall impression was identical. You'd have thought so, Roy. I'm sure you would . . . Can we go back up there so I can show you?'

'Tonight? You're off your trolley, girl.'

'No – tomorrow. In the morning. Please.'

'I don't see the point. He'll be hundreds of miles away by now, anyway. Maybe even out of the country.'

'But at least the police should be told. It may affect their strategy in some way. Please say you'll have a look, Roy. You're much better than I am at identifying mechanical things.'

'If it stops you nagging, yes. Now shut up about it. What's for dinner?'

'There's mince in the fridge. I could make spaghetti bolognese quite quickly.'

'Chilli would be better.'

Men! 'I'm sorry, Roy, we've no kidney beans.'

'The shop's open till nine. You start the mince, I'll go and buy a tin.'

Bonnie, quite taken aback by this unexpected offer, said nothing to jeopardize Roy's contribution. Perhaps there was hope yet. But as she stood by the cooker, browning the meat in the large frying pan, her head was full of Jeremy.

12

'Where *is* this famous bike, Bonnie? I'm beginning to think you must have imagined it.' As Roy stood to one side to let yet another noisy family erupt along the waterside path, his impatience and lack of genuine interest were evident.

'Don't be silly.' Bonnie's own voice was sharp; she was baffled and frustrated. After some difficulty with surface reflections she had found the rusty pram, and felt confident that the bike would be located within minutes. Now she prowled up and down the same stretch of path, peering at the silt with an increasing sense of disbelief. There was no sign of anything resembling a bicycle. Either she was going mad, or . . .

'You've got the wrong place,' said Roy.

Bonnie sighed. 'It wasn't this far beyond the pram, I'm sure. And we've checked every inch in between. I just don't understand. It *was* here, Roy. I swear it.'

'You said the bike was in good condition?'

'For its age, yes. I don't think it had been in the water long.'

'Someone's nicked it, then. Some young lad.'

'Since *yesterday*?'

'Why not? What's the time now . . . eleven fifty, the best part of a day since you were up here. And if you spotted it, why shouldn't someone else?'

'I suppose that's possible . . .' Bonnie stared doubtfully at the water. Apparent depth four feet, real depth nearer five. Whoever had removed the bike would have got very wet. But if they were motivated enough . . . Yes, it was just possible.

'Let's go home,' said Roy.

'Don't you want to stay and have a proper walk?'

'Not with all these screaming kids milling around.'

'We don't have to confine ourselves to the reservoir – we could head up into the hills.' Bonnie was desperate to avoid another dull, fractious Sunday cooped up in Clegg Street.

'Okay,' said Roy. 'You can show me where you got the blackberries.'

Bonnie's heart gave a horrible lurch. Jeremy! While his home was at least three miles away over rough terrain, there was no guarantee that he might not at this very moment be taking his own Sunday walk in the direction of the reservoir. She should have thought of that before. Supposing they met him? Then Roy would know her for a liar – by omission, if not by commission.

'Maybe it's not such a good idea,' she amended. 'My legs are quite tired from yesterday. Let's go back and read the paper.'

As the Escort wound down the road past the derelict mill and turned into Jubilee Lane, Bonnie's heightened senses once more told her that something in the locality had changed. They were past in a flash, though, before she could define it more specifically.

'Roy . . . Please can we turn round?' she asked. 'I think there's some work going on at the other end of Jubilee Lane.'

'So what if there is?' he said wearily.

The car swung into Clegg Street; Bonnie knew better than to persist.

'No heather?' echoed Hazel the next day. 'I'm not surprised. This moorland's too wet as a rule. The Yorkshire moors, now, they're different. They're on the east side . . .'

'There's 'eather up near Burnley,' objected Jayne. 'And over on Longridge Fell. Masses of it, all purple. We 'ad a picnic there last year. Ace views. Yer can see clear across ter Pendle 'ill.'

'What about whinberries?' asked Bonnie.

'Winter Hill,' pronounced Hazel. 'Out near Bolton. That's the best place I know.'

A strangled cry in the corridor interrupted their deliberations. Hazel and Jayne exchanged knowing glances.

'Mr Fisk,' said Hazel in answer to Bonnie's expression of alarm.

'Reckon 'e's seen that spider in the corridor,' said Jayne. 'It's a right monster – the size of a walnut, and that's just the body!'

Hazel nodded in affirmation. 'They always come indoors in

September. They start appearing in the sinks and baths . . . You all right, Bonnie?'

That evening Bonnie alighted from the bus at a later stop than usual, and took a back route to the far end of Jubilee Lane. Things had undoubtedly changed here. An entire row of houses from the Clegg Street side of the road had disappeared. Open cellars filled with rubble were all that remained to mark their passing. Beyond this area had been the house with the 'hanging mantelpiece'. This, too, was now gone, and in its place had sprung up a compound bounded by metal fencing which bore the welcoming notice DEMOLITION SITE. KEEP OUT.

Active demolition, thought Bonnie. The empty houses of Jubilee Lane were being rolled up like a carpet. Once this momentum reached the junction with Clegg Street, it would be perilously close to her own home. At best, there would be noise and nuisance. At worst . . .

Bonnie circumnavigated the fenced-off compound, but all was quiet; the workmen had clearly downed tools for the day. She called out 'Hello' near the small wooden hut guarding the entrance to the site; there was no reply.

It was only Roy's evasiveness which had made her uneasy. Something guilty in his manner whenever she broached the subject of Jubilee Lane had niggled with Bonnie for some time; she resolved to find out for herself what was really happening.

The next day she reached the site at five to five, having worked through her lunch break in order to appease Gradwell's. A man wearing overalls and a hard hat was climbing down from a huge mechanical digger; another man stood in the entrance to the hut.

'Excuse me,' she called to the latter, and he walked towards her.

'Yes?'

'I live just up the road. Can you tell me your, er, schedule, please?'

He grinned, showing tobacco-stained teeth. 'Don't worry, lass,' he said. 'We finished our last contract early, so we're just clearing Jubilee Lane while we've got a few days. But Clegg Street will be after Christmas, as planned.'

Clegg Street . . . Bonnie felt the blood draining from her face and stepped away for fear of making a fool of herself. Murmuring 'Thank you' she stumbled towards her home with constriction in her chest and a numbness in her brain. On the corner she paused, reluctant to face Roy, who was presumably lounging on the premises. He knew about this; of course he did. He had let her become attached to the house, make small repairs, decorate, create a real home, all the while knowing it was due for demolition within a matter of months. But why had he bought a doomed building in the first place? It didn't make any sense – unless he hadn't known at that point. Had Roy tried to save on solicitor's fees, and made a ghastly error . . .?

Sudden renewed fears for their financial situation made Bonnie feel ill. She *must* have misunderstood. That foreman, or whatever he was, probably meant that a few houses at the very bottom of Clegg Street would be affected. That was it.

As she dragged herself ever more slowly towards number 14, Bonnie saw Wayne Schofield, Darren's elder brother, trundling her way on his mountain bike. She could ask him, perhaps . . . A surly youth of twelve, he passed her without greeting, and Bonnie had no heart to call out and stop him. Her ignorance would appear ridiculous, anyway. But she *had* to know before confronting Roy . . .

Madge would be able to tell her.

'I thought yer knew!' Madge gaped at Bonnie as they sat on threadbare armchairs in her dingy sitting-room. 'I mean, it's been in the papers an' everythin'. I reckoned yer were squattin', the pair o' yer. It were nowt ter me. Bill 'Eaton were doin' the same.'

'Do you own this house?' asked Bonnie.

'We pay rent. It's the landlord's problem, not ours. We've got another place lined up – we're movin' on November fifteenth.'

'But . . . why is Clegg Street being demolished?'

'Need you ask?' Madge rolled her lizard-lidded eyes. 'Another road – another bloody swath o' concrete. It'll swing round the 'ill an' link 'Oldendale with the M62. All the properties round 'ere are under a compulsory purchase order. 'Ave been fer the last two years.'

Roy's face was closed and hostile as Bonnie recounted her discovery to him.

'Did you really buy this house?' she finished up.

'I told you I did. With Ivor, as it happens.'

Ivor, whom she had never met. 'Truly, Roy? We're not just – squatting?' Ambivalent before, now Bonnie needed to hear that they had no binding financial stake in this blighted pile of bricks and mortar.

'We bought it from an old man who wanted to live in Somerset with his sister. He was confused by the situation here, and didn't know if he'd receive an adequate amount of compensation; he was glad to sell.'

'Compensation?' Bonnie felt a surge of hope.

'Of course. The council have a legal duty to compensate us. We'll do quite nicely out of it.'

'Oh . . .' Somehow she hadn't thought of this. 'You mean, make a profit?'

'Yes. That was the whole point.'

'Roy. Did you con that old man?'

'We took a load off his shoulders.'

'But did you give him a fair price?'

'He thought so at the time.'

Roy's lips were narrowing, a warning sign Bonnie knew she should heed. Nevertheless, she was troubled. Roy was lazy, uncouth and drank too much, but none of these characteristics affected anyone except herself. As such, she could manage to cope. But this latest affair smacked of dishonesty, a con. She had a mental image of an elderly, semi-senile man, frail and vulnerable, signing away his birthright for a mess of pottage . . .

Another realization struck her. If Roy had bought the house

with Ivor, she had no rights at all. The deeds would be in their names.

'What was your arrangement with Ivor?' she asked hesitantly.

'Half the stake, half the proceeds.'

'But you don't know where he is.'

'He'll send me his address in Newcastle when he's sorted out. There's no hurry. What *is* this, Bonnie, this interrogation? You've got a roof over your head. Is there some problem?'

Bonnie steeled herself against the instinct to back away. 'No,' she said mildly. 'It's just that . . . I thought when we got married . . . I thought we'd be buying a house together.'

'But you know you haven't signed any mortgage documents.'

It was true. 'I've never understood these things,' she admitted. 'I didn't have occasion to. I – I imagined you'd signed the contract on my behalf. You'd always spoken about *our* house.'

'Well, it is ours. We're living here, aren't we? I really don't know what you're bitching about. You had nothing when we married; I arranged all this for us, and when the money comes in we'll be able to buy a better place.' His jaw began to jut aggressively. 'I don't ask much from you, you know. Just a bit of cooking, like any other woman can manage. But lately it's been nothing but pap.'

Bonnie was shocked. 'I'm sorry, Roy. I was just trying to save money. I thought you liked the food.' He had done, she was sure. Only on Friday he had asked for seconds of a vegetarian dish she had created, a medley of carrots, celery, courgettes, chickpeas and tomatoes with a cheese crumble topping. And he had wolfed down potato pie the night before. Now, she felt, he was spoiling for a fight in order to deflect her attention from the house.

'I want *meat*, Bonnie!' He thumped his fist on the kitchen table to accentuate the point. 'Steak and chips, pork chops, steak and kidney pie. You get it?'

Can we afford it? 'Yes.'

'You're sure?'

'Yes.'

'What are we eating tonight?'

'Er . . . I hadn't quite decided.' Bonnie made a lightning mental inventory of the contents of the store cupboard and fridge: nothing there would appeal to Roy in his current frame of mind.

'We'll have fish and chips,' he decreed, and she began to breathe again.

'I'll go up to the chippy,' she said, heading for the door. 'I fancy a bit more of a walk. What can I get you?'

'The usual.' Haddock, chips, mushy peas – and curry sauce. Ugh.

Bonnie was glad to leave the house. She walked numbly up the road, wondering if this was really to be the pattern of her life for the next six decades. Would she ever be able to trust Roy to make the right decision, the honest decision, in important circumstances? It seemed not.

The conclusion was so desolate that she couldn't bear to dwell on it. Later she would have to do some serious thinking. For now, she would simply buy fish and chips and close her mind to everything else.

There was a large queue at the shop, dour-faced people with hands in their pockets. Bonnie squeezed inside and breathed the steamy fat-laden air; for a moment she was transported back in time to her first day in Clegg Street, to the frying smells in the passageway between her house and Lorna's, to the slowly whirring fan . . .

No, she vowed. I won't look back. There must be some way forward for Roy and me which will let us both be happy.

The queue shuffled towards the counter, and Bonnie found herself in a corner where a pile of cheap magazines and newspapers had been left for waiting customers to read. She riffled through the magazines, each a riot of primary colours, ankle-deep articles and humanoid interest stories, then pulled out a newspaper. It was a *Holdendale Evening Gazette*, dated a week previously. Idly she turned the pages. National news – 'Rebel MPs Brought to Heel', 'Sunday Shopping still a Shambles' – gave way to local items – 'Fund-raisers Beat the Bounds' and 'Neighbourhood Watch Success' – none of which caught Bonnie's interest.

Her gaze glided down to the foot of the page, resting briefly on 'Pedestrian Killed': 'A woman died today in collision with a car on a pelican crossing in Deansgate, Manchester. The victim has been named as Miss Cassandra Kershaw, a prominent feature writer with the *Manchester Herald*. She was taken to the Royal Infirmary immediately following the accident, but was certified dead on arrival. The driver of the car involved was treated for shock . . .'

Bonnie's fingers tightened around the newspaper as a cheerful voice behind the counter sang out to an invisible assistant for more chips. Cassie – dead. Vibrant Cassie. It couldn't be true. No . . .

Deep inside, she knew that it was.

13

As the queue edged forward, Bonnie kept the newspaper in her possession.

'May I take this?' she asked when her turn came. 'There's an article about someone I know.' The proprietor nodded, and she left the shop with the paper tucked beneath her arm. Once outside, however, she deftly folded it around the white package of fish and chips; for reasons not yet fully formulated, she wanted to withhold her discovery from Roy.

He hovered in the kitchen as she unwrapped the food. 'Newspaper?' he queried. 'Is the shop going back to the old days?'

'Oh, I just asked for a bit of extra wrapping to keep our supper hot,' she said, crumpling the paper and dropping it into the nearby pedal bin.

Later, she retrieved it and cautiously smoothed out the creases. The news item was very brief; it had been filed on the day of the accident when facts had been in short supply. But Cassie had been a journalist, albeit with a rival newspaper; they had surely covered the story more fully later in the week. And the *Herald* itself would doubtless have made a thorough investigation.

The scanty information tantalized her. *Collision with a car on a pelican crossing* . . . what did it mean? Had the driver not seen the red light? Or had Cassie been in a hurry and taken a dangerous risk? No . . . she was cool and competent. A silly misjudgement on a pelican crossing was not how someone like Cassie would have died.

Muffled gunfire and shouting American voices filtered through the wall from the living-room, where Roy was watching television, his feet on a frayed Dralon pouffe. Bonnie rolled the paper into a tight ball and thrust it once more into the bin. She dried the few dishes on the draining-board and made a pot of tea.

'I'm going to bed,' she told Roy, placing his mug within reach of his hand.

His eyes flickered towards her. 'I see.'

'I thought I'd read my new library book.'

She didn't. She lay in the orange-tinted darkness, the book unopened on the bedside chest-of-drawers. *Daniel Deronda* was there, too, and formed an extra focus for her growing unease.

First Lorna, then Cassie. The only two people in Holdendale who had taken more than a passing interest in her were dead. It was an outrageous coincidence – so outrageous that it was inconceivable. But these were two women who had never met, who had had vastly different lifestyles, and who had died in sudden, separate, unpredictable ways . . . Only Bonnie herself formed any kind of link between them. And to a lesser extent, Roy.

Roy . . . She shivered and curled up in the bed, trying to warm her icy limbs. She couldn't help but remember how Roy had tried to discourage her from developing any friendships with their neighbours. And that wasn't all. After an initial period of naïvety she had come to know him as a deceiver with a thuggish streak of barely suppressed brutality.

Don't tell Roy, Cassie's note had said. Bonnie had respected this instruction, but what had been the reason behind it? Horrible possibilities paraded through her brain. Perhaps Roy had pursued a long career as a con artist, and Cassie had found some newspaper report to his discredit.

Bonnie thought back to her own handling of the note. She had hidden it in her underwear drawer – a perfectly reasonable guard against *accidental* discovery, but a poor choice of location if the note's existence was already known. Roy had spotted it earlier protruding from her dressing-gown pocket; supposing he had not believed the shopping list story, but had instituted a search in his own time? She had so few possessions, he would have found it with ease.

Suddenly alarmed, Bonnie swung her legs out of the bed and padded barefoot to the light switch. Jeremy's telephone number was tucked between the leaves of *Daniel Deronda* – another obvious place. She curled the paper into a thin cylinder and pushed it down the narrow neck of an ornamental porcelain vase she had bought at the market. Tomorrow she would tape it under the bed.

Back beneath the covers, she drew her knees up to her chest, colder than ever. What was all this mistrust leading to? Was she really suggesting that Roy had taken the Escort and deliberately mown Cassie down *en route* to her rendezvous at the Exchange? No, the idea was madness. Marrying Roy had been a mistake, she knew, but not one of *that* magnitude. He wasn't the stuff of murderers . . . surely . . .

Bonnie rolled and fidgeted as the pernicious doubts refused to disperse. Could one marry someone and not *feel* evil in them, sense it beneath the friendly façade? Maybe one could. Some notorious serial killers had wives who apparently knew nothing of their dark activities . . .

With an effort, she tried to remember what had attracted her to Roy in the first place. He had offered fun and companionship just when her spirits had reached their lowest point, and his knowledge of Madeira had shown his character to best advantage. That was the bleak truth, but it was far from proof that Roy was a killer. If she put his recent actions under the golden spotlight of generosity rather than the blue one of suspicion, kinder interpretations emerged. So he didn't encourage local friendships – he was probably afraid she would learn about Clegg Street's demolition prospects before he was ready to tell her. Why hadn't he explained to her at the start? Because the deal *had* been shady, and he was ashamed of her knowing. He couldn't have been the driver who hit Cassie – the Escort was unmarked. And as for Lorna's death, not only had Bill Heaton guiltily run off, but Roy had been here at home at the time of the murder. So that was that.

Perversely, Bonnie's cramped limbs still refused to relax; indeed, when she heard the click of a light switch in the hall her muscles tensed all the more. As one of the landing floorboards creaked under Roy's feet, she closed her eyes and tried to breathe steadily.

He entered the room and spoke into the half-light. 'Still sulking, Bonnie?'

She gave no reply.

'You can't be asleep yet.' He sat down heavily on his side of the bed and pulled off his shoes. 'Look, I know why you've been quiet all evening. I shouldn't have been rude about your cooking when you've been trying hard to save money . . . Let's not quarrel. I'm sorry for what I said.' He leaned across and laid a hand on her shoulder; she could sense him peering at her face.

'It's all right,' she murmured, blinking. 'I'm sorry, too.' Continuing to feign sleep would only have antagonized him, she knew.

Within minutes Roy was in the bed alongside her. 'Stone the crows!' he exclaimed. 'It's a bloody ice-box in here. Your feet are like two bags of frozen sweetcorn.'

'Sweetcorn?'

'Niblets,' he said obliquely.

He seized her right foot and chafed it between his hands, then repeated the action for the left. Soon she felt him pressing closer with unmistakable intent.

'Thank you, Roy,' she said. 'Good-night.'

'You can't mean that. You need warming up. We're newly-weds, remember.'

Newly-weds! It felt like a million years. 'I've got a headache,' she told him. 'I'm sorry.'

He gave a snort which fell somewhere between amusement and disbelief. 'That's not very original, Bon.'

She made herself twist round and touch his cheek. 'I *do* have a headache,' she said. 'I'm sorry. Things'll be better tomorrow.'

To her relief, he sighed and subsided. Bonnie kept very still, staring at the diffuse light of the street lamp as Roy moved again, settled and finally began to snore.

Thank heavens . . . She knew her revulsion would have been plain to him, and then what would have happened? But this was a new and worrying phenomenon; she had never felt such an acute physical shrinking before, even those times when Roy was drunk. It was as if her body was reacting to all the unresolved misgivings in her mind.

New questions crowded into her brain, demanding attention. Who was Ivor? Did he really exist? And if he did, why hadn't they heard from him? *Was he still alive?* And what about the 'old man' who had sold Roy the house? Did he really go to Somerset? Was *he* still alive?

Bonnie lay helpless in the grip of these appalling ideas. The 'case for the defence' she had attempted to construct seemed dangerously flimsy; now she tried to shore it up with additional fragments of logic. If Roy was a crook, why had he involved her at all? She was simply a liability, someone who might stumble upon one of his schemes and give the game away.

If he had plans which needed a contribution from her, he would have confided in her by now. But he had done nothing of the kind. That made no sense. *Unless . . .*

There *were* no plans. Bonnie gave a small smile in the gloaming and nodded a mental approbation. It was the only conclusion. Cassie's death had upset her, that was all, and everyone knew how distorted a person's thinking could be at night.

Gradually her breathing slowed, became deep and regular in a pattern to match Roy's. She thought about the way he had warmed her feet. Poor Roy – unskilled, narrow-minded, none too bright (and who was *she* to complain about that?), but not criminal.

Not criminal . . .

Just as Bonnie was on the point of dozing, Jayne's coarse, eager little voice burst through into her consciousness: Jayne bubbling with motives for someone to embark on a loveless marriage. *'I've got it! It's the life insurance . . .'*

'Morning brings counsel' . . . Aunt Rachel, a fervent exponent of improving mid-nineteenth-century American family stories, had often proffered this quotation when Bonnie suffered mental turmoil after dusk. The context had usually been that of exam revision; in Bonnie's experience, morning had merely brought confirmation of her intellectual limitations, plus the added dread of their imminent exposure.

This morning, however, there was 'counsel' of a sort. As Bonnie sat on the lurching bus to Holdendale town centre, she found her brain was working with increasing clarity. It was as if every mile of distance between her and Roy served to disperse the muffling emotional effects of his presence: the fears, the suspicions, the resentment. Now the fog had lifted, and she could more dispassionately consider the implications of the recent dark events.

Jayne's hypothetical suggestion really did embrace the facts. Workshy Roy, doubtless a veteran of several minor 'scams', had come across a girl adrift in the world without any family support. He had married her, whisked her away from her few friends, and planted her in a community which was about to be dissolved. He had then taken out massive insurance policies on her life, giving himself householder status with 14 Clegg Street as his bona fide British address. And when they moved from Clegg Street to an area where they knew no one at all, she would meet with an 'accident' and Roy would become wealthy.

She remembered his air of suppressed impatience, of having to bide his time. Like her, he had started off with a job, but had abandoned it as soon as he could, doubtless hoping she would never find out. *'I liked you better when you were stupid,'* he had told her once – one of few occasions when Roy had been sincere.

She had played ball at the start, pathetically grateful for his assumption of responsibility for her future. She had concentrated on being a good wife, and left the paperwork to him. But slowly, nevertheless, she had begun to break the rules – his rules. She had formed a friendship with Lorna. She had asked Roy awkward questions. And she had invited Cassie, an alert woman of the world, into their home . . .

Bonnie stood up as the bus jolted to a halt with loud squeaks and the hiss of air brakes. She suspended her ruminations until she had fought her way through the masses thronging Holdendale bus station to the stand where she could queue for the connecting bus to Gradwell's. Once aboard, she doggedly took up the thread again.

If the theory was correct, then Roy must have viewed Cassie as a threat. Even if the meaning of her note had been entirely benign, he had interpreted it in the light of his own guilty past. Roy had met Cassie, and could therefore easily recognize her as she walked between the *Herald* offices and the Exchange at the appointed hour.

'Action this day,' Churchill had urged his Ministers. Bonnie pondered what practical steps she could actually take. She could try to acquire more newspaper coverage of Cassie's accident – the central library in Holdendale subscribed to both local and national papers. She could also make discreet enquiries with a view to clearing up her burgeoning peripheral suspicions of Roy. Realistically, she knew that 'Ivor' would be impossible to track down without some lead from Roy himself. The matter of 14 Clegg Street's previous owner, however, was more tangible.

The edge of the industrial estate swung into view, and Bonnie gripped her bag in preparation for leaving the bus. What if her enquiries proved that a woman of sixty-five had blundered into Cassie, and 14 Clegg Street's former owner was alive, happy and living in Somerset? Would that be enough totally to dispel every last doubt about Roy's intentions towards herself?

Bonnie wasn't sure.

'The library closes early today,' said Hazel in answer to Bonnie's query. 'But if it's local newspapers you're after, I can help you.

I've got a pile of them at home waiting for recycling. I can bring some in tomorrow. What exactly were you looking for?'

'A girl I knew at school was knocked down last week. I've only just heard.'

'I'm sorry, love.'

'It's all right: we weren't close friends. I went down south and she stayed here. She became a journalist on the *Manchester Herald* – Cassandra Kershaw.'

'Cassandra Kershaw! I've read some of her articles. There was one on the Manchester Ship Canal. It was quite detailed – more the depth of a Sunday supplement than a local paper. I must admit I got the feeling she preferred reporting hard facts to human interest stories.'

Bonnie gave a wry smile: that was Cassie.

'I'm sure I've got the odd *Herald* lying around,' went on Hazel. 'I'll bring those in as well.'

That evening, as Bonnie approached the junction of Barlow Road and Clegg Street, she debated the pros and cons of asking Madge if she knew anything about 14 Clegg Street's previous owner. On the one hand, Madge knew a lot about the area. On the other hand, she had looked at Bonnie very strangely when they had discussed the compulsory purchase order: she might interefere in some way, or tell Roy. On balance, Bonnie felt she would prefer to question someone else.

Responding to an impulse, she turned off the street early and took the narrow boarded passage which led to Clegg Street's cobbled back alley. Sometimes the younger children were out playing after tea. One of them might know.

As she walked cautiously along the alley, she saw Darren Schofield with his brother and two girls outside number 18. Wayne was deep in a 'cool dude' fantasy, a cigarette between his twelve-year-old lips, a baseball cap worn back to front, and a Walkman personal stero pouring flat, tuneless rap into his ears. His mountain bike leaned against the wall nearby; one hand rested lightly but possessively on the saddle.

The other children stood slightly apart. Bonnie decided to

start with Darren; the lone Wayne, just over half her age, intimidated her.

'Hi, Darren,' she said. 'Have you got a minute?'

He nodded and joined her.

'You know the old man that lived in Number 14 before Roy and I came?'

'Yeah?'

'Well, I've lost his name and forwarding address, and I need to contact him about something. Can you remember what he was called?'

'It were Walter.'

'That's great, Darren. What about his surname?'

'Sorry, Bonnie, I dunno. Wayne might, though. 'Ere, Wayne!'

Drat, thought Bonnie as Wayne fixed them with an insolent stare. Clearly this was par for the course, as Darren continued unabashed, 'Bonnie wants to ask yer summat about old Walter.'

It was time to be firm with this young man. 'Yes,' she said crisply. 'I wondered if you could spell his surname for me.'

Wayne gaped, as if it were a novelty for anyone to imagine he could spell anything.

'I'd be greatly obliged,' she prompted him.

He lifted the smouldering cigarette in his hand, and drew deeply. 'It were a daft name,' he mumbled. 'Tizzy, or summat. Nah, it were Tisley. I don't know 'ow 'e spelled it, though . . . an' I don't f – well care!'

Bonnie felt her face burn. The Schofield parents were nice people, if a bit rough around the edges like Roy. They didn't smoke, hence Wayne was lurking in the alleyway. As a newly enrolled adult, Bonnie felt it her duty to give them a little support in the thankless job of rearing youngsters.

Instead of retreating, she leaned towards Wayne so the two girls wouldn't hear. 'Wayne – have they told you at school that smoking can give you awful chest trouble?'

He drew in another lungful and eyed her speculatively as he exhaled. 'Listen, sister,' he said at last. 'Round 'ere, sayin' "'ave a pear drop" to the chicks don't do nothin' for yer cred.'

Bonnie retreated to her own back gate with as much dignity as she could muster. As she slipped into the yard, she reflected that Aunt Rachel might usefully have stressed, *'quit while you're ahead.'*

'Here,' said Hazel the next day, producing a Tesco carrier bag full of newspapers. 'Nine days of Holdendale dailies plus a few *Heralds*.'

'Thank you,' said Bonnie. 'That's really good of you.' Her heart was already thumping as she placed the stack on her desk and began to leaf through the Tuesday issue. Would they describe the driver who had been 'treated for shock' after the accident? Since first learning of the tragedy, Bonnie had tried to recall Roy's demeanour that Monday, but it was impossible. All the drama of the jammed float valve and the discovery of his absence from the timber yard had taken centre stage that evening.

She found a more detailed report, and sat down to read it. Cassie had 'stumbled' into the road when the lights were against her, and been hit by a silver Audi driven by a Mr Peter Green, 58, of Byrnes Drive, Holdendale. She had died of multiple injuries, including a fractured skull.

Sifting through the other papers added little. The funeral had been held on Friday, and the *Herald* had run a touching obituary for its erstwhile feature writer.

Just an accident, thought Bonnie. Perhaps Cassie was wearing stilettos. What a waste.

At lunch time, she turned her attention to the question of Walter Tisley. No mail addressed to that name had arrived at 14 Clegg Street since Roy and she had begun their occupancy. Presumably, then, it was being forwarded by the Royal Mail, either at his own behest to Somerset or – appalling thought! – at Roy's instigation to some collection point, probably local.

Bonnie was alarmed to find how readily she still suspected Roy, despite the evidence of the newspaper report. Nothing less than proof that Walter Tisley was still alive would now satisfy her. Hazel and Jayne were out buying the pies: she didn't have long to act.

With a guilty glance over her shoulder, Bonnie picked up the office phone and dialled the Royal Mail's advice number. Eventually she was connected to the right department, where she gave her name and address. 'I wonder if you can help?' she went on. 'Mr Tisley, who owned number 14 before us, paid to have his mail redirected, but one or two items have slipped the net. I'd send them on to him, but we've lost the address he left behind.'

'Just put them back in the post, love. We'll sort it out.'

'Actually, we would like to contact him ourselves about a gas bill, and he's in Somerset now . . . I don't suppose you could let me have the address? . . . That's very kind. Thank you.'

After a considerable delay, the precious address was relayed as Bonnie scribbled on a notepad. When she hung up, Mr Fisk was frowning at her from his newly opened office door.

'Bonnie,' he said, 'I'll thank you not to make personal calls on the office telephone.'

'I'm sorry, Mr Fisk.'

'And kindly refrain from reading newspapers in work time.' He began to close the door again, then paused. 'I'm surprised at you.'

Bonnie was too distracted to reply. Besides, she could hardly tell him that she had very little small change and the nearest public phone box was half a mile away. Information which was vital to her peace of mind would seem mundane to the disinterested observer. But she had made real progress: the address was Frome.

That evening, she stopped at a telephone box in the bus station. She fervently hoped that Walter's sister was neither married, widowed nor divorced, since Directory Enquiries would be unable to provide the telephone number in the absence of a surname. Bonnie could write a letter, of course, but their reply might take weeks, time she could not afford. It might also fall into Roy's hands.

She kept her fingers tightly crossed as the operator said, 'What name?' A few seconds later she was copying down a number, hardly able to believe her luck. The pips sounded just as she reached the last digit. Glancing up, she saw that a small queue had already gathered outside the box: they would hear everything through the glass. Hating her moral cowardice, she replaced the receiver and slunk away to catch her second bus.

She tried again closer to home, changing two pounds in a shop and taking possession of a vacant phone box at the far end of Barlow Road. Mentally she rehearsed her tale, then, with a deep breath, dialled the number she had been given. As the ringing tone went on and on, she found her hand was trembling. The fact of Walter's post being redirected to Frome, though encouraging, did not in itself constitute a guarantee that he was there.

'Hello.' It was a woman with a warm West Country burr.

'Er, hello. This is Mrs Judd speaking. May I speak to Mr Tisley, please?'

'Who's that again?'

'Mrs Judd. I'm ringing from Holdendale. My husband bought the house from Walter.' Now Bonnie could feel all the worst effects of adrenalin. Was the woman about to say that Walter wasn't there, they didn't know where he was but they were looking after a couple of letters for him . . .

'He's just having his tea at the moment.'

'Walter?' The good news felt as much a hammer blow as the expected bad.

'That's right. I'll fetch him if it's important, but it'll take him a few minutes to get to the phone.'

'No – don't bother him, please. I'm sorry to have disturbed your meal. I'll ring again another time.'

'You're not disturbing me at all. It's only salad. Perhaps you'd like me to take a message?' The woman sounded eager to talk; perhaps she didn't receive many telephone calls.

'It was just a query about some furniture. You see, Mr Tisley left some pieces behind by agreement with my husband Roy . . .'

'That's right. He didn't need them, coming to live here.'

'Well, just recently I went up to the attic to track down a water leak, and I saw a little spiral-legged table and a carved wooden bookcase. I wondered if Mr Tisley had forgotten they were there, and might have wanted them.'

'I'll go and ask him.' Bonnie heard various noises: the clunk of the receiver as Miss Tisley laid it down, cutlery, a television, but she was unable to discern Walter's voice. She sincerely hoped they wouldn't want the furniture; it was in very poor condition, and would cost a fortune to send to Frome as a removals part load.

Clunk went the receiver again. 'Mrs Judd? Walter says keep the furniture. He says it's the least he can do after your husband came forward to help him out. Such a good price he gave, no quibbling. Walter had been wanting to live down here for years . . .'

Bonnie murmured her valedictions in a daze. Whatever else she might have expected, it was not Roy the Hero.

In Clegg Street her steps slowed as the green door of number 14 came closer. Walter Tisley was alive and flourishing in Somerset, and a middle-aged man in a silver Audi had killed Cassandra in an unfortunate accident. Why, then, did she still feel a sense of primitive dread, a reluctance to face Roy? He was innocent: indeed, Walter Tisley had just lauded him . . .

Two young boys began shouting at each other on the pavement ahead. They joined together in a scuffle, then broke apart violently as the boy nearest the houses flung the other away from him. His friend staggered backwards into the road, which was luckily empty of all but parked cars.

Bonnie stopped. Of course. Her new-found incisive reasoning had been an illusion, a mass of flaws. How could anyone driving a car in one of central Manchester's busiest roads hope to be in just the right place when Cassie chose to cross? Even if the plan had been to plough into her when the lights were allowing pedestrians right of way, it was still fraught with difficulties.

No. How much more likely it was that someone on the pavement had jostled her at the crucial moment, causing her to 'stumble' into the path of the Audi. And if it *wasn't* an accident, that someone could well have been Roy.

14

At home, the atmosphere was stifling. Bonnie concentrated on making her persona even paler, more mouse-like, anything to avoid irritating Roy. At work she would sit in a fugue, wondering whether her perception of Roy as a dangerous criminal was accurate or the product of fevered imaginings, trying to determine whether there were any more practical investigatory steps left to take.

Mr Fisk tutted, Hazel jollied her along, Jayne remained oblivious. Bonnie knew she had to buck up, or her job would be in jeopardy. If only there was someone to talk to, someone who wouldn't laugh, spread gossip, or recommend a psychiatrist.

Meeting little resistance, Jeremy's image floated into her brain. Bonnie smiled ruefully. If only they had managed to spend a bit more time together . . . but she didn't know him well enough. She couldn't possibly ask him for a rendezvous and spill an elaborate tale like this – could she? No. But she wanted to – badly.

'Call me if you ever need a friend,' he had said. She did, she did. But something – was it pride? – was standing in the way. Was she actually embarrassed because he would guess she had clung slavering to the first person who had shown any interest in her?

Bonnie picked up her pen, dithered with it, laid it down again. In many ways her relationship with Jeremy had been that of pupil and mentor. If she kept things strictly on that footing, regarded any meeting as a form of consultation, she might be able to ask him for advice. There was no one else.

At dinner that evening she made up her mind. Roy was morose and surly, fielding her well-meaning questions about the job hunt with sarcasm. He had nothing gracious to say about her steak and kidney pie. As he slouched into the living-room, Bonnie felt an overwhelming desire to escape from the confines of Clegg Street, even just for a few hours.

'Er, I meant to tell you,' she began as he scanned the television schedules in the newspaper, 'Hazel from the office invited me to her house tonight to look at some dress patterns. I can get there on the bus – she lives near the town centre.'

'You want a lift?' He didn't sound keen.

'Thanks, but there's no need. The bus goes straight past her road . . . See you later, then. Have a nice evening.'

Bonnie washed her face, cleaned her teeth and slipped a perfume spray into her bag. She ducked under the bed, where she had taped a copy of Jeremy's number – reversed for security – and committed the digits to memory in their correct sequence. Minutes later she was fidgeting impatiently outside the red corner telephone box as a teenage girl recounted to a friend every detail of her latest date.

At last the girl finished, and Bonnie stood alone in the stale, cramped cubicle as darkness pressed against the glass panes all around her. Cellophane from a cigarette packet crackled underfoot. The receiver was heavy and greasy.

Taking a deep breath, she dialled Jeremy's number. If he wasn't there, she would walk the streets, go to the cinema . . . anything rather than spend the time with Roy.

'Hello?'

'Jeremy?'

'That's right.'

'It's Bonnie.'

'Bonnie! How nice! I was just thinking about you – I've been eating stewed blackberries and apple . . . How are things with you?'

She felt suffocated. How could she just *invite* herself to his home without notice? Yet she had already disturbed his evening, and he was waiting for her explanation. If she funked this now, she could never call him again.

Out of the tail of her eye she saw a figure approaching the phone box from the Clegg Street side. To her horror, she recognized Roy. Was he coming to ring the elusive Ivor, or one of those other 'mates' she had yet to meet?

Bonnie hunched her shoulders and turned away, making herself as anonymous as possible. She held her hand over the receiver, stared at the floor and waited for the first squeak of the door behind her. Three seconds . . . five . . . nothing happened. Cautiously she straightened her back and glanced towards Barlow Road. Roy was just turning right at the corner. Presumably there was nothing he fancied on television, and he was heading for the Taphouse.

'Bonnie? Are you there?'

'Yes. I'm sorry about that – there was a strange man outside the telephone box, but he's gone now. I was wondering . . . may I come and see you?'

'Of course. You know you don't need to ask. When did you have in mind?'

'I . . . would tonight be possible? If you're not busy, that is?'

There was a fractional pause, but when he spoke any surprise he may have been feeling was carefully expunged from his voice. 'I'm not busy at all – having quite a lazy evening, in fact. Come on over. Would you like me to pick you up?'

'No – there's a bus in just a few minutes . . . Are you sure you don't mind?'

'Go and get your bus, Bonnie. I'll meet you at the bottom of the lane.'

The sitting-room in the farmhouse was even more cosy than before, with a fire flickering in the grate and the satinweave curtains tightly closed against the blackness of night. Bonnie perched on the sofa, her hands wrapped round a large pottery mug of coffee, while Jeremy regarded her quizzically from a nearby chair.

'This tastes like coffee but somehow – enhanced,' she was saying.

'I added a dash of Tia Maria – my answer to nippy October nights. Now, Bonnie, we've been exchanging platitudes for the last fifteen minutes, and very pleasant it is, too, but I'm sure it's not what you came for. Are you going to tell me what's wrong?'

She took another sip of the coffee and felt the sweet, sharp warmth of the liqueur diffuse across her tongue. 'I just wanted to see you,' she said.

He smiled, a slow and heartbreaking smile. 'Oh, I should be flattered. You certainly have excellent taste. But a newly married young woman already itching to spend time away from her beloved? No, Bonnie, you have your reasons – I say, don't cry! Tears aren't allowed in here: they ruin the upholstery.'

Bonnie turned away as her face twisted into a taut square of anguish, but in a moment he was beside her, his arm round her shoulder, rocking her in a gentle soothing rhythm. 'Shh,' he whispered. 'Shhh. It's all right. Nothing's worth getting upset about. Whatever's wrong, I'm sure we can sort it out.'

She felt his cheek against her hair, and made an enormous effort to control herself. Crying like a baby had not been on the agenda, but Jeremy's innocent choice of the description 'newly married' had suddenly summoned all her piercing sense of failure. Never before had she felt it so acutely.

'Guess what!' he said. 'I haven't got a clean, white folded handkerchief to offer you. Only this crumpled blue thing. Oh, it *is* clean, but that's about all . . .'

She gave a hiccup of laughter as she accepted the square of cotton, and attempted to blow her nose daintily. 'Thank you. I'll wash it and let you have it back.'

'I should hope so.'

She laughed again, then sobered as his face grew serious.

'Is Roy the problem?' he asked.

Battered loyalties still tried to block the path to disclosure, but they had grown thin and querulous with each new discovery Bonnie had made. 'Yes,' she said.

'Nothing you tell me will go beyond this room.'

'I know. It just feels – wrong to talk behind his back. But I need advice, Jeremy . . . I'm scared.'

Pulling away from him on the sofa so she could glance periodically at his face, Bonnie told him everything. She hadn't intended to do so, but some combination of his reassuring presence and her own shattered psyche militated against her original plan of offering a selective account. Jeremy gave her absolute attention, a thin line deepening between his surprisingly well-marked brows.

'. . . So I don't know what to think,' she finished up. 'I'm too involved to see things clearly. Whereas . . .'

'. . . I can provide the outsider's view,' said Jeremy with a wry smile.

'If you don't mind. I think you have a logical brain.'

'It has been said. Right, Bonnie . . . there are two aspects to what you've told me: the general and the specific. In a way, they're separate, but being realistic, I think your view of one must inevitably colour your view of the other.

'Let's look at the general first. You're unhappy with your marriage. You feel you jumped into it without sufficient consideration, and to your dismay you've found you have little in common with Roy. Is this too blunt, Bonnie? Good girl. So . . . there's been a sense of disenchantment right from the start. Next you discover that Roy has lost his job and hasn't told you, and finally you find that even the roof over your head can't be relied upon. Result: you feel confused and insecure.

'Now let's turn to the specific. Your friend Cassie is killed in Manchester and you think Roy might have had something to do with it. You've found no proof that he did, but none that he didn't, either. You think she may have been about to tell you that Roy is a con merchant who has married you in order to insure your life for a huge sum . . .'

Bonnie felt herself blush. 'Talking about it here, the idea sounds ridiculous. But back in Clegg Street, anything seems possible.'

'You don't know what's real and what's imagination, is that right?'

'Yes.'

'And you're sure you want my perspective?'

'Please: my own is hopelessly distorted just now.'

'Okay . . . from what you've told me, I think there's been a knock-on effect between all the factors we've discussed. If you'd been happy with Roy, and felt that mutual trust existed between you, you wouldn't have interpreted Cassie's death in the way that you did. But that wasn't the case, so you found it easier to believe that he was involved. Now, I'm treading on dicey ground here because we're talking about your husband, but if you're asking me whether he's criminal or simply weak, then I have to say I don't know, but I would suspect the latter. You said your neighbour died violently only a few weeks after you'd moved into Clegg Street – that's bound to have coloured your view of everything else that's happened.'

'I heard her die,' said Bonnie, staring straight ahead. 'The detectives were cagey, but I know I heard her die.'

Jeremy's hand strayed towards her, but withdrew as if the time was not right. 'Whether you stick with Roy in the long run has to be your decision, Bonnie,' he said. 'I can't advise you on that. But for your short-term peace of mind, there is something you can do. Have you thought about finding out definitively where Roy was when Cassie had the accident?'

She was startled. 'I – I don't see how. I can't ask him point-blank where he was on that Monday.'

'Why not? Have you discussed Cassie's death with him?'

'No.'

'Then he won't know anything about your suspicions. Can you not devise an indirect way of getting the information, or some convincing excuse for quizzing him about his movements?'

'I suppose – yes, it might be possible.'

'I strongly suggest that you do. Because otherwise, you're always going to wonder.'

'You're right. I can't thank you enough for listening to me, Jeremy. I thought I was going crazy.'

He shrugged off her praise with a gesture of dismissal. 'I'm glad you felt you could tell me, Bonnie. I don't want to interfere, but I hope you'll keep me informed. Let me know how things are going; ring me in a week or so. You promise?'

She nodded.

'Good. For now, though, I think we'd better be getting you back home before you make poor Roy even more paranoid.' He grimaced. 'Seriously, if I thought for one moment he was a mad axeman out to harm you, I'd keep you here.'

'Oh, he's definitely a mad axeman.'

Jeremy's eyebrows rose.

'I like this farmhouse,' she explained.

'I see.'

They both laughed, and he helped her into her jacket. 'I shan't listen to any nonsense about the bus this time,' he said as he locked the front door and led the way across a patch of bare ground to the tall bulk of an old barn. 'You must let me drive you home.'

He switched on a small flashlight and tinkered with the padlock which secured the double doors. Bonnie heard the rattle of a chain, then the creak of hinges as he pulled the doors open. The light beam picked out wisps of straw on the floor before steadying on a blue saloon car. In the background was some kind of elderly pick-up truck.

'Hop in,' he said, unlocking the saloon. Soon he was negotiating the rutted lane between the dry stone walls, while above the valley stars hung like frigid crystals in the indigo sky.

They spoke little until the car had breasted the rise and the lights of Holdendale lay in a random filigree before them.

'You'll have to direct me,' murmured Jeremy. 'I don't know Holdendale too well: I do most of my shopping in the village.'

Bonnie was already worrying about Roy spotting the car in Clegg Street. 'It's straight on down this road, then left at the first intersection after the abandoned mill . . . I hope you won't mind if we don't go right up to the door. I don't want Roy to hear your engine.'

'Whatever you think is best.'

Bonnie felt guilty, knowing her instructions would keep him away from the immediate vicinity of Clegg Street. She had a vague impression that he might decide to check up on her at some future date, run into Roy in one of his drunken tempers and end up injured. She couldn't bear to be the cause of that. 'Here will be fine,' she said. 'You'll be able to turn round in the car-park of the King's Head, just up the road. Thank you *very* much for the lift, and for everything.'

The engine idled and the nearside indicator light flashed with a steady monotony on the dashboard.

'You're sure you'll be all right from here?' asked Jeremy.

'Yes; it's very close.'

'Fair enough.' He squeezed her hand. 'Be kind to Roy, Bonnie. Give him a chance. I think he needs your strength.'

No one had ever told her that before; it was a whole new perspective.

'Take care,' he went on, and leaned towards her cheek at the precise moment her face turned to kiss him. Their mouths locked together and for a moment there was nothing but sweetness, the subtle taste of Tia Maria and the firm pressure of his lips.

She broke away with rending reluctance, her skin burning. 'Good-night,' she whispered, climbing out of the car.

'Good-night.' He winked, gave a little wave, and was lost in the desultory late night traffic of Barlow Road.

Bonnie crossed the street and hesitated; if she took the quickest route home, he would see her on his return journey. She didn't want that; better to step into the shadows and wait a few minutes. A nearby alley ran parallel with Clegg Street but much further down the hill – that would provide temporary concealment.

Twenty feet inside the alley she shrank against a rough brick wall and watched the entry for passing cars. A Mini, a small van . . . ah! That was Jeremy. Now she could go home.

Suddenly she caught a whiff of alcohol on the air. There was a presence in the blackness behind her, coming her way – no, right here, looming out of nowhere, and intent on her . . .

Bonnie tensed every muscle for the sprint to the alley entrance, but her reactions were too slow. A hand shot out of the Stygian passage and clamped around her wrist.

14

'Don't go, Mrs Judd. I want to talk to you.'

The voice in the darkness was thickened and slurred, but the grip on her wrist was tight. Bonnie stood petrified, forcing down the nausea of terror. Her initial fear that Roy had caught her was groundless – but this was much worse. The voice sounded like that of the man she had come to think of as Brown Raincoat – and he knew her name.

'Let go of me!' she choked.

The clamp was released. 'I'm sorry.'

She backed away towards the relative light of Barlow Road and he followed, so close that the hanging flap of his coat brushed against her knee. As the gloom lifted, she saw his face: seamed and raddled, bitter and bowed. It was indeed the man from the King's Head.

'That's far enough!' he ordered.

She stopped. They were still ten feet or so inside the alley, too far for comfort, but there was rough steel behind the miasma of alcohol, and she knew she must obey.

'Is it *really* Mrs Judd?' he asked with a sarcastic sneer.

'I don't know what you mean.'

He swayed. 'Perhaps you don't, perhaps you do. What's he offered you?'

'Please – you're making a mistake. I think you've got the wrong person.'

'How long have you known Roy?'

'That's none of your business . . . If you'll excuse me, I'm going home now.'

'You'd be better advised to hear me out . . .' He grimaced and belched, turning slightly away, but Bonnie resisted the temptation to run. 'Whatever he's promised, he'll double cross you,' he went on. 'Take it from me.'

'I really don't understand what you're talking about,' she said helplessly.

The man swayed, and was silent for several seconds. 'First time I saw you,' he said, 'you reminded me of my daughter. She's small and blonde, like you. But these days she doesn't want to know her old dad. I don't even know where she's living.'

Was he a harmless nutter after all? 'I'm sorry,' said Bonnie.

'Yes, so am I. *Bloody sorry.*' After this brief surge of aggression he appeared to calm down again. 'Let me see your face,' he said.

'The light's better up there.' Bonnie gestured towards Barlow Road.

His lupine leer signalled contempt for her transparency, but nevertheless he shuffled forward a few steps before seizing her by the chin. She willed herself not to recoil as he exhaled stifling fumes inches from her nose and mouth. Pain stung her palms as her fingers curled into involuntary fists.

When he released her he looked shabby and shrunken, despite his bulk. 'Run along, Mrs Judd,' he said flatly. 'Just remember, though . . . when you cross the line, things can get ugly. And then there's no going back.'

Thankfully, Roy seemed to have no inclination to grill her about the 'evening with Hazel' on her return. Neither did he notice how shaken she was. Lying in bed as the hours crawled by, Bonnie could not fathom the intentions of the man she called Brown Raincoat. Was it a threat she had just received, or a warning? Should she even have been the recipient . . .? She recalled him staring at her in the pub, making a disturbance outside the house on the night Lorna was found, loitering in Madge's side passageway . . . Yes, he had been watching her for some time. Why?

Roy twitched and grunted; Bonnie contemplated his shadowy shape in the bed with fear and dislike. *You* are the cause of all this, she told him silently. Tonight, just for a few hours, I was ready to give you the benefit of the doubt, but not any more. I shall follow Jeremy's advice and ask questions. Whatever scheme you are hatching, I shall find out.

The next evening, Bonnie had decided on her approach. 'I've just seen Madge,' she said to Roy on arriving home from work. 'She says she called round at lunch time last week to bring us some spare milk, but no one answered the door. Were you out?' It was thin, very thin, but she hoped her casual tones would allay any suspicion.

'What day?' asked Roy vaguely. He was crouched over the power lead of their standard lamp, fixing a new plug with deft little rotations of the screwdriver.

'Monday, I think.'

He paused to tighten the last screw. 'Monday and Wednesday, I was in the Taphouse.'

'Oh. Drinking.'

He looked up. 'No, Mrs Holier-than-Thou. I wasn't, actually. I was *serving* drinks – behind the bar.'

'You've got a job?'

'Scarcely. It was just a few hours as a fill-in. I'm still looking. In fact, there's a chance of some construction work across town; the foreman's asked me to go along next Tuesday.'

'You might have told me, Roy. Well done!'

'I just did. I'm glad you're pleased. If you're in a good mood for once, you might care to come into the kitchen.'

Swallowing her indignation at being made the villain of the piece, Bonnie followed him through the hall. Her nose twitched as she passed the cellar door: *something* unsavoury in the vicinity was proving very resistant to her efforts with air fresheners and aromatic plants. Perhaps it was a dead rat.

'Da-da!' trumpeted Roy with a showman's gesture.

The kitchen table was laid with a clean linen cloth on which rested a vase of carnations, a bowl of salad and two dinner plates containing something pink.

'Salmon poached in lemon juice,' he said. 'I cooked it myself. And these are potatoes in mayonnaise . . .' Coming from Roy, who liked his fish fried in as much grease as possible, this was sacrifice indeed. '. . . It might be a bit premature as a celebration, but I thought we needed cheering up. Look, there's white wine as well . . .'

'Thank you, Roy. It's lovely – especially the flowers.'

'Oh, I saw those on the Texaco forecourt when I went to fill up the Escort. Here, sit down . . .'

Be kind, Jeremy had said, and Bonnie did her duty. Kindness and love, however, had for her become very distant cousins.

'Excuse me.'

Bonnie nervously approached the bar of the Taphouse at lunch time the next day, aware that the regulars – a motley collection of oddballs, retired men, and workers downing a 'quick one' – were all staring at her, having little else to do.

'Yes?' The man behind the bar, a tall individual with an ex-NCO look about him, gave her a brief moment of his attention as he prepared the various drinks for a large order and placed them on a tray.

'I'm trying to find Roy Judd. I believe he does bar work here.'

He frowned at her. 'You from the DSS?'

'No – Roy's my husband.'

'Ah; well, I'm sorry, lass, but he's not here just now, unless he's popped in as a customer . . .' He peered over the heads of the regulars lining the bar and scanned the smoky interior, giving Bonnie a few heart-stopping moments. '. . . No, he doesn't usually drink at lunch times. Evenings, now, that's different.'

'But he did work for you?'

'Just a couple of sessions last week, filling in while Lily here went to help out her mum.' A woman in her forties with blonde-streaked hair turned from the small bar sink and nodded at Bonnie.

'Which days was he here?' pressed Bonnie.

''Scuse me a moment. Twelve pounds forty pence, please . . . Right you are . . . What did you say?'

'Which days did he actually work for you?'

The suspicious look was coming back. 'Monday and Wednesday. That was all.'

'Lunch times?'

He sighed. 'Yes, lunch times.'

*

'Fisk was looking for you,' said Hazel when Bonnie slipped back behind her desk at Gradwell's. 'I told him you were in the Ladies, but he's beginning to carp about your attitude to working hours . . . A word to the wise, Bonnie.'

'Thank you.' Damn, she thought. She had spent scarce resources on a taxi and been absent barely ten minutes over the hour, yet her boss had noticed.

'*I* knew you weren't in the loo,' chirruped Jayne. 'There was one of them whopper spiders on the door – you'd've come out shrieking.'

'That's one area where my feelings are entirely in accord with those of Mr Fisk,' said Bonnie with a shudder.

'But they can't 'urt you, so what's the problem?'

Bonnie sighed. It was impossible to explain to someone with no imagination that phobias were crippling phenomena which didn't respond to ready logic or the recital of cold facts. Spiders had been her *bête noire* – literally – for as long as she could remember.

'They say if you read about them, their habits and whatnot, they become interesting rather than objects of fear,' said Hazel.

'I did that once. I went to the library and pored over tarantulas, Mexican bird-eaters, funnel webs, trapdoor spiders, fenland raft spiders . . . you name it, I read it. I'm afraid the close-up photographs just made things worse. They looked uglier than ever.' Only in the garden could certain spiders be called beautiful, she thought, remembering slender, variegated bodies on dew-dropped webs at dawn.

'They do therapy for phobias,' said Jayne.

'They "do therapy" for everything these days,' said Hazel sourly.

'But they do! They give you what they call "flooding", which means they expose you to the very thing you're afraid of. Have you heard of that, Bonnie?'

'Oh, yes.' At the age of nine she had picked up one wriggling black monster bare-handed at the behest of her father, who thought that a direct approach would cut through the 'nonsense'. Moments later she had been left holding a single one-inch leg while the rest of the creature darted across her slippered foot and vanished beneath a skirting board. She had never tried again.

'So you pay good money to be frightened out of your wits,' drawled Hazel, nodding judiciously.

'I believe the NHS has some clinics,' said Bonnie. 'But let's face it – if you weren't a mass of neuroses when you went in, you certainly would be when you came out!'

In Clegg Street, however, her phobia was not a laughing matter. It seemed to be true that spiders colonized old houses, and now that autumn was well established, Bonnie was encountering them every other day. In the field of arachnid removals, Roy was indeed the unchallenged hero, though he often spoiled his good deeds with a careless remark.

'There are over six hundred species of British spider,' he told her that evening after carrying another one out into the yard. 'I just read that in the paper. Look – here's the article. This cardinal spider found in Wiltshire had a five-and-a-half-inch leg span. They call it *Tegenaria gigantea*.'

'*Thank* you, Roy.'

'Just thought you might be interested.'

'Riveted.' God. Five and a half inches. The cellar was probably full of them. And she was tired of asking Roy to investigate that smell . . .

It occurred to Bonnie that if Roy *did* have any dark secrets – insurance documents or even stolen property – he could hide them down the cellar secure in the knowledge that she would never interfere. She still didn't know what to think about Roy now that it was clear he was innocent of Cassie's death. If Brown Raincoat had not uttered his cryptic warnings, she would have quashed her remaining doubts and applied herself once more to making her marriage succeed. But he had addressed her by name, watering the seeds of mistrust at the very moment they were about to die from lack of nourishment.

In the course of her general housework, Bonnie had already

kept alert for suspicious items hidden in the rooms she shared with Roy. Roy had very few possessions, however, and she had seen nothing untoward among them. His few personal papers – passport, cheque book, car MOT, a handful of photographs – were loosely mixed with household bills in a cardboard wallet he had made no attempt to hide. The deeds to 14 Clegg Street presumably rested with the bank.

Where else, apart from the cellar, might Roy keep incriminating evidence? Of course . . . the car. Bonnie didn't drive, and he always kept the keys about his person. Perhaps there was something in the boot – a box file, a briefcase . . . (Or then again, she thought wryly, perhaps he's been *really* sensible and lodged his secrets in a safety deposit box.)

The idea of checking the car boot refused to go away, even though it was scarcely feasible during daylight hours: Bonnie had no faith in her ability to extract the keys undetected from Roy's jeans while he was wearing them. That left only nighttime, when the jeans lay across a chair. Exhausted with anxiety, Bonnie knew that the first challenge would be to stay awake until Roy was deeply unconscious. There was no virtue in delay: she would do it tonight.

It was almost one thirty when Bonnie slid out past the front door, clad in a jumper and trousers, the keys alongside the flashlight in her hand. The nearby street lamp was more a curse than a blessing: if for any reason Roy awoke and looked out of the window, he could not fail to spot her.

She had no excuse, no contingency plan. As she did her best to minimize the click as the boot lid opened, Bonnie was well aware that her situation was one of a hiding to nothing. If she found no evidence, would her suspicions truly lie down and die this time? And if she *did* find evidence . . .

The street lamp's lurid orange glow picked out several shapes in the boot, and after guiltily glancing in all directions, Bonnie ducked under the lid and switched on the flashlight. Inside there was a tartan travelling rug, a set of overalls and a box in which car tools nestled between oily rags. The only other item of any size was a plastic lunchbox with a red cross crudely painted on top.

She lifted the lunchbox to the front of the boot well; it was surprisingly heavy. Peeling off the top, she delved beneath a layer of lint and plasters and within seconds had found the reason for the disproportionate weight.

Wedged together in the bottom of the box were two items. One was a mobile telephone. The other was a brown glass bottle labelled TEMAZEPAM SYRUP.

16

Traffic snarled past as Bonnie stood by the pelican crossing in the tall shadow of Deansgate's Lincoln Building. Directly opposite was the soot-stained pink stone of the old John Rylands Library, while to its left, discreetly set back, was the more modern façade of the *Herald* offices.

Was this, she wondered, the crossing where Cassie had been killed? Deansgate was an important arterial for the west of the city; certainly the traffic flow was otherwise unimpeded at this point. Or had Cassie perhaps strolled up to Kendall's to admire the window displays of enticing new clothes, then waited by the adjacent lights as a queue built up around her?

Bonnie reached out and pressed the button; half a minute later she was entering the glassed-in foyer of the *Herald* offices. A smartly dressed receptionist greeted her.

'I was a friend of Cassie Kershaw's,' said Bonnie nervously. 'There's something I need to sort out, connected with her work, and I wondered if it might be possible to have a few words with one of her colleagues . . .?' She felt guilty as the woman offered sympathetic commiserations.

'I'll see who's in.' After making some telephone enquiries, she turned back to Bonnie. 'Jill Beale says she'll come down. She's another journalist – she'll just be a few minutes.'

'Thank you.' Bonnie migrated to a distant corner of the foyer where bound copies of the *Herald* lay beneath a notice stating REFERENCE FILES ONLY. She had just unearthed a new report on Cassie's accident when she heard the rustle of someone approaching.

'Hello, I'm Jill Beale.' A plumpish girl with brown hair.

'Er . . . Bonnie Judd.'

'Let's sit down. You wanted to ask me something about Cassie?'

'Er, yes. I knew Cassie at school. We met up again when I came back to live in this area after some years away in the south. She was going to have lunch with me on the day she was knocked down . . .' She paused; Jill showed interest, but made no move to supplement the statement herself. 'Cassie had sent me a note, asking to see me urgently. She didn't explain why, although I have some ideas . . . I don't suppose she told you anything about it?'

'Sorry, no.'

'Did she mention me at all – or anyone called Roy?'

Jill smiled, but shook her head, and Bonnie realized with dismay that she would have to resort to subterfuge.

'We were doing some research together,' she said, 'because a friend of mine who teaches humanities was looking for similar material: industrial heritage, that kind of thing. Cassie had some of my notes, and – it's awkward to ask, but I need them back. Are her files still here?'

'I'm sorry, her desk was cleared last week . . . Wait, though – I'm being stupid. Simon took everything home. That's her boyfriend; they were sharing a flat. He might know something about that message she sent you. You've met Simon?'

'No, but Cassie mentioned him, of course.'

Jill glanced at her watch. 'He'll have been out today on the usual assignments, but he may well be back by now. Let's go to Photographic.' She led the way through several corridors until they reached a room with a large central table, long peripheral worktops and a bank of computers. The walls were covered with glossy prints in both colour and black and white: human faces, sporting action shots, a Chinese dragon, a demented-looking ostrich . . . each was a triumph of creative balance, of light and shade, of communication. Jeremy was right, thought Bonnie suddenly, when he had said he was no photographer. In the hands of professionals, even static scenes smouldered with life.

As did this room. All around was an air of contained chaos: men in shirt-sleeves punched the computer keys, muttering, while others leaned over the table offering *risqué* captions for a photograph. A tall individual loped across the floor toting a heavy camera bag.

'No,' murmured Jill in answer to Bonnie's expression of enquiry. 'That's not Simon.' She raised her voice. 'Anyone know where Simon is, please?'

'He was doing a court snatch,' said someone. 'Don't know if he's back yet.'

'Yes, he is; he's in the dark room. Number three.'

Jill beckoned, and Bonnie followed her past a baleful red light into a series of narrow right-angled passageways, like the entrance to a wartime bunker. In the deep gloom at the end was a door; she heard Jill rap and ask for Simon.

'Hold on . . .' A few seconds later the shape of a man emerged, while behind him someone snapped, 'Close that bloody door!' Bonnie tried to make out his features while Jill explained her mission, but she had no success. All she could sense was impatience.

'You've picked the wrong end of the day for asking questions,' said Simon, turning her way as Jill headed back to her desk. 'I'm printing up today's shots, but if you want to stick around I dare say we can find a bit of time somewhere.'

Bonnie took 'sticking around' literally, and was soon a silent shadow in the inner sanctum while Simon and his faceless colleague stood in front of enlargers, deftly skimming negative strips through the holder beneath the light source as they selected the best shots for further processing.

'Too yellow,' she heard him mutter. The other man wandered across. 'That Conway?' he asked.

'Yeah.'

'You've got him pin.'

'Some of us do have the gift, you know.'

'If you pull up that section there . . .'

'Bugger off, Robert. What have you got?' He craned across and snorted. 'Ah: the Industry Award at the soft toy factory. Junior DTI minister in earnest conversation with stuffed frog. No, wait, that's a mirror . . .' Belatedly he half turned to Bonnie. ''Scuse us; I'll be with you in a minute.'

As she stood back, loath to crowd him, the lights went out. Even as her eyes adjusted, the enlarger lamp flashed on again in a timed signal; Simon waved his hand above one area of the print. 'Just dodging off this bit.'

'Dodging?' she murmured.

'Holding back the exposure. It'll print too dark otherwise.'

'I see.'

Under the muted glow of the safelights he carried the picture across the room and dunked it in a tray of developer. 'Okay,' he said. 'So you're a friend of Cassie's?'

'That's right.' Bonnie thought this was the worst possible time to talk, but presumably Simon regarded the creative part of his task as finished. 'She had tea with me about three weeks ago when she was doing some research on the fate of the Lancashire cotton mills. Did she tell you?'

'Holdendale, wasn't it?'

'Yes . . . I wondered if she made any comments to you when she got home?'

He agitated the print in the liquid. 'What kind of comments?'

Something like: I've just recognized a petty criminal; he's married to an old class-mate of mine, would you believe? 'Just comments. She wrote to me shortly afterwards, asking for an urgent meeting. I didn't know why, but I thought the Holdendale visit must have been the trigger.'

He transferred the print to the next tray, and shrugged. 'She didn't mention anything untoward to me. But I had to go to Marseilles that weekend. I got back on the Monday.'

The day of Cassie's death. What a devastating welcome home.

Bonnie said nothing as Simon lifted the print from the stop

bath and immersed it for the requisite time in fixer. 'Jill said you'd lent Cassie some notes and needed them back,' he stated, reaching for the print with tongs.

'Yes. I'm sorry to ask so soon after her accident.'

'Life must go on.' He seemed perfectly composed. 'So . . . what were these notes about?'

Oh, heavens! 'Various things . . . It would be easier for me to point them out than to describe their contents.'

She detected the mendacious edge to her own voice and wondered if he had heard it, too. He stood frowning at her, the print hanging limply from the tongs like a wet fish. 'Cass's stuff is at my place: all her files, her computer discs . . . If you've time you can come back with me and have a look. But I've work to do here first. I've got to get this dried and cropped, and write up a few captions.'

'I can wait as long as it takes,' she said. 'Thank you very much.'

Simon's flat was part of an unexpectedly modern block tucked in behind the tall, faded Victorian terraces more typical of the Rusholme area of the city. Platt Fields Park, a mature recreation ground wearing its desolate October face, was just across the main road they had driven down.

'I sometimes walk up to the Whitworth Gallery from here,' he said, unlocking the outer door. 'There's a good collection of paintings. But the flat was too small for both of us and all our gear . . . we were planning to move out to Salford Quays. They've developed the whole area; it's full of photogenic scenes. All those watery reflections . . .'

Upstairs, he admitted her to the flat. Like the *Heralds*'s photographic department, the walls were festooned with prints, predominantly black and white, and mainly of Manchester.

'Ah!' said Bonnie, homing in on an ornate pagoda incongruously sited across a narrow city street. 'That dragon picture must have been yours.'

'Yes,' he agreed. 'I covered a festival in Chinatown. Essentially that means Faulkner Street. It's full of restaurants and grocers' shops with wonderful names like "Wing Fat" written in both English and Chinese.'

Bonnie moved along to another picture, where an imposing metalwork bridge seemed to be surrounded by water. 'Is this Salford Quay?' she asked.

'No – that's the Barton Swing Aqueduct. It actually carries the Bridgewater Canal over the Ship Canal: astonishing feat of Victorian engineering. When a tall ship wants to come through, the water inside the aqueduct is sealed off and it swings aside like a road bridge. Cass was doing a centenary feature on the Ship Canal last year, and we took pictures all along its length. That's thirty-six miles of inland waterway for sea-going ships, Manchester's answer to Liverpool's monopoly of port facilities. In its day it was almost as newsworthy as the Channel Tunnel is at present . . . Now, Bonnie, which notes of yours do you think might be here? What were the topics?'

'Er, some of them were to do with cotton mills and weaving sheds . . . If you don't mind, it would be easiest if I could just take a brief look at the files . . .'

'I'll see what I can find.' He disappeared into a room off the large central living-room, and emerged with a stack of wallet files. 'Cass kept stuff all over the place,' he said, 'but this is the main nucleus, as it were. Here you are – *King Cotton.*' He handed her a file, but kept the others with their labels towards him. 'Anything else?'

'Er, yes, but I'll check this one first . . . Gosh, I'm thirsty. Could I possibly have a drink of water?'

'I'll make some tea, if you like.'

'Yes, please.' That would take longer, and she desperately needed to see those other files. She prayed that Simon hadn't selected only those he thought would be relevant . . .

As soon as he had left the room she swooped on the stack and ran her fingers through it as if playing a lightning chromatic scale. *Hypermarkets, Hallé Orchestra, Pendle Witches, Co-op 150 Years, RPC Raid*? This sounded promising, but the file felt disappointingly thin. She had just perched on a nearby chair with the wallet in her lap when she felt a change in the atmosphere. She turned her head; in the doorway stood Simon, watching her.

His gaze moved deliberately to the abandoned *King Cotton*, then back to her face. His own face was taut and hostile.

'I thought there was something odd about you,' he said, striding forward. 'What's the game, Bonnie? Are you just another sensation-seeker after all? Did you really know Cass?'

'Yes!' she burst out, but a rampant flush was searing her cheeks. 'I did.'

He swept the file from her lap. '*RPC Raid*. Strange material for a humanities teacher – I believe that's what Jill said your friend is.'

Bonnie sat curled in misery, unable to think of a single helpful thing to say. Her face still throbbed with the agonizing heat of shame, and she sensed that Simon would offer no quarter.

'I'm sorry,' she said at last. 'I was just curious.'

'Not good enough.'

'I . . .' How could she tell him that she suspected her husband of villainies as yet unspecified? That she was not entirely convinced that Cassie's death had been an accident?

'Try the truth,' said Simon, his eyes hard.

'All right.' She cleared her throat. 'Cassie did visit me in Holdendale. She said she'd been gathering material on a criminal case for one of her "anniversary" articles, and then a relative of my husband's came in, a man we've always regarded as rather dodgy . . . Cassie seemed to think she recognized him, although I don't think she could remember exactly from where . . . It was only two days later I got her urgent message to meet her in the Exchange. I had the gut feeling that the two things were connected.'

'Go on.'

'I didn't feel I could explain this to strangers, because it was too nebulous and reflected badly on my husband's family. So I made up a story. I'm really sorry, Simon. I shouldn't have abused your trust like that.'

He gave a small grimace. 'There wasn't all that much to abuse. But I still don't see why it matters if Cass recognized some minor crim, or why you need her files.'

'I thought it was just a possibility that something in her notes for the article had triggered the recognition. A photograph, or whatever. And as for the man, my husband's cousin . . . well, he's a fraudster, and he's very unstable. His wife's in constant fear of violence. I thought if he was wanted for something, if he'd been involved in a serious crime . . .'

'You could turn him in.'

'Yes. But I have no evidence.'

He sighed. 'Even if Cass did recognize him, that doesn't necessarily connect him with her research. It could have been any old story in the *Herald* that had caught her eye.'

'I know, but I have to try. Please . . .'

He hesitated, then held out the file. 'Go for it,' he said, 'but don't expect too much. This case is five years old – and it was big-time stuff.'

She took the slender cardboard wallet with trembling fingers and tilted it so the contents slid out on to her lap. There were two photocopied articles about a robbery, one very brief with no illustrations, the other comprising three pages stapled together. Bonnie glanced at the first page, then turned to the next.

Under the legend 'Slaughter in Saddleworth' was an artist's impression of a man with a moustache and longish hair. She bit her lip, but couldn't quite stifle the groan. The glowering face behind the excess hair bore a startling resemblance to that of Roy.

17

'Is that the cousin?' Simon leaned forward curiously.

Bonnie didn't reply. She was transfixed by the detailed sketch, by her own husband's face seen in this context. The planes of the cheeks, the set of the eyes . . . yes, they were Roy's. Yet it had to be acknowledged that this *was* only a drawing, presumably culled from the recollections of witnesses. Scores of other men could have features like this. Had a sketch really formed the basis for Cassie's actions, or had she collected other, more definitive material: an actual photograph, a name, even?

'It's very similar,' she answered at last,' but he doesn't have a moustache and it's hard to be sure.' She turned to the final page, but the only photograph was that of a body lying on a distant grass verge. Cold hands began to claw at her heart. This was something very serious, a level of evil she had not been expecting. She tried to read the article, but the words ebbed and flowed in a viscous grey gel. She felt catatonic with shock.

'Do you have any more on this story?' she asked him, laying down the pages on top of the wallet.

'I'm sure there was plenty more,' he said with a puzzled frown. 'Cass must have had the papers out and left them somewhere. I'll take a look.' He searched the study, but returned empty-handed. 'Sorry,' he said. 'They're not in any of the obvious places. Would you like that cup of tea now?'

'It's all right,' said Bonnie, scrambling to her feet. 'I ought to be going. Thanks for your time. I'm sorry to have intruded . . .' Her brain was beginning to work again now, and she needed to think in peace. It wasn't fair to involve Simon with her renewed suspicions of Roy. For all his cool demeanour, Simon was mourning the death of his girlfriend, an event he still had every reason to regard as an unhappy accident. 'Could I possibly borrow this file, just for a few days?'

He shrugged. 'Take it. Cass has referenced everything on the computer. I'll let you know if I find any more. What's your phone number?'

'I'm afraid I'm not on the phone, but I'll leave my address, if you don't mind.'

'Sure.' He handed her a notepad, and she scribbled her name. After a second's hesitation she added '18 Clegg Street, Holdendale', and the post code. The danger of Roy's intercepting the message was too great. She would have to prime the Schofields with a suitable cover story. 'Thanks again, Simon,' she said, after declining his offer of a lift to the city centre. She wanted to walk – and think.

The Exchange cafeteria was filling up with the evening's theatre-goers, but Bonnie was able to secure a table in the snug raised area behind the gleaming octagonal bar, where she could study the *Herald* article undisturbed. She read it again, this time absorbing every detail, feeling with an ever-sinking heart that this ran true: this crude, violent robbery was indeed Roy's kind of crime.

A consignment of industrial platinum from Thomson Plathey had been hijacked at the point of unloading at Runcorn Petro-chemicals (RPC). The masked four-man gang, who had menaced employees with a sawn-off shotgun, had escaped in a white Bedford van, which was found abandoned two miles away.

An hour and a half later a routine police patrol in the Saddleworth area found that a blue van they were following on a country road began to proceed erratically, speeding and weaving, and finally crashing on a bend. The two officers, Sergeants Collet and Brewer, went to investigate and found three men in the cab, one injured and agitated. Moments later, a fourth man appeared from the back of the van with a shotgun, and ordered the police away from the vehicle. Collet, reacting slowly, was blasted where he stood. In the confusion, Brewer managed to regain the patrol car and drive away, calling for assistance. When reinforcements finally reached the scene, Sergeant Collet's body lay on a grass verge at the roadside, but there was no sign of the blue van.

National publicity and an extensive police search led to the van's discovery three days later. It was found in an old lock-up garage in Holdendale, abandoned except for the corpse of the driver lying slumped across the front seats. There was no trace of the two-million-pound platinum haul, but at the time of writing an assiduous search was under way . . .

Brief descriptions of two of the men accompanied this account. One had been tall, dark and clean-shaven, the other of medium height and build with longish dark hair and a moustache. The artist's impression related to this second individual . . .

Bonnie laid aside the three-page photocopy, sipped her tea and turned her attention to the second article. It was a fragment, really, just a couple of paragraphs, but it provided a useful update. Someone called Ted Granville was in custody awaiting trial for the 'RPC raid', as it was now called. Also preparing to stand trial was the 'mole', an RPC employee who had provided the gang with details of the prospective delivery. Neither the platinum nor the other two gang members had been found . . .

Just suppose, thought Bonnie, that one of those two *had* been Roy. He had probably fled to Spain initially, but as time went on he had allowed himself to worry less about extradition. Perhaps he had set an arbitrary five-year limit, after which he would feel he dared return to England. Not only to England, but to Holdendale itself . . .

There could be only one reason why he would run that kind of risk. The platinum was still here in the north-west, waiting. And she knew where: Clegg Street.

Abruptly Bonnie returned to the counter and bought a savoury and a large glass of red wine. So she would be late home? Tough. Unless she resolved all the uncertainties here and now, she would give herself away once she was back in Roy's vicinity. Sitting down again, she took a huge swig of the wine, ignoring the startled glances of a couple at the next table. The café, its noise, bustle and smell of food receded to a thin peripheral blur as she focused her imagination on Roy and the consequences of a murderous five-year-old robbery.

If the platinum was indeed hidden in or near their home, then there lay the *real* reason for Roy's choosing to buy a condemned property. The reason, too, for his giving up the timber yard job. He must have hoped that after a suitable period of exemplary behaviour he could extricate the platinum from its place of concealment while Bonnie was out at work. But fate, in the shape of Bill Heaton, had intervened. The murder of Lorna had brought police swarming round the area, forcing Roy to keep a low profile for much longer than he had planned.

No wonder he had been irritable. Cooped up in 14 Clegg

Street with the bulldozers coming nearer, unable to act – and living with a prissy little madam who shared none of his interests. Bonnie gave a cynical smile as she recalled her naïve anxieties about life insurance fraud. She should have known that that was the wrong sort of crime for someone like Roy. He wasn't a smooth conman oozing superficial charm: he was a working-class thug with limited imagination.

She felt a shadowy understanding now about his motives for involving her. She was his respectable façade, genuinely ignorant, a buffer to shield him from police, neighbours and other busybodies. Instead of a solitary, shifty-looking man moving against the flow into number 14, people saw a pair of newlyweds making a temporary home. Bravo, Roy: a master-stroke. '*I liked you better when you were stupid . . .*' I'll bet you did.

Bonnie's jaw tightened as she remembered exposing the real contents of the 'first aid box' in Roy's car. Temazepam syrup – a sleeping draught. Presumably there to keep her quiet if he had to act at night. Mixed with a sweet wine like Madeira, it would arouse no suspicions . . . In fact, it was conceivable that Roy had already tested the drug. She could recall feeling inordinately hung-over on each occasion he had given her wine in the late evening. He would show no respect for therapeutic doses. And what of the mobile phone? It was there so that he could communicate in emergencies with – whom?

She knew the answer to that, as well. Brown Raincoat. He was tall and dark, for all that he stooped to hide it. He knew all about Roy. He was the nearest thing in flesh to the mythical 'Ivor'.

She sensed that they were unwilling partners. Maybe Roy knew something he didn't – the exact location of the platinum, a code, a combination – heaven knew what. Perhaps Brown Raincoat, able to stay in the vicinity because his description had never been clarified, had spent years trying to find it alone. But in the end he had been forced to contact Roy and tip him off about the impending demolitions . . . Perhaps, too, the man Ted Granville was up for early release; he could well have been the brains behind the operation.

Yes, thought Bonnie, they don't trust each other but they're in this together. When Brown Raincoat saw police activity near 14 Clegg Street on the night Lorna's body was discovered, he had to find out what was happening. So he pretended to be drunk and plied the police themselves for information. What a nerve! The man wasn't pathetic at all . . . Perhaps he always pretended to be drunker than he was.

A chill rippled down her spine as her mind swung back to the dark alley where he had accosted her. Brown Raincoat didn't quite understand why Roy had involved her, how much she knew. And Roy was keeping him guessing. Perhaps the man was now satisfied that she was an innocent dupe; certainly her resemblance to his daughter had given him pause. But he was highly dangerous, nevertheless. Either he, Roy or the Granville man had blasted a policeman to death and . . . yes, Brown Raincoat must have murdered Cassie.

A tall man edged past the table, and Bonnie recoiled as if he had menaced her. She grabbed at the glass and swallowed the remaining wine in one gulp; the couple at the adjacent table darted nervous little glances at her, evidently concluding she was a recipient of the 'Care in the Community' programme.

Back in Clegg Street, Bonnie scanned the clusters of children loitering in the half-light for a glimpse of Darren Schofield. She could see Wayne sitting on the wall of number 18; if absolutely desperate, she would have to speak to him.

'Hi, Bonnie.' Darren leaned out from behind a group of small boys and gave her a wide grin before turning back to his companion. '*That* were the 'ouse,' she heard him declaim. 'I went in the back gate, an' the kitchen door were open, so I went inside. She were lyin' on the linoleum, all purple in the face, an' 'er neck were all bruised . . .'

The little brute was conducting murder tours! Mere weeks ago, Bonnie wouldn't have known whether to laugh or cry, but a new harsh mood had seized her. Lorna's was not the only unnatural death Holdendale had seen in the last five years; somewhere in this sprawling town was a lock-up garage where another body had lain undiscovered for days – and if her suspicions were correct, the site was not far from here . . .

'Tell them about the other body,' she said loudly. 'The robber. Or were you too young?'

'Were I 'eck, Bonnie. I saw that one, too.'

'Did yer Buxton!' sneered Wayne, strolling over. 'Yer were four, yer little twerp.'

'It was near here, wasn't it?' prompted Bonnie.

'That's right.' Wayne struck a pose of authority; Darren scowled. 'It were in one o' them lock-up garages be'ind Barlow Road. I remember our mum an' dad talkin' about it. 'E were one o' the RPC raiders, an' 'is mates did 'im in so's 'e wouldn't squeal.'

The other children gasped; Darren looked more petulant than ever. When Wayne had sauntered off again, Bonnie leaned confidentially towards Darren. 'Can you keep a secret?' she whispered.

He brightened. 'Yeah.'

'An old friend of Roy's is going to send me something for his birthday, and I've given him your address so that we can keep it a secret from Roy. Could you tell your mum and dad? Ask them if a letter or packet arrives with my name on it, could they please hang on to it and catch me when I'm on my own?'

Darren nodded vigorously, and she doubled back to number 14. 'Remember,' she said, pressing a finger to her lips.

What an accomplished liar I've become, thought Bonnie as she took the passageway to her back yard and saw Roy's shadowy figure through the faded net curtains of the kitchen window. But just now perhaps that was no bad thing. Living with Roy was going to need all the subterfuge at her command.

'Will you be actually starting work on Tuesday?' she asked Roy as they sat in front of the television set after dinner.

'I doubt it – it's more of an interview with the foreman, discussing experience and the like. But I've done some labouring on a building site before, so there's no reason why they shouldn't take me on. I expect to be hard at it by the end of the week.'

'Where's the site again?'

'You wouldn't know the area. It's across town, a mile or so beyond Gradwell's.'

'Ah – you could give me lifts!' She laughed.

'Site work starts early.'

'Just leave me near the pie shop . . . What time's your interview? We could go in together on Tuesday.'

'Afternoon, for some reason. Two o'clock.'

'Never mind. I'll know when to keep my fingers crossed.' Bonnie was already doing so. She lay back on the threadbare sofa in an attitude of relaxation, but every muscle was taut and twanging from the sheer effort of trying to sound casual. She needed to know when Roy would be out of the house; this weekend was no good because his soccer team was playing in London. Tuesday was the only possible time – if he was telling the truth.

Pretending to concentrate on the raucous comedy programme Roy was enjoying, Bonnie considered the reliability of his job-seeking claim. If he had secured the platinum, he would have vanished long ago. There was therefore some difficulty; either that, or he was still maintaining a cautious front, making no attempt at all to disturb the status quo until the very last ripple emanating from Lorna's death had stilled. He would need a job to maintain the fiction of their lives and keep the questions at bay. Thus, she concluded, he probably *was* going to a building site on Tuesday. He could always throw in the job later.

She yawned, and sighed. 'I'm for bed,' she said. 'Thank goodness it's Friday.' She forced herself to kiss Roy's stubbly cheek then glided quickly from the room. Upstairs, she changed from her day wear of plain skirt and blouse to a thin lawn nightdress. She slumped on the bed, exhausted from feigning a neutral demeanour in front of Roy, and wondered how she could possibly maintain the act for a whole weekend.

It had occurred to Bonnie in the Exchange that she could simply run away, but she had firmly rejected the idea. Roy was her husband, her problem; if he was indeed a murderer, or the accomplice of one, she had to find proof for the police.

How assiduously he had tried to keep her away from the

cellar! From dangling a spider over her head to hiding the flashlight, from ensuring that the cellar light never functioned to locking her in with the blackness and terror . . . yes, he had done his best. And there could be only one reason . . .

Sick and drained, Bonnie dragged herself to the bedroom mantelpiece and picked up the gaudy Portuguese cockerel. She sat on the edge of the bed, cradling it in her hands. Jeremy . . . I wish you were with me. I wish I'd known you for years, so we could fight this thing together . . .

Mentally shaking her head, she lay back, still holding the bird. Good old Bonnie. Looking, as ever, for someone else to solve her problems. But this one was hers alone. Squirm as she might, there was no escape from the unwelcome plan she had been incubating ever since she had left the cafeteria.

On Tuesday she would force herself once more down those worn stone steps into the cellar and examine every cranny for signs of digging. Because somewhere in that black hole, buried behind or beneath the brickwork, was the proof she needed – a hoard of precious metal worth two million pounds.

18

On Tuesday morning Bonnie didn't go to work. She had always despised those individuals who planned in advance to 'go off sick' on a specific date, but now she found herself employing the same tactics. There was too big a risk of being detained if she turned up at Gradwell's.

Having telephoned Hazel with a story of stomach pains, she set up camp in the small branch library on Nuthall Street. There was a single table at the back with a rickety chair; Bonnie produced a folder of papers and spread them out, then chose a reference book from the shelf nearby and pretended to consult it.

Within half an hour she was tense and restless. The time was passing so slowly. For the fourth time she reviewed her simple plan: return to the corner of Barlow Road and Clegg Street at ten to two; check from this distance that Roy's white Escort had gone; enter number 14 via the back alley in case Brown Raincoat was watching the house; lock herself in. Then, creep down to the cellar and examine it as rapidly as possible. When she had last ventured below ground, many of the nooks and crannies had lain in deep shadow, but now she had her own torch, bought the day before; this expedition was not going to founder on whether or not Roy had hidden the red flashlight again. Her shoulder bag also contained a chisel, a small trowel and a plastic carrier bag.

Bonnie stood up, moved back to the reference section and seized another volume. The woman at the desk, bored, gave her a brief smile and Bonnie did her best to respond. The tome she had selected, *English Nature*, was heavy; she eased it down on to the table and opened it at random.

A nightmare of splayed-out spiders covered the illustrated page. As she stared in repelled fascination at the lifelike drawings they seemed to shimmer and quiver with a life of their own. 'The zebra spider can leap many times its own length . . .' she read, and hastily pawed at the leaves of the book until a page of peaceful country flowers appeared. At this stage, she thought edgily, the last thing she needed was a reminder of the creatures in the cellar. Only by pretending that they didn't exist could she steel herself to go down there once more.

At ten to two exactly Bonnie stood behind the telephone box, peering down Clegg Street. The Escort had gone; Roy was on his way to his appointment. Good. Well . . . good in a manner of speaking. Bonnie knew that her mind had been harbouring a tiny, treacherous splinter of hope that the mission might have to be aborted. She doubled back to Barlow Road, sidled down the narrow, board-flanked portion of the alley and glanced about her as it widened and the cobbles began. No one was about.

As she stepped on to the cobbles she heard a faint clanking sound behind her.

'Mrs Judd!'

She scrambled to one side as Wayne Schofield erupted from the ginnel astride his mountain bike, like a cork from a bottle. He squealed to a halt on the cobbles with a dramatic flourish.

'That parcel's arrived,' he told her conspiratorially.

'What . . . oh, good!'

'Darren said it were a secret. If I give it ter yer now, then yer 'usband won't know about it.'

'Thank you, Wayne.'

He strolled down the alleyway with the bike, swinging his hips in a carefree manner, and Bonnie wondered why he was home at nearly two o'clock on a school day. 'Bunking off' for the afternoon, she assumed, and kept the thought determinedly to herself. Now was not the time to spark an altercation with Wayne.

They reached the back gate of number 18, and he leaned his bicycle against the adjacent wall. "Ang on,' he said.

She watched him cross the yard, fumble for the key in a niche behind the dustbin, and let himself in. A nerve-stretching five minutes elapsed before he reappeared.

"Ere. It came yesterday.' He handed her a thick A4-sized package.

'Thanks very much, Wayne, for looking after it for me.'

"Sorright.'

As Bonnie crept into her own back yard, she was aware of precious time trickling away. Much as she longed to examine the package, she knew that it would have to wait until later. Thrusting it into her bag she paused, irresolute, by the back door. Supposing Roy had returned prematurely while she had been waiting for Wayne? With gnawing anxiety she juggled the stiff bolt on the side gate and padded down the passageway. Clegg Street stretched quiet and dull in both directions. A grey car was parked down the road, and behind it a black one, but there was no sign of Roy's white Escort. She released her pent-up breath in a silent gust of relief.

With the side gate bolted once more and the kitchen door locked behind her, Bonnie was careful to disturb none of the more visible household items. The shoulder bag would go below ground with her. So would the drab navy skirt and blouse she was wearing, which Roy had seen at breakfast time. Her coat, however, was best hung in her wardrobe.

Descending from the bedroom, Bonnie found herself once more gripped by doubts. If the platinum was here, in a situation remotely accessible, Roy could surely have vanished with it long ago . . . And did a sketch of a man with a moustache make Roy an armed robber? Perhaps after all this whole thing was a farrago of circumstantial events, whipped into substance by her own neuroses . . .

The hall was still scented with the clean, sharp smell of lemon from a polish she had sprayed over the hall stand the previous evening, but beneath this high note lurked a grumbling semi-chorus of something undeniably rank. It reminded her of a mess of raw meat trimmings she had left in Aunt Rachel's kitchen waste bin for two days one hot summer; the resulting noisome stink had hung in her nostrils for hours.

Aunt Rachel . . . Bonnie paused in front of the cellar door, her heart thudding, and found her mind quite devoid of pithy aphorisms. Aunt Rachel would have produced something uplifting about strength and courage for this occasion. Bonnie strained to recall even a fragment of one of her maxims, but to no avail. Even efforts to conjure up her aunt's face were doomed: she seemed distant and insubstantial, a spent force whose time was gone.

With dismay Bonnie felt her frail resolve ebbing away – then suddenly, there was Jeremy, his face aglow with approbation, and he was saying, 'You did *that*, little Bonnie? Well done!'

Determinedly she picked up the bag and opened the cellar door. The foetid smell intensified. Out of curiosity she flicked the light switch, but as she had expected, the hole beneath her remained darkly obscure. She glanced at her watch – two thirteen. Holding the web-covered latch through a duster, she pulled the door gently to behind her, switched on the torch and began her descent.

At the bottom she stood very still, taking her bearings. The thin, dreary light from the heavily begrimed window limned the cellar's general contents in faint outline, but her torch could spotlight individual items. Slowly she played its beam along the wall to her left, which encased the stone steps: all she saw was a century of undisturbed brickwork. Beneath the window the wall told a similarly blank story.

Bonnie trained the light on the alcove corner, and felt herself tense again. This recess – perhaps the most obvious site for hidden valuables – was choked with black dustbin sacks and bags of Coalaflame, some burst open as before; Roy appeared to have made no effort to tidy their scattered contents. Lying randomly amongst the heaps of fuel were various tools, including a spade. A nearby bucket was filled with a lumpish powder resembling old mortar. Two more bags of Coalaflame lay against the right-hand wall.

A faint scampering sound made her gasp, and for a second the torch-beam wobbled away from its target. Bonnie caught a fleeting glimpse of something narrow bisecting the fourth cellar wall before she steadied the beam again. *Rodents*, she thought despairingly, then pushed the unwelcome confirmation to the back of her mind. If she dwelt on that, she would be unable to continue.

Illuminating the strange linear shadow, she identified it as a piece of brown wiring attached to the wall. With the beam she followed this conduit up to the ceiling, where it terminated in the central light fixture. A surge of anger replaced the dismay as Bonnie saw a new-looking bulb hanging there. In seconds she had traced the discreet switch at the other end of the wire and jabbed at it with her finger.

The cellar lit up as sixty watts of power probed all its darkest corners. In the same moment, it seemed to shrink. Bonnie gratefully fed on her fury – how *dared* Roy secretly fit up a light for himself whilst keeping the switch by the door defunct? That *proved* he was up to no good. She scanned the wall where the new switch was: once again, the brickwork was neat and solid, innocent of disarrangement, the joins patchily draped with spiders' webs.

Then she saw it. Behind the two leaning bags of Coalaflame,

something was definitely wrong with the wall. Some of the bricks were out of true; there was even a suspicion of a gap around them . . .

Bonnie picked her way across the uneven carpet of Coalaflame pieces and grasped the nearest bag. With a heave, she slid it to the right. A similar effort shifted the other bag leftwards. She stepped back, breathing rapidly, and stared at the triangular defect she had just uncovered.

It was a hole, two feet high at the apex, where the bricks had been removed then loosely repositioned. Perhaps that was their mortar in the bucket . . . Cautiously she lifted out the top three bricks; a few inches behind she could see another wall of dusky terracotta. Reaching through with her hand, she pushed against its rough surface; there was movement.

This must lead through to Bill and Lorna's cellar, she thought. Another creepy, claustrophobic chamber to investigate! Again she checked her watch: two twenty-one. Technically, Roy could be on his way back already. She should turn off this light, and yet – it would be so much quicker to work without having to hold the torch . . . She only needed a glimpse of the platinum, then she could restore everything to its former state and hurry back to ground level . . .

Briskly she began to remove the bricks from the hole, stacking them in a double column nearby. When the second layer had been suitably breached, she crouched down on her hands and knees and inched forward through the gap to the cavity beyond. Yes, it was the cellar of number 16. She could see the dull brickwork of the wall opposite, the deeper shadow where the stone steps began their ascent . . . Whispering encouragement to herself, Bonnie slithered right through the opening and rose stiffly to her feet. Now what? This cellar was bare except for a few bags of Coalaflame. She was no further forward, unless . . .

Three bags lay close to where she stood, but two more lolled, apparently randomly, against the wall which supported the steps. Acting on instinct, she crossed the cellar and hurled them out of the way. The crudely rebricked opening thus revealed was no surprise. As she dragged the bricks from the hole, a mounting excitement lent her vigour. This cavity beneath the stairs was a perfect place to hide stolen valuables . . .

Bonnie was both disappointed and alarmed to find nothing but the now-familiar signs of a roughly camouflaged exit hole beyond. How far must she crawl before she found the definitive evidence she was seeking? With anxiety once more gnawing at her stomach she ducked through this second aperture, and then a third, to find herself standing between piles of old furniture and fishing tackle in the Schofields' cellar. It was very dark; their grating was boarded over, and the homing beam of her own cellar light was now no more than a distant gleam. There was a rich smell of apples.

Bonnie flashed her torch-beam around the chamber, then steadied it on the ceiling, where a bare bulb hung. The switch, as expected, was up by the door. Once there she paused, breathing rapidly but as noiselessly as possible. Were any of the Schofields in their home? Wayne? His mother? She couldn't hear anything on this side of the sturdy barrier . . .

Gritting her teeth, Bonnie disengaged the latch through a handkerchief, hoping to ease the door open a few cautious inches. Nothing happened. She tried again: it wouldn't budge. Presumably the door was bolted to protect the younger children . . . With decision she pressed the switch and flooded the cellar with light.

From the bottom step she slowly scanned the room. It felt different from the other two cellars . . . At first, she thought that this was just because of the clutter: the bench in the corner, the fishing nets against the wall. Suddenly, however, she realized it was *structurally* different. The alcove was missing. It was completely filled in.

Having secured her attention, the wall needed no close examination to confirm that the brickwork in the would-be alcove area hailed from a more recent era than the foundations. Both the bricks and the mortar were discrepant in hue from those of the adjacent walls. Excited now, Bonnie slid aside a table and some boxes of apples which were obscuring the lower façade; there near the floor was a roughly hewn hole. It wasn't triangular this time, but more of an irregular square. Maybe the shape didn't matter in a non-load-bearing wall . . .

Transferring the loose bricks into a stack to the left, Bonnie peered through the opening. Inside stood a tall bag of something – no, several bags. She prodded at the nearest one: it gave very slightly, as if it were full of flour.

Perhaps the gang had hidden the platinum inside sacks of meal, or whatever! That would make sense . . . But without actually seeing the pieces of metal she had no evidence for the police. For the first time, Bonnie realized that she didn't know exactly how the platinum should appear. Would it be in sheets, or wires, or ingots, even? She tried to drag the first bag through the gap, but the hole was too small. Neither could she manoeuvre it to gain access to the top. Panting with frustration she looked about her. Her own chisel and trowel were still in the shoulder bag, which lay on the floor in the cellar where she had started. On the bench here, however, was a comprehensive collection of Mr Schofield's tools . . .

Once more she padded up to the door to listen; still there was silence above. Hopefully Wayne was out – or slumped somewhere deafening himself via his stereo headset . . . Bonnie went to the bench and gingerly weighed in her hands a chisel and a large mallet. Positioning them, she gave an experimental tap at the mortar. To her ears the ensuing sound was a ringing cavernous echo; she paused, head tilted, but no one came.

Minutes later she had removed a further two bricks, and this time the sack scraped through the opening. Trembling with anticipation, she emptied the apples from one stout cardboard box into another, then turned back to the sack. It was composed of some kind of strengthened paper, and had 'Portland cement' stamped on one side. The top was stitched down; she seized a Stanley knife and sliced across it.

She reached inside, and her hand came out covered with fine greyish powder. If part of the platinum cache was hidden at the bottom, she would need to scoop away all this cement . . .

'Necessity is the mother of invention.' Thank you, Aunt Rachel. Using an old cracked mug and a dustpan Bonnie managed without her trowel, decanting the cement into the apple box

with mounting impatience. When two-fifths of its contents remained, she was able to lift the bag and pour the rest of the powder away. All she found was a small flat red plastic oblong trailing two strange tailpieces. Nothing else was left inside; the empty bag keeled lightly over as she relaxed her grip.

Dismayed, she repeated the process with another sack. Empty . . . but why hide bags of building materials behind a false wall? Was it a double-cross, a twisted joke waiting five years to explode? Or had Roy already found the spoils and left these bags as a message for Brown Raincoat? Where had Roy really gone today? Was he coming back . . .?

With a pang of trepidation Bonnie looked at her watch. Three o'clock. It couldn't be! Here she was amidst all this chaos and the Escort could be cruising down Clegg Street at this very moment!

Half blinded with panic, Bonnie clawed at the dustpan, then realized that any attempt to restore the previous status quo would take far too long. She thrust the two empty cement bags into the hole, replaced the bricks then pulled the powder-laden cardboard boxes in front. Finally she lifted the boxes of apples on top.

Wiping her hands on a nearby rag she climbed the steps, switched on the torch and extinguished the main cellar light. Immediately the room became an obstacle-strewn dungeon. She picked her way past the clutter and crawled through to Lorna's cellar. A thin pool of light still shone from her own property, making her deeply uneasy. That glow, such a comfort to her, might be seen through the rear grating.

This unpleasant thought spurred her to wriggle onwards into her own cellar and hasten to the little brown switch on the wall. For a moment she stood, breathless with exertion, a band of foreboding squeezing her guts; the air was thicker again here, gaggingly pestilential . . . something scampered in the corner where the black bags were.

With a stifled sob she turned out the light. She could almost feel her pupils flare, adjusting to the new deep gloom. The small high window muted the afternoon sky into a feeble filtering of grey.

Even as she looked upward, the grey darkened. A pair of ankles was walking past the grating.

19

Bonnie stiffened. A surge of such choking terror had seized her that her limbs were paralysed. That was Roy in the yard: she knew it with primitive certainty. And if he had seen the light, he could be down here in less than a minute.

She wanted to curl up and quiver, like some small frightened animal, but that way lay sure discovery. Then came the urge to run – if she slithered her way back to Lorna's cellar she might escape, but what if the door was locked, like the Schofields'? Roy would see the gaping hole she had left behind, and follow . . . She would be trapped.

Sick with fear, Bonnie propped her torch along the top of the shoulder bag and piled the bricks roughly in the triangular aperture. She dragged back the two bags of Coalaflame, then paused to listen. With the thundering of her heart it was difficult to hear extraneous sounds, but then a distant creak pierced the muffled cacophony inside her head. Someone was above her in the house – perhaps even in the hall itself. Clenching her teeth to stop them rattling, Bonnie seized the torch and bag, and turned towards the only hiding place this cellar could afford.

At the entrance to the alcove her foot slipped on a piece of coal and she stumbled; her upper body hit one of the split bags of fuel with a painful thud; coal trickled softly to the floor. She had to get behind those black dustbin bags . . . The thought of large hairy spiders, disturbed and running pell-mell, made her want to scream, but her inner sense of doom was insisting she make an effort to survive.

She heard the scrape of the latch. Roy was about to enter the cellar. She couldn't breathe . . . panic was strangling her, and the smell in this corner was unbelievably putrid . . . A faint glow reflected from the wall opposite. The hall light must be on:

it was too diffuse for a torch. She fought to control her bursting chest, a hand cupping her nose and mouth. Perhaps he was standing there, listening. Perhaps he wouldn't come down . . .

There was a faint click and a new circle of light fixed on the wall. Slow footfalls echoed flatly from the stone steps; the light twitched and wavered.

Bonnie scrabbled, desperately and silently, for concealment before Roy turned the corner into the cellar proper. Half shielding her own torch-beam, she crouched behind two bulging black dustbin bags. A third bag lay on its side; to her unspeakable disgust she could hear tiny squeaks within.

The feet had almost completed their descent. Bonnie's thumb was tightening over the torch's on-off switch when the thin swath of light picked out something protruding from the bag. Partially obscured by torn black plastic, it looked like a bunched-up shirt. Old clothes for a jumble sale? But wait . . . the pattern was oddly familiar. Surely the red and white squares were identical with those on Bill Heaton's lumberjack shirt . . .?

As she plunged the recess into darkness at the last possible moment, an image came dancing on to her retina. She saw a blackened claw emerging from the checked cotton, half hidden in coal. It was gnawed, but still recognizable as a human hand. And suddenly she knew the truth in all its malign clarity: Bill Heaton had never left Clegg Street.

'Hello? Anyone there?'

Roy was calling from the bottom of the steps. His voice boomed around the small chamber, and Bonnie could feel his physical presence very strongly. Could he also sense hers?

'Hello?' He walked forward, and she saw the beam of his flashlight sweep along the wall ahead of him to hover where the two coal bags stood. There it paused for several seconds.

Bonnie squeezed herself into the tightest of balls, dry-mouthed and quivering. She closed her eyes and prayed he would go away, but even as she did so, a furtive rustle came from the nightmare object at her side.

The light swung her way. 'Bloody rats,' she heard Roy mutter, then the beam slid away again. She heard the crunch of his feet in the coal which covered the floor – not approaching, but growing fainter. Silently she exhaled and took another lungful of air. The stench was nauseating; she fought against the seething urge to gag. Inches away, light sounds of scampering culminated in more rustles, a tearing noise and a gleeful squeak. Hold on, she thought. You can do it. He's leaving. He really is . . .

The cellar light came on.

'Bonnie.' Roy's voice was like carborundum. Her eyelids fluttered open, but she couldn't move. 'I thought I saw a light,' he went on, 'but I wasn't sure. What are you doing?'

Infinitely slowly, she rose to her feet. Any explanation she could cobble together would be useless, she knew. He would kill her, like Bill Heaton . . . *and Lorna.* 'I – I came home early because I didn't feel well,' she slurred. 'I thought I heard a cat down here, so I came to see in case it was trapped. But instead I found . . .' She indicated the thing on the ground. It was impossible to pretend she hadn't seen it. Indeed, she would have to step over it to leave the alcove. 'Then I heard someone coming. I didn't know it was you – I thought it was whoever had done this. So I hid. I was frightened.'

'You f— little liar!' His mouth was working now, and his eyes flashed back and forth as if helping his brain decide what to do. With a snarl of rage he kicked aside the nearest Coalaflame bag; the random huddle of bricks behind seemed to answer his question.

'Roy . . . please.' Bonnie held out a hand towards him, knowing in her gut that this was the end. She lifted her feet over Bill Heaton's body and stood among the scattered coals, defenceless.

He glared at her, chest heaving. 'You shouldn't have interfered, Bonnie!' he shouted, then pulled something from his pocket. There was a glint of steel: it was a flick-knife.

'Don't come near me,' she warned through lips gone numb. She bent down to the heavy spade and grasped the handle. 'Don't do it.'

Ignoring her pleas, he rushed at her; she swung the spade horizontally, catching him on the forearm. With a stream of vile curses he staggered to his knees, but as she tried to run past he seized her ankle. Frantic, she jabbed at his shoulder to make him let go; as his grip relaxed she saw him turn and stretch towards the fallen knife.

I'm not going to make it, she thought. I've got the spade, but he's stronger than I am. This contest will never be equal. Unless . . .

With a wild surge of energy she whirled the spade upwards and smashed the ceiling light. Roy's flashlight lay on the floor beneath the second switch, giving narrow illumination to a limited section of wall. The rest of the cellar, except for the stairs, was in deep gloom.

Bonnie tensed for action. He might even throw the knife. Sensing movement nearby, she stepped back and swung the spade at hip level in a wide defensive arc.

Tbere was a dull thud. Roy screamed, a sound so bone-chilling that she dropped the spade and staggered backwards, fetching up at the bottom of the steps. She sank down on the cold stone, trembling with horror. Seconds passed. There was a low groan, then another, weaker, one. Then – silence.

'Roy?' she quavered. No one answered. She felt something wet trickling into her left eye and brushed at it tentatively with her fingers. In the faint light from the hall she saw a dark smear across the pads.

'Roy?' She was shaking so much that the voice could have come from a ninety-year-old woman. Was he acting? Or was he dying? She couldn't leave without finding out, but both the torches were in there with him. If she tried to reach them, he could grab at her foot . . .

Still trembling from head to toe, Bonnie dragged herself up to the kitchen, where she rootled beneath the sink for a candle and matches. Keeping her mind studiously blank, she descended to the cellar again and held the candle aloft.

Roy lay motionless, his head turned to one side, his mouth slightly open. She began to step towards him, then recoiled: a deep gash had laid open his forehead to the bone, exposing a skein of blood vessels and nerves; a viscous pool of blood was soaking into the coal-dust all around like a Satanic halo.

She took a ragged breath, and forced herself forward once more. He was very pale. She couldn't tell if he was breathing. Stretching out a reluctant finger, she touched his neck where she thought a pulse might be. The flesh was warm, but nothing throbbed beneath it. 'Roy?' she pleaded, her voice cracking. Still he lay there. Sobbing with fear, she scrabbled to get away again, and almost fell over the spade. Its broad blade was splashed with blood. 'Oh, God,' she murmured. 'God . . .'

She had killed him. How could she go to the police now? Would they believe it was self-defence? And if they did, would she still be clapped in jail amongst all those rough, streetwise women who somehow managed to cope so much better with adversity than she did?

She would have to run away. Anywhere. Roy was right: she had interfered, and everything had gone wrong. Yet she had thought morality was firmly on her side. *What now?* yattered the blood surging in her own skull. *What now?*

She had gained the steps before she realized that her shoulder bag was still in the alcove. With grim determination she picked her way back to the corner and retrieved it, grubby and web-strewn, from the depths. That other bag, the black plastic sack with its rotting burden, still lay across the entrance, more tangible as evidence than the elusive platinum. For a moment she wondered if the secret of the platinum had died with Roy, then knew that it no longer mattered.

Can you be certain the body was that of Bill Heaton? echoed a voice in her head. Well, almost certain. But what if it was to disappear? What if Brown Raincoat came to investigate and removed all the signs? Bonnie stared at the protruding arm. Slowly she picked up Roy's flick-knife through a handkerchief, and with a shudder, slit open the rest of the bag. Coughing in disgust, she reeled away. As far as one could humanly say, that had been Bill Heaton.

*

Upstairs in the kitchen, she sat sipping water. Everything was clear now, starkly so. Following that disastrous armed robbery, the cache of platinum had been hastily bricked into the cellar of number 18. Five years on the nearest house which could be rented or bought had been number 14, belonging to poor, confused Mr Tisley. The Heatons were never a part of the plan. But one of them must have surprised Roy while he was burrowing through their cellar wall. Who? Bonnie felt that Roy must have done most of his careful chipping during the day when the houses were empty, so that meant Lorna.

Her eyes strayed up to the fan on the wall, and suddenly she understood. Yes . . . Lorna had returned to her home unexpectedly at lunch time that Friday. She had heard a noise in the cellar, gone to investigate – and had been strangled by Roy. In the early evening he had lain in wait for Bill Heaton, murdered him (using the knife, presumably; Heaton was big and strong) and bundled the body into the plastic sack forthwith, to circumvent the problems of rigor.

The next day, she remembered, they had gone out to buy all that solid fuel, and while Roy was down in the cellar 'stacking the bags' Bonnie had heard the furious shouting from next door . . . *Fiend*, she thought, shaking her head. You told me to make tea. You knew I'd be right behind the extractor fan. Then you left it to me to spill my theory to the police, thus fixing your alibi.

She felt calm now, calm and cold. She could recall quite vividly watching *Jungle Warfare* with Roy on the Saturday evening, eating the Chinese meal, drinking Bual as Roy became amusingly amorous. Bual . . . he had almost certainly spiked the sweet Madeira with temazepam syrup. Then while she slept he had reversed all his painstaking progress in the cellars, replacing the old bricks whose integrity he had preserved, mixing their distinctive cream mortar with quick-drying cement, and brushing coal-dust over the cracks. He had carried Lorna's body to the kitchen, positioned it appropriately, and left through the back door. Finally, he had taken Bill Heaton's bike, strapped it to the roof-rack of the Escort, and driven off to dump it in the reservoir.

A bike was one thing, a body quite another. He must have decided that the cellar of number 14 was the safest place to keep Bill Heaton in the short term. Nevertheless, Bonnie must have given him some awkward moments when she spotted the bike in the water. He must have rung Brown Raincoat that evening, instructed him to relocate the bike. Yes . . . that was the evening Roy had volunteered to go out and buy chilli beans . . .

Bonnie lifted the glass once more to her lips. A vast weariness was seeping through every limb. If she didn't act soon, she would slip into some kind of indefinite fugue.

Her first instinct to run away had now passed. But the thought of coolly ringing the police, locking herself into some inexorable system from which there was no realistic escape, was abhorrent. Was there any other way at all? Who could advise her? Who would know?

Stop kidding yourself, she muttered as she walked to the hall stand and scooped silver coins from the little dish kept there for telephone money. *You know you want to ring Jeremy.* But should she involve him in something so sordid and complex? He had asked for an update, but he could scarcely have envisaged *this* . . . She stared at her reflection in the mirror; the face gazing back at her was cadaverous, dead white with purplish circles around the eyes. Her hair was matted with blood; a streak had dried in her left eyebrow. *Ring me if you ever need a friend.* Just for advice, Jeremy. That's all. And if you tell me to go to the police, I will . . .

Slinging her shoulder bag into position, she pocketed the front door keys, released the lock and turned the handle. The stout door creaked open.

There on the path stood Brown Raincoat.

20

He looked more ghastly than ever in daylight. His skin was a dirty yellow, the face seamed and drawn. Even as she gasped with the shock of his sudden presence, he lunged forward, scowling intently.

Bonnie span back into the hall and slammed the door shut. She hurtled through to the kitchen and out into the yard. There was no choice: she dared not be trapped in a house with no telephone. He would smash the rear window and enter with ease.

As she scampered across the rough paving slabs she heard a fierce rattling sound behind her. One glance over her shoulder was enough: Brown Raincoat, teeth clenched in either fury or concentration, was working at the stiff bolt on the side gate. Thank God Roy had only oiled it once! It was giving her precious seconds of respite . . .

She heard a grunt from her pursuer as he heaved a leg over the recalcitrant gate. Darting into the alleyway, she paused and tried to formulate a plan. She could hide in the Schofields' yard until he had gone, or in Lorna's; she could run up to Barlow Road or down towards Jubilee Lane . . . He was so close behind that none of these options seemed feasible. She could stand and scream, but what if no one came? The alley was quiet and dead, a thin dreary finger pointing out to the mist-shrouded hills . . .

As she hurried towards the possible haven of number 18, her feet sliding on the gleaming cobbles, she heard her own back gate crash open. Fear lent her speed: the Schofields' gate was ajar – perhaps someone was at home? Even Wayne might prove to be of some use.

The yard was empty, the back door closed. If she ran to knock on it, she was committed . . .

Torn by indecision, Bonnie suddenly glimpsed Wayne's bike

propped against the side wall. There was no sign of a padlock . . . In a flash she had seized the handlebars and wheeled it at a run towards the exit. Brown Raincoat was just appearing as she charged out into the alley; the front wheel caught him a glancing blow on the knee, and he fell heavily on the cobbles with a grunt of pain. Bonnie carried on running, wondering if she dared mount the juddering bike and ride it down the steep slope to Jubilee Lane. She glanced back – yes, already he was following. Biting her lip, she swung her leg over the top tube and perched on the saddle.

It was ten years since she had last ridden a bike, a sedate machine with three gears and small, neat wheels. This ATB, Wayne's pride and joy, was a much hardier animal altogether. Darren had boasted that it had eighteen gears . . . Bonnie could identify the thumbshift controls easily enough, but was loath to experiment with Brown Raincoat so close behind. The bike was moving; that was good enough for the present . . .

The junction with Jubilee Lane rushed up to meet her and she slammed on the brakes. With a squeak the bike stopped so abruptly that she was nearly catapulted into the road. *Don't do his work for him,* she muttered to herself. She waited as a car passed by, then wheeled round to the right and pedalled with increasing speed along Jubilee Lane.

As she approached the main road leading to the reservoir, she spotted a white car parked on the wasteland between the mills. It was Roy's Escort! The implications of this tortured her as she turned left and struggled to find the correct gear for the hill. Why hadn't he parked in Clegg Street, as usual? Had he suspected something? Had she given herself away with all those questions about his interview?

The ruined mill skimmed past on the left. Ahead, the swelling uplands were crowned with a cold haze, but already sweat was oozing from all her pores. She wasn't fit for a five-minute jog, let alone a gruelling Pennine cycling challenge on an unfamiliar bike. Her shoulder bag made it difficult to maintain a proper balance in the saddle; she was wearing the wrong shoes. Her calves ached; her heart thundered; she gasped for air.

Eventually, she was forced to pull over and rest until her

pulse rate slipped back to the merely pathological. She stood in the grass by the side of the road and craned round to scan the route back to Holdendale. There were no pedestrians at all: Brown Raincoat had been left far behind.

Still panting, Bonnie allowed herself some thinking time. She had been unable to reach the telephone to ring Jeremy, but was now less than four miles from the farmhouse. She would press on. Even if he were not at home, he would arrive back eventually. He would have told her if he was terminating the lease. Surely he would . . .

Down the road behind her, a small black dot was slowly getting bigger. Suddenly Bonnie remembered the black car parked in Clegg Street. It had been here on that previous occasion when she had sensed she was being watched – and she could feel danger now. It was facile to imagine she had shaken off Brown Raincoat. He had simply returned to his vehicle and was now tracking her at his leisure as she rode ever further from houses and people.

Clammy tendrils of mist began to float around her face. There was no cover here at all, not so much as a stone wall, but if she could get above the false cloud-line, she might be able to evade him.

Scrambling back into the saddle, she pedalled furiously uphill. The track to the reservoir was near here, she was convinced. As the mist closed behind her, she resolved to take that track. She could wait in the car-park area until Brown Raincoat had driven past . . .

Five minutes later she stood lank and dripping in the gully where the picnic tables were placed. It was eerily quiet. The reservoir, only partially visible in the rolling gloom, was a flat dull grey and the sliced wooden slats of the deserted tables were dark with moisture. There were no people to be seen; on a late Tuesday afternoon in October they were all sensibly enjoying more comfortable surroundings.

It occurred to Bonnie that she had propelled herself into something of a cul-de-sac. While she could ride around the reservoir indefinitely, even a mountain bike couldn't cope with the open country leading to Jeremy's valley. At least, not in her inexperienced hands. So she must wait, and listen, and hope that each of those cars, whose engine sounds carried faintly through the mist from the main road, would continue to pass in distant oblivion.

Ten minutes passed, and she began to shiver. At fifteen minutes she climbed back on to the bike and made a slow return to the road. Soon the ride would be all downhill, and she could turn into Jeremy's lane without exposing him to risk. She prayed he would be at home.

Drained now, she pedalled doggedly until she had reached the crest of the hill, then began to freewheel down the other side. There was very little traffic. Bonnie was thankful to rest her limbs, but too weary to feel the usual cyclist's exhilaration when accelerating downhill. As she flashed past a gateway set back behind a dry stone wall a glimpse of black clawed at her attention.

Tears stung her eyes as the bike hurtled down towards the valley floor. Damn you, she raged silently. Damn you for the cunning bastard that you are. She wanted to scream at the unfairness of it all. Why was she here, fleeing from a murderer, and open to the grim charge of murder herself? How had it happened? She had only wanted to be a good wife . . . nothing more.

A lump rose in her throat. *You said I look like your daughter*, she whispered. Don't you remember? Doesn't that count?

Not with someone who had already pushed another young girl in front of a car. Someone who may well have pulled the trigger on that shotgun five years ago in countryside mere miles from here . . . She had seen the hard resolve in his face. So, no, it didn't count. He had warned her once and she had paid no heed.

A steep bend forced her to concentrate entirely on the bike. She was swishing down into the valley now, and could see Jeremy's farmhouse on the shoulder of the hill opposite. It was so close, but if the black car appeared she would have no alternative but to pedal on into the village and seek refuge in the shop.

Jamming on the brakes once more, she juddered to a halt just beyond the bus shelter, which was constructed like a small wooden hut. She pulled the bicycle against its side wall and peered back at the mist-wreathed hills, runnels of sweat coursing down her face. There was no sign of the black car. Perhaps it hadn't been Brown Raincoat's vehicle lurking near the reservoir, after all . . .

Before she could change her mind, she ran with the bike across the road and steered it into Jeremy's lane. Further delay would have ensured a self-fulfilling prophecy. She held grimly to the handlebars as the bike leapt and jolted over ruts and potholes; after fifty refractory yards she was still in clear sight of the road. She paused: unencumbered, she would be at the farm in three minutes or so . . .

Sorry, Wayne, she muttered as she reluctantly heaved his precious ATB over the stone wall into the field of sheep. She couldn't leave it in the lane: it was too obvious. For a moment she visualized Wayne himself capering with outrage and felt a hysterical laugh bubbling up in her throat, but when it reached her mouth it had turned into a strangled sob.

Please be at home, Jeremy, she begged, bending low into the shelter of the dry stone wall as she ran. Please be home. Because if you're not, I don't know what I shall do.

The tall doors to the barn were open. Jeremy was leaning over the exposed engine of the pick-up truck, wiping a metal rod with an oily rag. In the dank October drabness, only the bright gilt of his hair shone like a monarch's crown. She called his name; he stared at her in astonishment.

'Bonnie – what on earth has happened? You look terrible!'

She paused in the entrance, panting. Part of her longed to collapse in a luxurious wash of tears, to dump the problem squarely in his domain – but another part of her, newly mature, urged her to remain calm. He was. She had seen the flash of concerned speculation in his eyes, but now he stood by the side of the vehicle, casual in old denims and a roll-neck jumper, waiting for her to explain her dramatic appearance in her own time.

She swallowed and stepped forward. 'I've killed Roy,' she said.

'Drink this,' he insisted as they sat on the comfortable sofa. She had asked for a cold drink, but the mug he thrust into her hand contained tea. It was hot, and revoltingly sweet.

'Now, tell me again. Are you *sure* he was dead when you left?'

'I think he was . . . I couldn't feel a pulse, and there was such a lot of blood . . .'

'It must have sprayed out. There's some in your hair.'

'Yes. It was on my face, too, but I think that was washed away as I cycled out here.' She shuddered. 'I'd like to scrub it all away, but I suppose it's evidence.'

'Your story will be the best evidence. I'm sure no jury would convict you once they'd heard the facts.'

'You think so? Really?'

'Absolutely. It was self-defence.' He wandered to the window and looked out from behind the curtain. She knew he was checking to see if Brown Raincoat had followed her right up to the farmhouse, but typically he wasn't going to worry her by saying so. He had grasped the bare bones of her story very quickly, and concentrated on the essentials. Was she hurt? Was she certain Roy was dead? Did this other person tail her as far as the lane? She had hardly mentioned the platinum, the root cause of all this carnage.

He came back to her, his handsome face thoughtful, and sat down with a sigh. 'I'm going to have to ring the police,' he said. 'You know that, don't you?'

'Yes.'

He took her hand. 'It'll be all right, Bonnie. I promise. And if this Brown Raincoat fellow is hanging around, they can deal with him before he does any more damage. Now, I'll go and ring from upstairs. Are you comfortable here for a few minutes?'

'I . . . could I possibly use your bathroom?'

'Of course.' He walked with her to the hall. 'Go on up. It's just at the top of the stairs. Dusky pink, I'm afraid.' As she trod zombie-like up the creaking stair treads, she heard him slide home the bolt on the front door. Yes, she thought – for all his cool demeanour, Jeremy was taking the Brown Raincoat threat very seriously indeed.

She waited on the landing. 'Jeremy – I'd love to have a wash. I got so hot riding that bike. If they take me into custody, I might not have a chance for days . . . Do you think it would matter if I just have a little wash? A sort of sponge bath?'

'Well . . .'

'I feel so filthy.'

'You'll find you don't want to put those clothes back on. Wait, though . . .' His face cleared. 'I can lend you one of my shirts. It'll be more like a dress on you if it's secured with a belt.'

'Oh, *please*.'

'As long as you don't get your own clothes wet or do anything with your hair.'

'I won't. Thank you, Jeremy. I'll be very careful.'

He gave her the clothes, a cream checked country-style shirt, a leather belt and a baggy green jumper, and pattered downstairs again to make his telephone call. She heard the *ting* of the bedroom extension as he lifted the sitting-room receiver.

Bonnie sat wearily on the edge of the bath, unable to do anything at all for a few minutes. Then she ran a basin-full of lukewarm water and washed her face with an iris-scented soap. That was better . . . but with the release of immediate tension came the first intimation of a thundering headache. This was bad; she needed a clear brain to put her case. Perhaps Jeremy had some aspirins in the medicine cabinet?

She opened the attractively carved pinewood door with its inlaid mirror, and rummaged guiltily among the packets inside. He wouldn't mind, she was sure. As soon as she found some aspirins she would close up the cabinet . . .

There was nothing among the throat pastilles and sticking plasters on the upper shelf. The lower shelf held items of personal toiletry – after-shave lotion, toothpaste, shampoo. Her eye was caught by the label of a bottle she assumed to be more shampoo. 'His Secret,' it said, and below, 'Platinum Gilt.' She blushed with shame at her own prying and smothered a giggle.

So men dyed their hair, too! The instructions made the nature of the product quite clear. That accounted for Jeremy's dark eyebrows beneath the blond hair. What colour was he really? At least he didn't wear a wig!

Beneath the amusement Bonnie felt a flat little core of disappointment. There was a flavour here of something false, insincere, as if she had struck a venerable bronze bell and heard a hollow note. Perhaps the bottle belonged to the farmhouse's owner . . . she was not convinced.

Next to it stood a tall brown bottle which looked vaguely familiar. Unable now to quash her curiosity, Bonnie pulled it from the shelf to read the label. Cough mixture might ease her fiery throat.

TEMAZEPAM SYRUP, she read. Oh, no. Not here. Surely, surely not. With shaking fingers she replaced the bottle, while through the wall the telephone went *ting*.

So they met in Madeira, she found herself murmuring. So what? Roy was asking him the time. That's all, just the time . . . Since when has the possession of a watch been a criminal offence?

Suddenly she was on her knees on the dusky pink carpet. She clawed Simon's packet out of the shoulder bag and tore open one end to pull out a great sheaf of papers. Clipped to the front was a handwritten note. 'Found these under the bed,' Simon had scrawled. 'Cassie must have been reading them. Hope they're of some use to you. Good luck. Simon.'

With a feeling of dread, Bonnie riffled through the various photocopies. Within seconds she was staring at Jeremy's face, a dark-haired, smugly laughing Jeremy standing in the grounds of someone's ancestral mansion. BARONET'S SON IMPLICATED IN RPC ROBBERY, screamed the headline; the article beneath went on to describe how Rupert Bannerman, maverick son of Sir Edwin Bannerman, was now thought to be the prime mover behind the infamous RPC 'heist'.

She tried to read the rest, but her brain was crowded with horrors. The sense of sick betrayal would come later, she knew, but just now blind fear was careening out of control.

Next door, the telephone began to ring.

21

Bonnie crept across the landing to the top of the stairs, and leaned over the banisters. The sitting-room door was open. She could see Jeremy clearly as he picked up the receiver and gave a guarded 'Hello'. If she tried to leave that way she would cross his line of vision.

The bathroom window, she knew, was too small to be of use . . . She padded to the grey square of light in the bedroom: this window had a funny little lock and would not budge. Besides – where could she run to? She would be caught within minutes.

She glanced at the beige telephone on the bedside table. Who was talking to Jeremy? It might not be the police, but it might still be some neutral person who could help. Should she break in on their conversation, shout that she had been kidnapped? She padded across the room, praying that the floorboards wouldn't squeak. Gingerly she lifted the receiver and held it to her ear.

'. . . little bitch nearly sliced my head open,' someone was saying. Her heart jolted at the familiar tones – Roy was alive!

'How bad is it?' That was Jeremy – no, Rupert.

'Bloody sore . . . I was out for half an hour, and I still feel dizzy. Won't stop bleeding, either. That f— little bitch!'

'Oh, stop whining. You've only yourself to blame. Christ, Derek, you've screwed up all along. You should have lifted the goods weeks ago, not embarked on a one-man killing spree. You didn't even have the wit to dump that bloody bike at the other side of town. You're a f— liability. Now get over here and we'll sort out how to shift the stuff tonight.'

'I *can't*. I keep collapsing.'

Bonnie heard a snort of contempt. 'I'll come to you, then. But there's something I have to take care of first . . .' Abruptly the dialling tone clicked in. Bonnie replaced the receiver as delicately as she could while sweat started out once more on her forehead.

Her heart pounded in great soggy thumps. *He's going to kill me,* she thought. *I'm about to join all the others . . .*

She reached the bathroom just as Jeremy began to climb the stairs.

'You still in there?' he called.

'Yes.' Her mouth was so dry she could hardly articulate the word. 'I'm nearly ready.'

'Good. I thought you'd died, or something . . . sorry, that's not very funny. Come out whenever you like.'

Where was the pain? she wondered. When a loved one had gone away, there was usually pain. But Jeremy had never existed. There had only ever been Rupert, with his dazzling good looks, intelligence and charm, and a soul of unredeemed corruption . . . For a brief moment she was reminded of Madeira on the ocean-floor map: the lush, inviting pinnacle above the waves, the stark black rock below.

She felt her panic subside, leaving nothing but a deadly weakness in its stead. The fight was over. With just one friend, she would have gone on struggling, placed a soaring price on her life, dared them to end it. But no one cared. No one would mourn her; no one would know.

She walked down the stairs with leaden legs. Jeremy looked up from the sofa where he was elegantly sprawled. 'Oh – didn't the shirt fit?' he asked.

'I thought I'd better put these back on, after all. When are the police coming?'

'Soon.'

She nodded. Everything was peculiar and muffled . . . unreal. While her brain wondered if anyone could ever be totally resigned to death, her emotions remained anaesthetized.

'Bonnie – you look worse than you did before. Come and sit down.'

'No, thank you.'

'What is it, Bonnie?'

She took a deep breath. 'I want an honest conversation with you.'

'What?' His face went slack.

'You knew I was in love with you. You must have found that highly amusing, especially since you'd already allocated me to Roy. At least it gave you another factor to manipulate.'

Lithely he sprang to his feet, his powers of recovery far superior to hers. He looked every inch a dangerous animal, yet she remained unmoved. 'Why are you telling me this?' he demanded.

'Because I want you to know that I know. Because thanks to you, I've spent these last few weeks using people, lying to them. Just in little ways, but it's something I'd never done before. And it's easy, isn't it, after the first couple of times . . .? But now I want just one piece of truth before I go.'

'You're mad,' he said quietly.

'There was no house in Hertfordshire, was there? No Helena, either.'

He shrugged.

'You're not a writer . . . but you have travelled, and learned a lot. Was that purely from necessity?'

'You don't understand a thing.'

'Explain it to me, then.'

'To see the world properly, you need money.'

A chink, she thought. There could be hot yearning behind even the coldest action, as long as you knew how to keep them in their own sealed compartments. With the chink came the first sting of feeling as her torpor began to thin.

She saw him make a gesture of dismissal, as if to devalue the answer he had given. 'Conversation can be a big mistake,' he said, and leaned casually down behind the sofa. He emerged with a length of chain in his hands, similar to that which held the barn door padlock.

Bonnie gasped. Suddenly she *did* want to live, badly. But he was stepping towards her, and his eyes were pitiless. Once that chain was round her neck no sound that she could force up from her throat would ever translate into a persuasive argument to stop. She had seconds left to communicate.

'The platinum wasn't even there,' she blurted out.

He hesitated, his mouth narrowing. 'What do you mean?'

'It wasn't there. I saw the place where it should have been, behind the bricks in the cellar alcove . . . Roy must have taken it. Or maybe the man with the brown raincoat . . .'

She saw his features swell with rage and disbelief. 'Do you think I'm that stupid?' he yelled, seizing her by the shoulders and shaking her. The links from the chain he held in one hand bit into her flesh.

'It's true!' She saw a flicker of doubt cross his face and took a sharp breath ready to speak again, but suddenly he lunged. He pulled the chain across the back of her neck in one rapid movement, then swung it round her throat to twist in a knot. Stepping smartly behind her he began to tighten the knot as she fought to insert her fingers beneath the chain.

Bonnie sank to her knees, throbbing crimson pressure rising in her eyes and ears. Her chest was bursting to release the air she had sucked in, even in the hoarse gargle of death, but the unyielding metal was crushing her larynx. Wildly she fought, but the strength was draining from her limbs . . . In her head the crimson darkened to mulberry . . .

There was a shattering explosion nearby. Dimly she realized that shards of glass were flying all around her, then a dull *thump* reverberated across the room. She heard Jeremy swear, and the cruel grip on her throat slackened. Then there were more sounds of breaking glass, and she became aware that someone else was in the room.

Bonnie emptied her lungs in a long sigh and began to crawl towards the shelter of the sofa. The expected tug on her neck never came. Instead, there were curses and thumps, grunts and panting as Jeremy and the intruder grappled fiercely together in the sitting-room. She curled up into a foetal ball, harsh breaths whistling up and down her raw larynx. On the carpet nearby was a large chunk of stone. Behind her the frenzied sounds went on, but they were more distant now, as if the antagonists had whirled out into the hall.

Now was the moment she should telephone the police – but

she had no voice. She put a hand to her throat and tried to squeak 'Help'; nothing happened.

Suddenly the cursing stopped. She heard a soft thump somewhere out of sight, then only the sound of someone else whooping for breath. A minute passed, then Brown Raincoat staggered into view. 'He's dead,' he said.

She tensed, uncertain as to his intentions.

'Don't be afraid, Bonnie. I'm on your side. I always have been – though I haven't always known it.' He collapsed on to the sofa, dishevelled and deeply exhausted.

Bonnie slowly unlocked her limbs and climbed to her feet. She coughed. 'Who are you?' she croaked.

'My name's Stan Brewer.'

Brewer . . . for a moment she couldn't identify the context, then the contents of 'Slaughter in Saddleworth' rushed back into her mind. 'Sergeant Brewer,' she said.

'Former sergeant. But I blew it. I couldn't handle what happened to my mate Mike Collet. I went off the rails in a big way.' He gave a rueful grimace. 'Booze . . . and more booze. I lost my wife and my daughter, and I don't blame them, either. And my job. I was a security guard for a while, but I couldn't even manage that.'

'You've been watching us since the summer.'

'Yes. I always thought the raiders would come back. We never knew the exact location of their emergency hide-out, but we felt it wasn't far from that lock-up garage. I've been patrolling the streets around Barlow Road for five years, just looking for something unusual. My mates at the station thought it was a waste of time. They said the platinum had long gone. But I reckoned the gang had been unnerved by the unprecedented police activity which followed Mike's death, and had made a temporary cache of the platinum. So I kept looking – and one day I *did* see something unusual.'

'A couple moving into a row of condemned houses.'

'Almost. I didn't spot you in the actual act of moving in, but I did notice that number 14 was suddenly under different occupancy. I asked around; no one knew you; people assumed you were squatting. One night I got a good look at Roy in the King's Head. I thought he bore some resemblance to Derek Ventnor, one of the wanted men, but I wasn't quite sure. I cased the pub for weeks after that, but he never reappeared.

'I'd just resigned myself to its being a false alarm when I saw police buzzing around your house one night. I'd had a skinful, but it was obvious that here was something else out of the ordinary. I waded in to demand details from the young bobbies on your doorstep. They all knew about my obsession, but they assured me that this was a domestic incident next door, and was most unlikely to be connected.'

'*Sir to you,*' remembered Bonnie. Yes, they were constables, and hierarchies die hard.

'I still thought it was a curious coincidence,' went on Stan Brewer. 'I focused my attention on Clegg Street, and the more glimpses I had of Roy, the more I could visualize him in alternate guise as Derek Ventnor. But I didn't know whether you were involved, or not. So one night I asked you.'

'You terrified me,' she said.

'I'm sorry. I'd sneaked into the alley to cut round to Clegg Street when I saw you getting out of some bloke's car; it was a surprise when you entered the alley yourself.'

'What about today?'

'Today? All my instincts were aroused. I saw you peering out furtively from behind a phone box, then again from the passageway next to your house. When Roy returned home, he came on foot from the direction of Jubilee Lane, a place with no garages where he might have left the Escort. He was acting oddly, too – creeping about, glancing in through the bay window . . . After half an hour, I just couldn't wait any longer, so I invented a pretext and crossed the road to knock on your door. I'd just set foot on the path when you appeared, blood all over your face. When you ran, I had to find out where you were going . . . What happened, Bonnie?'

Briefly she told him about her search in the cellars, and Roy. 'I didn't shake you off,' she reflected. 'I thought I had done. Thank God I didn't.'

'No,' he agreed. 'I pulled in again near the cloud-line and

watched the valley. It was all laid out like a child's farmyard set. You couldn't see me, but I observed you riding into the lane. There was only this property at the top.'

'And only one tenant,' said Bonnie. She knitted her fingers together as Stan Brewer suspended the halting narrative to catch his breath. 'I must see him,' she announced.

'Are you sure? I promise you he's dead. We were grappling in the kitchen and he went for the carving knife . . .'

'I'm sorry; I must.' She walked to the kitchen doorway, looked down, and wondered how she could ever have imagined that she had killed Roy. The crude copiousness of the blood was the same, but the bodies were profoundly different. Only an empty shell lay here, she knew.

'I was attracted to him,' she explained on returning. 'He showed me round Madeira and knew so much about the land, its plants, and customs . . . It was only today that I realized he had been vetting me. He must have gone to the island to find Roy, tell him about the demolition plans for Clegg Street. Roy in his turn tipped him off that I was alone in the world, and rather dim to boot . . . I don't know if they cast lots to decide who would be lumbered . . .'

Stan Brewer held up a hand as her voice cracked in misery. 'It wouldn't have been like that, Bonnie,' he said. 'Rupert Bannerman was the boss; his were the orders. Someone had to move into Clegg Street, but it wasn't going to be him. His face was still on the wall in the local Cop Shop, and besides, someone with his voice and manners would have stuck out like a sore thumb in a working-class district like that. So Roy was the obvious choice.'

'Why did J – Rupert need to do it?' she mused. 'Surely he had everything going for him?'

'Too many privileges as a child. Gave him a taste for travel. But then his father belatedly decided to stop funding him and teach him the value of money. Rupert resented that. He couldn't decide on a legitimate career, and eventually turned to crime instead. He had plenty of intelligence, and some interesting contacts . . . We suspected he was behind a robbery at a Blackburn jeweller's six months before the RPC raid. It would have given him the means for a more ambitious enterprise . . .' His eyes moved slowly to Bonnie's face. 'Are you *sure* there was no sign of platinum down the cellar, Bonnie? It's worth about two million pounds, and there's still a big reward . . .'

'I found nothing,' she answered.

'Perhaps it was the wrong place . . . Did you see any plastic containers, like bottles?'

'No, only – wait. Plastic, you said. There was something.' She groped in her bag and withdrew the flat red oblong with the long plastic tails.

He beamed when he saw it, and reached out eagerly. 'That's a security seal,' he said. 'See – it's stamped with a seven-digit number. Those long pieces thread through holes in the neck of each container.'

Bonnie frowned, puzzled. 'I don't understand these "bottles". What does the platinum *look* like? Isn't it solid after all?'

She saw him flash her a speculative glance. 'Platinum for industrial use is sent around the country in the form of "sponge", a greyish powder. Were you hoping for a stack of shiny ingots?'

'Oh! Powder! Mr Brewer – it's there! It is! It's in some bags labelled "Cement". I had no idea that was the platinum!'

'Call me Stan, for God's sake,' he growled, then went on more ruminatively, 'The day after the raid was dustbin day. When the body of the young driver was found behind Barlow Road two days after that, I urged the force to check the council dump because the plastic containers could have been jettisoned in black binliners masquerading as domestic rubbish. They felt that was unlikely, and in any case there was insufficient manpower to follow existing leads. So it was never done. I reckon I was right, after all . . .'

'But what could the gang have done with the powder?'

'Ah . . . I told you that Bannerman had brains and contacts. They'd have set up a bogus company – all you need is an address – then mixed the platinum with some gubbins or other and sold it on in small aliquots as "platiniferous sweepings" . . . quite likely ending up back with Thomson Plathey themselves.'

'There's a laptop computer upstairs. It might contain evidence of the arrangements.'

He gave her a tired smile. 'Perhaps.'

Bonnie felt buoyant, a reaction to her earlier apathy. 'Just imagine if the Schofields had found the platinum!' she exclaimed. 'They might have used it to resurface their yard – or sold it to some builder. It could have ended up between the bricks of the new prison!'

He gave a snort of laughter, but subsided again as if the effort was too great. Bonnie felt a stab of alarm as she studied him closely for the first time since the violent scuffle. There was pallor beneath his habitual yellow, and a bluish-grey tinge around the mouth. He lay against the back of the sofa, every limb flaccid, his head lolling. Guiltily she noticed that his breathing, though quiet, was rapid and shallow. 'Are you all right?' she quavered.

'I just need a rest,' he said faintly. 'I'm not as young as I was.'

Everyone treated her like a child! 'You look ill,' she said firmly. 'Please tell me what's wrong. Shall I fetch you some water?'

'Yes, thank you – but don't disturb the kitchen if you can help it.'

'There's a glass upstairs.' She brought it to him and sat close by, waiting to assist should he need her.

'What is it?' she repeated, laying the glass down.

'Nothing much,' he said, but she saw him wince and shift his position.

'Let me look.' He tried to demur, but she pulled aside the raincoat, which was already unbuttoned, and lifted the thread-bare jumper below. An oozing oval stain marred the white shirt beneath. 'You've been stabbed!' she cried.

'I know.'

All that talking, and he'd been lying here injured! She must take charge, reassure him, call for an ambulance . . . 'There isn't a lot of blood,' she said in confident tones. 'It doesn't look too bad. I'll just get something to press on it.'

'No.'

'Why not?' She felt an uneasy twist in her own stomach. There was a pearly sheen across his upper lip, and his breathing now seemed more rapid. He was frighteningly pale.

'The bleeding's internal,' he said. 'I can tell.'

She leapt up from the sofa. 'I'll ring for help.'

'Don't!'

She looked at him in surprise. All his energy seemed to have gone into the shout; he slumped back, eyes closed, then the lids flickered open again. 'Please don't,' he repeated more quietly. 'I'm dying.'

Oh, no, she thought. No . . . you mustn't. 'But the hospital will save you!' she protested

He gave a faint smile, and slowly shook his head. 'You don't understand,' he whispered. 'I've got cancer. Gut cancer. It's spread to the liver and they can't do anything for me. They reckoned I had three months left, if that.'

'But – '

'Shh. If you call someone now, there'll be fuss and noise and chaos instead of peace. I'll die just the same, and even if it's not immediate, all I'll get will be more trouble and questions. I've just killed a man. I feel right about it, but the due process of law will still have to proceed in all its laborious majesty. I'm too tired for that, Bonnie. They can manage it without me.'

He shifted restlessly. 'I made my wife's life a hell until she left me,' he went on. 'And Ann, my daughter. God, you are so much like her! The same small hands and feet, the soft flaxen hair . . . Yes, I was a monster. I couldn't forgive myself for living when Mike was blasted to death. There must have been something I could have done. Instead, I ran away . . .'

His eyes began to roll upwards, but he rallied himself and clung tenaciously to his narrative. 'I wanted Rupert Bannerman,' he whispered. 'And today I got him. All that has happened is due to him.'

'Did – did he fire the shot?'

'That was Granville, but Bannerman was guilty all the same. When you hire psychotic thugs and put lethal weapons in their hands, the responsibility for what follows is yours . . . And remember what he did to you.'

Bonnie's fingers pressed lightly against the skin of her throat: it felt bruised and sore. *And Cassie,* she thought. Cassie, whose smiling by-line photograph had proved to be her death warrant.

'The reward will be yours, Bonnie,' murmured Stan Brewer. 'You'll use it wisely and make a fresh start.'

'Oh, I couldn't!'

'You must. You're a lovely young woman, pretty, capable and resourceful. You'll make someone a splendid wife one day.'

'I did marry Roy,' she said despondently.

'No . . . he's a bigamist. Derek Ventnor has already abandoned a wife and two children.'

'Really? It's not legal?' She felt a long-familiar weight start to rise from her chest.

'Not legal,' he muttered. He moved on the sofa, and grimaced.

'Would you like to lie down?'

'No . . . just stay, please. Val, my wife . . . give her my love. Tell her I'm sorry.'

'Where is she, Stan?'

'Don't know . . . but Tim, at the station, he knows . . . He helped her get away. He's all right, is Tim. Tell him thanks for looking after Val. Tell him it's all okay.'

'I shall. I promise.'

'And Ann . . .' His voice trailed away to a soft delirious babble. 'Rescued Ann . . . Chain around neck . . . my little Ann . . .'

Tears pricked Bonnie's eyes. She seized his cold moist hand. 'I'll tell her. Everything. They'll be so proud of you.'

The low muttering went on, and his breathing became more laboured. His skin was a translucent grey. As Bonnie crouched by the sofa, not daring to move, his eyelids suddenly opened and the faded brown eyes looked straight at her. 'Ann,' he said.

Carefully she squeezed his hand. 'We love you, Dad.'

He smiled, and the eyelids drooped once more. Something whispered away from his face, and was gone.

*

Outside the splintered window, the sky darkened to indigo and the distant bleating of sheep was stilled. Bonnie rose stiffly to her feet. She crossed the room and paused by the telephone.

She thought of 'Roy', waiting dazedly at home for Rupert Bannerman to come. Soon he would have more visitors than he had bargained for. She thought of Rupert, and Stan, and his dead colleague. And she thought of the platinum.

It was right that the focus of so much misery was not a gleaming treasure trove. The games and forfeits had been too adult for that. Let that nondescript powder bear witness to the fact that, when weighed against life, all possessions are but dust.

She picked up the receiver, and began to dial.